Jill Dawson was born in Durham, England. She is the author of three other novels: *Trick of the Light*, *Fred and Edie*, which was shortlisted for the Whitbread Novel Award and the Orange Prize and translated into several languages, and, most recently, *Wild Boy*, which is currently being developed for film. In addition she is the editor of five anthologies, including *Wild Ways: New Stories about Women on the Road* (co-edited with Margo Daly) and the recent *Gas and Air: Tales of Pregnancy, Birth and Beyond*. She has taught at Amherst College, Massachusetts and currently teaches on the MA in Writing at the University of East Anglia in Norwich where she was latterly a Creative Writing Fellow. She lives in the Fens with her partner and two sons.

'Lily walks between loneliness and defiance, wretchedness and quiet triumph; it's a delicate balance and Jill Dawson achieves it with style, humour and honesty'
Roddy Doyle

'Seldom has inner-city London been depicted with such passion, and peopled with such a disparate array of characters, all of whom remain totally convincing and linger in the memory long after the final page'
Caryl Phillips

'An enjoyable novel, its brisk prose infused by Dawson's warmth and sympathy for her well-observed characters.'
Edward Platt, *Sunday Times*

'Jill Dawson is excellent on the tragic details of life . . . [but] *Magpie* is funny too, and well-observed, on single parenthood, class and what you have to do to survive those inner-city blues.'
List

Also by Jill Dawson

Trick of the Light
Fred and Edie
Wild Boy

Jill Dawson

Magpie

SCEPTRE

For Meredith

Acknowledgements

I am deeply grateful to the Royal Literary Fund for help during a crucial time.

I would also like to acknowledge the assistance I have received from the Kathleen Blundell Trust Fund (administered by the Society of Authors), the London Arts Board and the British Council and to express my gratitude to all three.

A letter is an unannounced visit; the mailman the mediator of impolite incursions. One ought to have one hour in every eight days for receiving letters, and then take a bath.

Nietzsche, from *The Wanderer and His Shadow*

Pica[2] n.: a craving for unnatural food such as mud or cloth, as occurs occasionally in hysteria and pregnancy. (New Latin, from Latin *pica*, magpie (from its omnivorous nature).)

Reader's Digest Universal Dictionary

One for Sorrow

I collect things; I collect stones and fish. One time I had fish. I had Clown Loach and Black Ruby Barb. I had Blue Lumphead and Tiger Barb. I didn't have Rainbow Fish or Lantern Fish. They glow in the dark.

Mum has got a paper bag with some nice pastries in them. Mum says it's early Matthew, look, come here, I'll show you how high up we are. We are far up, we're like birds or aeroplanes, but we haven't got an aquarium in this house and we can't have one now. But we have got a gas oven in the kitchen with a blue flame but Mum isn't scared of it. And I'm not. If you don't have an aquarium in your house you can have cards with pictures of fish on them and your Mum can read you the names. Ghost Shrimp, Hairy Cancer Crab, Beach Crab, Rose Star, Peanut Worm. Sand flea. White Sea Cucumber. Your Mum can read all those words and you can have a book with them in. Your Dad can read you the words as well. Your Dad can say, Sea Gooseberry. Sea Dollar.

I like to say: Sea Willy Head.

Midnight and a police helicopter twirls its beam over the Flanders Estate like the blade in a liquidiser. Light settles for a short while on a black cab pulling up at the entrance to one of the blocks of flats; Bridge House. The slim figure of a young woman alights, pays the driver at the cab window and then pulls from inside the cab two small cases and a tumbling, dark-haired child. The woman pauses, and so does the helicopter, hovering like an expectant wasp, before she and the child disappear into the entrance of the flats and the helicopter climbs, a little unsteadily, makes a poorly executed turn (now a drunken wasp) and sets off in the direction of Bank: radio reports are coming in of someone with an Irish accent asking for directions in a Bedford van.

Lily Waite and her five-year-old son, Matthew, stand in sleepy silence beside the lift in Bridge House. Lily's heart is not sleepy, beating ferociously hard inside her ribcage, her hands in the pockets of her denim jacket tight as balled-up paper, her right hand clutching two brand new, sharp-edged keys. Lily sneaks a glance over her shoulder, trying to take in a little more of the amber-lit Flanders Estate. A small council block of lowrise flats, red brick, built in the thirties in square design, facing each other, clustered around a metal-fenced hexagon of grass, one large London plane tree. A handwritten sign to Lily's left announces a Tenants Meeting; a second notice offers the services of Madam Crystalle, clairvoyant. Pale blue tiles (mostly chipped) line the inside of the entrance-way. There is a smell of floral disinfectant, faintly underscored by the scent of overflowing bins.

The lift arrives at the ground floor with a whirr and a bump, a literal sound, the lift in a Hitchcock film. Lily and Matthew step hesitantly inside, Lily shuffling the cases in front of her.

'Would you like to press the button for our floor, the top floor . . ?' she asks. Matthew remains silent. Lily waits politely, then presses the button for floor five and the doors to the lift slide creakily shut.

No crows gathering. No gangs with knives, no welcome party of any kind, not even a net-curtain twitching. Lily smiles meaninglessly at her son, a habit she has developed of late, handy to disguise the fact that she is studying him; his celery-coloured woollen hat pulled low to his eyes, eyes which in the sharp artificial strip-light inside the lift are two dark contracting points, deeply suspicious.

'Here we are then,' Lily says, in the same smiling tone, quickly adding: 'Don't lean against the walls of the lift Matthew. Come over here, next to me.'

The lift arrives at floor five with a bump and the doors open on an identical hallway, blue tiles, same concrete floors, same smell. There is a flat on either side of the lift, and number 12 is to their left.

Lily takes a noisy breath, pulls the key from inside her pocket.

'Here we are,' she says again, but this time her voice is high-pitched, Matthew raises his eyes, attuned to nuances in his mother's tone. He is unsure if this voice means something exciting is about to happen, or something terrible. He stands close beside Lily, tugging at the collar on his coat, as she struggles with the key, bursting into the flat with a dramatic oh when the door gives way after much jiggling and fussing. The hallway is dark, but Lily, armed with a letter from the council informing them that the electricity won't be on until tomorrow morning, has come prepared, draws a mini Action Man torch from her back pocket, aims; flashes.

'Let me!' squeaks Matthew, waking up a little. In his hand, light strips bounce from ceiling to floor, from dangling bulb to uncarpeted corridor, and in these few moments, as she stands on the threshold of number 12, Bridge House, surveying her new home in tiny stripes, Lily's brio nearly deserts her, threatens to tip right over into something else entirely.

'Let me,' Lily insists, gathering herself with some effort, turning to Matthew and taking the torch from him, carefully closing the door behind them, shuffling until they and the bags are fully inside. Lily directs the beam unblinkingly at the long thin corridor and the five doors. The bare floor is the worst part, nests of fluff in every corner, the remains of an old rotten carpet; but it's clear at least that the walls have been recently painted. The flat smells of paint, a good smell, and the kitchen is big, reasonably clean, with plenty of surfaces, and at least the toilet is separate from the bathroom. The bedroom is wide and cold and outdoorsy; a window has been left open. Bringing the cases into this room, Lily begins unpacking, unrolling two sleeping bags on top of the narrow single beds.

'We need to buy lots of things, Matthew, don't we, we need to start from scratch: pillows, sheets, duvets . . .'

'Where's Pooh Bear?'

'Well now, love, you know we don't have Pooh Bear any more, but I can buy you a new one just as soon as I cash some money . . .'

Matthew says nothing, raises arms silently while Lily pulls his sweater over his head, slips his glow-in-the-dark Ghost Busters pyjama top in its place. Lily snuggles him into the cold, zipped nylon of his sleeping bag, kisses the top of his head.

'This place stinks,' says Matthew, into nylon, as loud as he can, but if Lily heard him, she doesn't take the bait. He can see her shadowy outline, sitting on the single bed nearest the window, holding the torch between her teeth, so that the circle of light falls in small pools inside their cases. She drops the torch when she finds her cigarettes, and even from his own sleeping bag Matthew can smell the funny gold paper they are wrapped in. He watches Lily cup her hand in front of her face, hears the snap of her lighter and then the familiar tiny red glow in the dark, which to him equals: Lily. When he closes his eyes that bright red spark dances on his eyelids for the longest time, chasing him down dark corridors into sleep.

Lily is wide awake, standing at the slightly-opened bedroom window, blowing smoke out over the estate, amazed to see so many lights still on at this hour, a car pulling in, a figure walking into the entrance of the flat opposite. Voices, the ping of a milk bottle kicked over. *Here I am in the inner-city.* She likes the sound of that. Inner. Inside. High up.

What's pricking her awake is excitement, she can feel her heart racing now, as if she just downed twenty cups of coffee. All through the train journey, the cab drive, she was steady, competent, asking Matthew in a sensible, calm voice – a voice which felt false to her, new – if he'd like a drink of orange juice from the buffet-bar? or a nice packet of crisps? Now, with Matthew sleeping, she can cast that self off, feel the bubbling just beneath it, the tiny voice muttering, *I've done it. I'm here. All by myself.*

It's only a few hours since Bob was driving Lily and Matthew to the station in Leeds, Brenda beside him in the passenger seat, an atmosphere so brittle, so tense, that no one seemed at all surprised when Brenda dropped and broke her compact mirror, shattering into tiny silver pieces at the bottom of the car. Lily, in the back seat, could tell her mother was crying, blowing her nose in her handkerchief and muttering, 'That's seven years bad luck, *seven years* . . .'

Lily and Bob were silent, knowing it was useless to try to reassure Brenda about one of her superstitions. *Don't open an umbrella in the house, don't walk under a ladder, don't look at the moon's reflection in the window.* If Brenda saw a magpie, she crossed her eyes so that the image would duplicate. *One for sorrow, two for joy.*

Well, Lily thinks, I'm dispensing with that claptrap. I've thrown out all the rules. I've proved that nothing matters at all, nothing is under our control, no matter what we do. Bob isn't superstitious, but he goes to church, he prays for things, the things he wants. As a child, Lily went with him often enough. Whispering between her hands *and can I have a Sindy wardrobe and could you make Susan Masters be my friend?* Ridiculous. Delusional, Lily decides. We might as well just allow ourselves to be buffeted around like flames in the wind, boats on a choppy sea. And we might as well enjoy it, set ourselves adrift. Perhaps it isn't even as terrifying as we think.

The tail-lights of a plane glide across the sky like Lantern Fish in a bowl, and she can hear noises, ordinary noises, nothing terrible; exactly the sort of noises you hear anywhere. In Yorkshire, for example. A dog barking. A baby crying. A car door slamming.

Light wakes Lily first, a slant of lemony-grey splashing

on her face from the curtainless window. For a minute she can't remember where she is, expecting to feel the straggly limbs and heat of Matthew lying beside her, sharing her bed like they did in the last few months at Brenda and Bob's. She glances over: Matthew's dark hair sticks out from the top of his sleeping bag like a paint-brush and he breathes raggedly, a sound like sobs subsiding. Above that Lily can hear the soft purring of pigeons, presumably in the roof. At any rate, very close.

Before Matthew wakes she has unpacked most of the things, folded their few clothes inside the one fitted wardrobe, placed the white fluffy slippers that Brenda gave her under the bed, the two cups in the kitchen, the other basic kitchen items, the two thin towels, the three books, the chopping board, the donated tea-towels decorated with a picture of the Castle Museum in York. When she has done this, swept the floors, scrubbed the bath and sink and inside the fridge, the flat smells less of new paint and more of the fresh coffee brewing in (Brenda's old) cafetière, but everywhere is still decidedly empty. Two whole cases. Strange how little they fill a home.

There is one bag, a plastic carrier, that she has kept secret from Matthew: she places this at the bottom of the wardrobe, without looking inside. It smells of smoke, an ugly, cloying smell that sickens her if she opens it. In this bag are the oddest things: a plastic comb, the ends black-ened and melting, a square of smoky red fabric, a child's diary with a great black streak across its silver glitter front and a broken lock. Also, the most remarkable thing, and this one not damaged at all: a tiny doll in a white crispy nylon dress with silver paper wings, blonde frizzy hair and a pale face, a thin line for a mouth. A Christmas-tree fairy, intact, ironic even; the sole survivor

– that's how Lily thinks of her. Amazing what survives a fire. Alan said this many times. Not the things you might think. Books, paper even. *Never ceases to amaze me*, was what he actually said, back then. Lily likes to remember things exactly, the phrases people use, the order of the words. She writes them down sometimes, the words. This is important.

Lily is wrong about the net-curtains not twitching at their arrival. She didn't glance sideways, at flat number 2, where Joshua Larkland Senior is standing, smoking, and listening with expert ears to the sound of an engine. The engine of a black cab. Joshua once worked under the railway bridge on Richmond Road, for a firm which fixes black cabs. Cabbies are crazy fools if you ask Joshua ('arks' is how he pronounces it); they love their cabs better than their women or children. One white guy he knew used to balance a fifty pence piece on the engine while it was ticking over and wag his finger at Josh, saying: That's how I want it. Sweet as a fucking nut.

But that was a couple of years back. And that isn't the reason Josh's ears prick up now at the distinctive sound of a black cab engine arriving at midnight at Bridge House. He is listening for Daphine. Of course, she isn't due back yet, she didn't give him a time to expect her, she hasn't rung. Could be a few weeks, a few months, a year. She left last Saturday to go to Portland, to see the family, after the worst year of her life. Portland, Jamaica. ('Porty', Josh calls it, but not lately. He's not been talking much, lately.) He has a letter, the one letter from Daphine he's received in twenty years of married life, but he hasn't got round to reading it yet.

What he sees, under the amber light above the

entrance to Bridge House, is a white girl, wiry, boyish, must be around twenty, with short tufts of blonde hair and a denim jacket, helping a boy from the cab, and then bundling him and two cases into the entrance-way. As she walks under the light and, for a moment, directly into Joshua's line of vision, he sees her lit up like a hare caught in headlights, and sees that he is wrong about her age; her face is a little too set to be so young, she has a small upturned nose, a thin line for a mouth. A glint of silver at each ear. He lets the curtain swing shut. He finishes the joint, and stubs it carefully out in the silver ashtray, on Daphine's side of the bed. She doesn't like him smoking, especially spliffs. He wafts his hand around the bedroom, fetches the Fresh Pine air-freshener from the kitchen, gives the air a generous squirt. Then he rinses the ashtray under the sink and polishes it with one of Daphine's brand new dusters.

When he looks out again the cab has gone and there is only the sound of Julie Weaver's dog, yapping like a damn-blasted maniac.

Lily needs to check if the phone is working so she phones Brenda and Bob.

'Oh hello love, thank goodness, I thought you might have rung last night when you first got in . . .' Brenda's anxiety raises instant hackles.

'It was late. The electricity didn't come on until this morning.'

'Oh, is it on now then? So, how's things, how's Matthew doing? What's the house like?'

'Flat. The flat's fine. Bit empty, but it'll be fine. Well Mum, I just needed to check the phone, I've got such a lot to do this morning . . .'

'Okay then, love. Your father wants a quick word – Bob, here's our Lily . . .'

Lily holds the phone away from her ear while Bob booms at her, various instructions, practical matters, setting up a direct debit to pay the services, that kind of thing. In the background she hears Brenda saying to Bob, why did they have to go so far, that's what I want to know, there are perfectly nice places near East Keswick; the council were perfectly happy to rehouse her locally, if she'd wanted. Her parents have the habit, preserved throughout her childhood, of holding a conversation with each other at the same time as talking to Lily and behaving as if Lily can hear only one of the conversations, the one they direct at her. She would like to answer their questions, she feels like bursting in with *I'll tell you why I had to go so far* but since they aren't addressed to her, there never seems to be the right moment.

She finally manages to finish the conversation by letting Matthew speak for a while, leaving him in the living room trying to bite the phone cord while Nannie asks him if his wobbly tooth is out yet.

Lily calculates, as she waits in the kitchen for the kettle to boil, that in her entire life (and that's twenty-five years of it) she has only spent two weeks living on her own, that is, without another adult present, and that they were the two weeks leading up to the fire.

When she was eleven years old Lily dreamed of living in London. She would go to sleep in her overwarm purple bedroom, mentally taking the road to the Boston Spa roundabout, that led to the A1. If she listened hard enough, past the sound of the owl hooting and Bob's snoring, she could hear trucks in the distance rolling towards London and she knew how easy it would be for a girl like Lily – a small girl that men at Bob's work called 'poppet' and 'darling' – to hitch a lift with one of these truck drivers, climb right up high in their smoky cabs, glow with joy on the black plastic seat beside them like a jittery yellow candle flame.

Of course, she knew better than to let slip any of these thoughts to Brenda. Brenda told Lily from as soon as Lily could remember that she is *her most precious darling child*, that Brenda lost two babies before Lily came along, and although this confused Lily, wondering for a long time where Brenda lost them, she got the message, the very strong message, that it was her solemn duty to take care of herself so that Brenda didn't lose any more.

Lily was a tiny girl, always a tiny girl, a good head and shoulders smaller than her classmates, easily intimidated by them. Her favourite book in primary school was *Thumbelina*; at breaktime when Miss Hansom sent the children to the book corner with the soapy-tasting milk and the soggy straws to suck on, *Thumbelina* was what Lily picked up, settled down with. The book across her knees was huge and flat, precarious to balance. The tiny girl in the story floated along in her walnut boat, then was proposed to by the ugly mole, who seemed well-meaning in the beginning but turned out to really want to keep her in his dark underworld with him. Eventually, Thumbelina was rescued by the swallow, a big blue bird taking up the whole page in the illustration, who swooped off with Thumbelina, with Lily, into the wide sky, to another life.

Always got her head in a book, our Lily. Or in the clouds. Lily heard this as a criticism, her parents suggesting she was in some way not right, different from them. Bob would take her to the library, at her insistence, but he would wait outside, whistling, shifting from one foot to the other, while Lily lost herself in Mrs Pepperpot, finally tapping on the library window, calling *Cmon lass* in a disgruntled tone until she ran out, hugging her choices. Books, not just the reading of them, but the feel of them; hard, their sharp corners, their scent of musty paper, the smudged and creased pages where other children's sticky fingers had traced storylines, were Lily's joy, Lily's lifeline, in her hushed existence at home, navigating the carefully phrased perimeter of Bob's world, Bob's version of things; tiptoeing outside Brenda's sickly bedroom.

Her fantasies of London were delicious, illicit, fed by books and cobbled together with images from *Blue Peter*. She always pictured herself on the top deck of a double-decker bus, feeding pigeons in Trafalgar Square, or strolling around Bloomsbury, the British Museum, staring at the mummies. London would be colourful, busy, lots of people, big old buildings. A bit like York only dirtier and with more strangers.

So now she's finally here and the guilt about Brenda is heady and intoxicating and though she couldn't say this to her mother she would like to say look, you were wrong: I'm charmed, nothing can touch me. I've survived a fire and losing a husband and here I am *right as rain*, as Bob would say.

'Come on, let's go out and do some exploring . . .' Lily suggests to Matthew when she puts the phone down, already holding out his coat to him. Matthew allows Lily to push his arms into the sleeves, keeping them stiff as wooden coat-hangers, and submits to his woolly hat, regarding Lily all the time in silence, chewing the plastic toggle on his coat.

'It'll be fun!' Lily insists, picking up her keys and nudging him towards the front door.

The morning is crisp, bright sunlight, cool. Out on the Flanders Estate, a couple of children, about

Matthew's age, are leaning from one of the first floor flats, throwing empty cans on to the roof of a car below. Matthew sticks his tongue out at them and they pull faces back. Music thumps from one of the other flats and the smell of something spicy floats over to them. Lily holds Matthew's hand tightly, her other hand reaching for a cigarette. They pass several people: adults hustling children into cars, an old man pushing a shopping trolley, a young man starting up a motorbike. Lily has a blank, casual expression, deliberately contrived to look as if she is ready to speak, to say 'Now then,' if necessary or whatever the Southern equivalent is. She soon realises that no one is going to greet her and relieved, concentrates on enjoying her cigarette.

Matthew kicks a bottle-top on the ground in front of him, aiming for the concrete bollards which dot the pavements in an attempt to stop cars parking on them (a failed one, Lily observes, as several have been knocked down and broken). Lily notices that every car she's seen in London has dents on it. She reads a sign saying *No Ball Games*, and *Liquid Petroleum Cylinders Must Not Be Brought Into This Building*.

Leaving the Estate, she notices that there are trees, that every street is lined with cars and every road has speed bumps. She notices buddleias in some of the gardens and a sign on a lamppost saying *Voting for Mans law is a Sin (Haram), The Voice, The Eyes and The Ears of The Muslims*. She notices Shari's Caribbean and English Restaurant. A kebab house. Mini-cab, dry cleaner. Ray's Video Club. Kayani's Food and Wine. It is compulsive with Lily, the reading of signs. A cataloguing, sifting, left over from her time in the library. Posters with *Vote for Diane Abbott* on them. Eden's Perm Centre for Hair Relaxing. Lennie's Hot Wings.

On the High Street Matthew spies a gobstopper machine outside one of the shops – 'Can I have one, can I?' – and Lily searches for a coin. The multicoloured sweets shine mouthwateringly while Lily searches all her pockets and the bottom of her handbag. Matthew stands very still, his eyes glued to the gobstoppers. The sweet machine, a glass dispenser, is covered in chains, a big heavy chain, with a padlock on it, something he never saw at home, or at Nannie's. Lily finally finds twenty pence and lets Matthew put it in, but after all that the machine is broken, no red ball of gum rolls out.

'Oh Mum, can't you get me some in Marks Expensive?'

'Marks and Spencer's doesn't sell gum.'

But she doesn't want Matthew complaining all the way home. She finds a newsagent, buys him some Bazooka Joe and they walk back in the direction of the flats with him sucking on it, making noisy snapping attempts to blow bubbles. Matthew notices a sign with a drawing of a fire engine, and he reads the word *Fire* on the ground in front of him, embedded in one of the flagstones. *Fire Something Beginning with H* but he can't read that word. He makes an effort to step right on it as they pass. *If you step on a crack, you'll fall and break your back, if you step on a leaf, you'll fall and break your teeth.* He doesn't know the one for stepping on fire. If you step on a fire, you'll fall into the fire. No, that's not right. He can't ask Lily, although he knows she's good at making up rhymes. Nannie told him to be a good boy and not to mention the fire or Daddy to Lily. He snaps his gum, finds a pebble to kick along in front of him, but the rhyme keeps going in his head anyway.

If you step on a fire, you'll turn into a liar.

Joshua is not watching Lily, but of course, given that his is a ground floor flat, he can't help but be aware in the mornings and afternoons of her comings and goings. Especially given that the morning ones are so noisy. The child's wailing echoes through the lift shaft as the lift descends and when the girl and child emerge on to the estate from Bridge House, the howls reach fever-pitch. Poor little pic'nee. Obviously hates school. Then he hears the girl's voice, the strange Northern accent rising and falling in exasperation, not the words but the tone; at first calming, then cajoling, then finally vexed, desperate.

One morning the boy takes off. Makes a dash for the tree in the middle of the estate, flings his arms around it, the screaming is enough to lick your head off. The odd part is watching her. She pauses for a second, then bolts after her son. Joshua moves closer to the window, pulls the curtain aside a fraction further. He is astonished to feel his body respond in the oddest way to the sight of the girl running. He thinks she is going to hit the child. His mouth drops open slightly, the jaw tense. He is aware of a rising discomfort that he can't make sense of; he adjusts himself in his shorts, lets the curtain drop.

Skinny white girl. She look like a boy. Joshua is increasingly late for work and he has to admit that he waits until Lily has left the building before he gets his tools and his work gear together and heads off for the garage behind the police station. Without Daphine to put his elaborate packed lunches together he has stopped avoiding meat, or salt. He has taken to eating at Jerk Chicken or even McDonald's and this last few weeks he's been going through money like water. He is not aware that he is depressed. *I don't care if Daphine never come. Don't feel no way if me lose me job.*

There is still the letter and he knows he will have to read it eventually. He has opened it now, seen Daphine's large writing, recognised her attempt to write clearly for his benefit, or the benefit of whoever it is she expects to read it to him. He can recognise his own name, that is, Daphine's name for him: Landy. The name he had back home, the one people here had never heard, the one his mother used for him. The problem with Daphine being in Jamaica is that images of it keep cropping up for him and they are not the wanted ones, not the expected ones. The long dusty road to school, the trees with the cocoa-beans he reached up and plucked, chewed on, the taste rich, strong as coffee and not sweet, but something else, deep powdery chocolate taste and powerful: it makes him think of Neville, how he never even took Neville to Jamaica and for how long he thought he had all the time in the world for that. Josh shakes those thoughts, he literally shakes his head, shakes Neville out of it. He's late for work. *The girl have a nice backside, that's all.* Apart from that, she's nothing special.

Daytimes are fine, daytimes are sustained by Lily's excitement, by a prickly energy, by being busy, keeping herself cheerful in the way that Bob always did, whistling on his way to the Brewery in Tadcaster where he worked for years, or sometimes walking Lily to school, holding her hand and whispering in her ear, *Keep y'sen cheerful lass, that's the way*.

Night-times are different. After Matthew has fallen asleep, after she has washed up, tidied up, she is seldom tired enough to fall asleep herself. She could phone someone, but she doesn't want to. She has books, a newspaper, which she flicks through. Finally she makes herself cocoa, lies in her T-shirt on her bed, vaguely comforted by the sound of Matthew's breathing, by the traffic and voices she hears outside, the thump of music from the flat below.

She dreads closing her eyes. She is afraid. Of remembering Alan. Of feeling things again. Or more specifically, of landing in the grip of her recurrent nightmare. It's not of the fire, she would have expected to dream about the fire, instead it's something banal – she dreams of taking Matthew on a trip to Mother Shipton's Cave in Knaresborough. This is not particularly scary, she went there herself as a child, she even remembers her mother saying she visited as a child too – it's a popular Yorkshire attraction – but in real life Lily never got around to taking Matthew.

In the dream the cave is longer, darker, there are no admission fees. Lily leans over the dropping well, with the other visitors, dutifully making her wish, hearing the drip drip of water at her ear, smelling the green dank rock, reading the signs forbidding visitors to drop gloves or handkerchiefs into the petrifying well, a favourite trick of her mother's generation. Then suddenly Matthew is falling, or he slipped, or Lily dropped him, she doesn't know which; he is already stiff, the petrifying has happened in an instant with no time to prevent it and instead of a living child, a crying, protesting, frightened child, Lily pulls out a slim piece of rock, shaped like a gingerbread biscuit, or Matthew, faintly green. She pulls him out, she dips him in again, but it's all too late; his form remains the same; solid, flat, only some indentations in places where the nose and eyes should be.

She always wakes from the dream sweating and tangled in the bed sheets, with the sensation of having dived down, over and over to try and bring up Matthew in another form, but without success; with a sense of knowing again something terrible that she always knew; here is her son held in her arms, a stone child, something ancient and unavoidable: a gargoyle.

To keep herself from sleeping, from dreaming, from remembering Alan, Lily is writing a list. Listing all the things she lost in the fire, all the possessions she had in the world, apart from the smoky bag of charred remnants, apart from the new things she has brought to Bridge House. She is up to three thousand six hundred and fifty-four. Big things and small things. How many things does a person amass in twenty-five years? The list-making is compulsive, both soothing and agitating at the same time, like pacing a room. She has filled one notebook already, she is not remembering in any particular order, just as they come. The essential thing is not to miss anything. Tea set from Argos catalogue. A chest of drawers. About sixteen pairs of cotton knickers from British Home Stores, with the lace mostly peeling. The answerphone, also from Argos. Axminster carpet from Thorp Arch Trading Estate. Navy spotted curtains that she made herself. A gold christening bracelet she wore as a baby and Brenda gave her when she was pregnant, in case Matthew was a girl. Six rustic looking brown cups on a plastic mug tree. Cuddly toy. Her wedding ring. When something snags at her she feels the bump but carries right on, like running an iron over buttons on a shirt.

So as not to wake Matthew, she bends the lamp on the bedside table to spotlight her list. Now they have bedside tables. Cheap painted wood, second-hand from a shop on Wishley Street called the Secons Shop. (Lily finds this hand-painted sign embarrassing. All the while standing in the shop paying for the tables and arranging delivery, she has to control an urge to bring the mistake to the owner's attention. She crushes these thoughts and tries consciously to replace them with others. *Don't be silly. What do they care?*)

The music from the flat below is thudding on, something about a train being bound to glory; the muddy undertones, not exactly the tune. She glances over at Matthew, only his hair sprouting from the sleeping bag, marvelling at his ability to sleep through anything. Stepping to the window in her T-shirt and knickers, she pushes the stiff metal-framed window wide open. It's not gospel but a kind of reggae she's unfamiliar with; she can hear it properly now. Something about a brand new Second Hand girl . . .

A cool delight finally creeps over her skin, cancelling the dread of her bad dream like icing covering mistakes on a cake. *Here I am, far from home, and nobody really knows where I am. I can do anything I want. I can start all over. There's no Alan, no Bob to tell me to take care, nothing to lose, nobody to please: just myself.* The thought is exhilarating, it zooms up her spine like electricity, making her shiver, making her draw in her breath in large gulps, reach for a sweater to wrap around herself.

Wishley School has the benefit of being close to the Flanders Estate, part of the playground can be seen from the flat, at least that's what Lily tells Matthew. When she tries this, however, a high brick wall around the Victorian school building means that she can only see one particular far corner, which has a single child in it. She wonders whether to suggest to Matthew that he should play in that precise area, but decides against it.

Enrolment was an adventure for Lily, she's never done that kind of official thing before, at least not on her own.

The headteacher is a woman called Ms Brightman, surprisingly young, chic, slim in a tight black and white skirt and DM shoes. She sits in the swivelling office chair opposite Lily and Matthew, reading the notes on a file on the desk in front of her. The office smells of strong perfume and plastic chairs.

'And Matthew is five, is that right, Mrs Waite?'

'Nearly six,' says Lily, politely.

'And he's already reached Key Stage 1, Level 3, it says here, for reading and maths. Remarkable.' Ms Brightman leans forward, raises her voice slightly as if talking to a deaf child.

'You're a clever boy then Matthew, is that right?'

Lily grins at Matthew in the seat beside her. Matthew chews on the collar of his sweater. He is dressed in the oddest outfit; the shoes are fine, they fit, they look new enough, apart from the different coloured laces, but it's the trousers, which are actually girl's leggings, dark green and baggy at the crotch, and a pale blue polo-neck sweater, with the sleeves way too long, that make him look strange. A tubby little vicar. Lily makes a mental note; as soon as she gets her Income Support book she must get him some decent clothes.

'Do you have family in this area of London?' Ms Brightman leans forward to ask this, pen poised. Lily wonders if she would actually write down the answer.

'No. It's all new to us,' says Lily, cheerfully.

Ms Brightman smiles. A professional smile. There is a little pause. Lily looks round the office, reading notices. *The Child Protection Act: Teacher's Checklist. Multi-Faith Assemblies: A Guideline.* Questions hover around them, Lily sees that Ms Brightman's pen is still poised. Little sounds of Matthew chewing. The head-teacher clears her throat.

'So.' Ms Brightman picks up the file. 'Matthew's form teacher is Mrs Jalil. Shall we take him along there now, to 2B?'

They stand up together, nearly bumping into each other in the cramped office. Ms Brightman leads the way out. Lily glances at Matthew. He seems to have shrunk in the last five minutes, the sleeves on the jumper longer than ever. Or else he is screwing up his hands inside them, drawing clenched fists, tightening his shoulders.

'He's small for his age,' Lily offers, to no one in particular. She could do with a cigarette.

'Don't worry,' Lily whispers, putting her mouth to Matthew's ear. They follow the purposeful stride of Ms Brightman in her air-soles. The shoes might be trendy, but Lily suspects that their trendiness in something of a ruse. Ms Brightman definitely chose them for their practical merits, for their virtually inaudible rubber squeak. Lily plans to share this thought with Matthew later, try a gentle send-up. *Ms Brightman, Private Dick.* The corridor is tiled, one wall decorated with a long caterpillar of paper plates. On each paper plate is a poem about food and beneath that a sign: *Visiting Poet: Michael Rosen.* The other wall has drawings in felt-pen of children's hands and the sign: *Welcome to Wishley Primary School. We speak twenty-six different languages.* Stuck over the hands are a lot of words which presumably are 'Welcome' in twenty-six languages. Lily recognises French.

Ms Brightman steps forward to open the door to class 2B. Matthew, who up until now has been tightly squeezing Lily's hand, suddenly breaks free and darts past both women, rushing back along the corridor.

Ms Brightman makes a small sound, a kind of surprised breathing out.

'Matthew!' Lily shrieks.

He speeds down the corridor back towards the Head's office and the door out of the school. Lily has to run fast to catch him. She snatches at the blue sweater, finds his arm thinner than she remembers, it's almost too light to catch, a piece of string, a strand of spaghetti. This frightens her suddenly – how did he become thin, usually so solid, plump even, one tug and an image of her child spins before her like a spool of string, unravelling . . .

'Matthew, Matthew, love, calm down, come on, come on, ssshhh now . . .'

He's crying, huge noisy sobs, the kind of sound much younger children make; howling. The hairs stand up on Lily's arms, her nipples prick up, it's primitive, she almost expects other children in the school to join in like wolves, sparking from classroom to classroom. She tries to hug Matthew but his body is rigid, he rests his dark head on her shoulder as she crouches beside him and she feels the dampness of his open mouth seeping into her jumper, she feels his teeth touch flesh through the wool.

'Now Matthew,' Lily begins, 'don't bite.' A warning tone.

She feels his teeth again, the beginning of pressure.

Ms Brightman has caught up, appears beside them in a puff of perfume. 'Now Matthew. It's not that bad. Mummy will be here for you at three thirty. Be a big boy now, I know you're very clever for your age . . .'

Matthew sobs afresh. The sounds muffled in Lily's shoulder come out as burblings. Lily wonders if Ms Brightman has notes on the Waite family, she wonders how much to say.

'It's hard for him. A new school, new friends . . .'

Ms Brightman nods, smoothing down her neat skirt.

'Yes, yes, I'm sure. Come along now Matthew, let's try again, shall we? Come and meet Mrs Jalil, your teacher. Mummy can stay for a little while . . .'

Matthew's sobs are dying to a shudder, he is mollified a little, and allows himself to be led back to the class-room, hand tight in Lily's. It's his lightness which is disturbing, the image of the string child. Now she has pictured it she can't shake it off. She used to make them herself as a girl; little dolls of string or wool, the knack was in the winding and tying but they were bright colours at least, you couldn't lose them. The picture she has of Matthew as a wool boy is the blue of his sweater, this pale egg-shell blue, a colour like a vein, like the whites of an eye; or a bruise fading.

'This is Matthew,' Ms Brightman announces, loudly, to the startled teacher in her small round glasses and long violet headscarf, as they make their second entrance to the classroom. Mrs Jalil tries her best to smile as if nothing has happened.

'And this is class 2B. Say hello to your new classmate. This is Matthew Waite.'

'Hello Matthew!' thirty perky voices yell, not quite in unison, and Lily hears football crowds, she hears her own schooldays, and shudders.

Two for Joy

Dreaming, waking again, finding sleep impossible, Lily is thinking of her husband, Alan, remembering. A week into their marriage and her astonishment when, still lying in bed, nursing a cup of tea that he has brought her, she watches Alan step into his jeans, put his uniform into his bag, preparing to leave for work.

He catches her stare, sits down on the bed beside her.

'Well you didn't think I could stay home for ever, you and me like bunnies in a warren?'

'But so soon, it's only a week—'

'I did well to get that, love. We're short of lads at the Station just now, you know that.'

'But the night shift, then, why do you have to do the night shift! You should tell them I'm pregnant, I worry about you . . .'

'Lily, nothing is going to happen to me. Play a bit of snooker, drink too much coffee, probably one call out to some late-night chip pan boiling over . . .'

e tea cold and passed to the bedside table, she
away from him, buries her face in the pillow. Lily
ls foolish, but she can't stop this panic, the flames that
url at the edges of Alan when she pictures him at work,
the smoke that forms in a deep obscuring cloud, any
more than she can stem her anger at being left, left in
bed, on her own, so soon after she thought she'd secured
Alan for ever.

Hearing the creak of Alan's knees as he rises to stand,
she struggles to sit up, pull herself together.

'I wish you had another job.' Her voice sulky, her
eyes fixed on his chest, the dark hairs curling at the neck
of the white vest.

'Down the mine in Balby you mean, like me Dad?'

'No not that of course. Something safe. Working in
a bank.'

He smiles at her, tucking his T-shirt into his jeans,
buckling his belt.

'Always armed robbers you know, always that.'

Lily doesn't smile. She flings back the covers, hops
out of bed in her nightie, plants a kiss on his neck.

'Don't try to be a hero, that's all. I don't need
that . . .' she whispers, her mouth brushing against the
bristle on his chin.

'And I thought that was what you married me for!'

He's grinning and swinging his bag off the bed,
closing the bedroom door gently behind him and Lily
hears each tread of his steps down the stairs, his bag
bumping against the banister, the front door closing. To
her annoyance, she can even hear him whistling.

Casual. Cavalier, even. How casual we all are, Lily
thinks, until it happens to us. And then what? She tries
saying it to herself, finding better words, seeing if it will
sink in. *We were in a fire. Our house burned.* We had a

fire. The house nearly burned down. Someone called the fire brigade. We were in a serious fire. We lost everything.

But it's no good. She can't believe in the danger, precisely because she survived it. The experience is ordinary, malleable, a story. It's less real than it ever was. Nothing about it has touched her.

Lily remembers something else but she doesn't know if it is real or a photograph or a story she has been told. She is in her pushchair, she is rolling on wheels between Brenda on the one side, Bob on the other. Tied to the pram is a flame-coloured balloon, bobbing on its string in front of Lily's face.

The balloon dances. Sometimes a wind tugs at the string and jerks it close to her face, so close that she can smell it, the strange rubber, birthday smell. She knows the balloon wants to be free. It strains and strains at its string, batting the sides of the pushchair in anger, a flickering, lively, swirling thing. A poppy. A fierce goblin. A thing protesting at being tied. She hears its voice, the odd squeaky sound when it rubs up against something. Lily is frightened for it. Brenda is frightened too, she has told Lily to *hold on tight to that balloon now girl otherwise you'll lose it*, and then it is Bob who comes up with the idea of tying it to the handle of the pram, reassuring her. *There now. Safe now*, Bob tells her.

Bob and Brenda walk on together, chatting. Bob is keeping Brenda company. Brenda would never walk Lily alone.

The balloon reminds Lily of the butterfly in the *Thumbelina* story. Tied to the lily-leaf by a tiny girl who wants to keep it, experience it, smile at it, for ever. That is, until a huge bird comes down and plucks her from the leaf, leaving the butterfly behind. She has to watch the white wings flutter helplessly on the green leaf, as it spins away from her, twirling downstream, feeling a great sadness to see that, despite all her efforts, it is gone from her.

The balloon and the butterfly, the red and the white, bat gently at Lily's childhood, produce desire in her. A hot taste in her mouth, the taste of wanting, the impossibility of ever really having, or keeping. Everything lovely, magical, desired, floats away from you. You have to hold tighter, tighter, as tight as you can. She's no idea why she thinks about this, or where the stories are from, only that she does.

She has dropped Matthew at school, she is returning to her flat with arms full of a bag of washing from the launderette on Wishley Street. The lift arrives at her floor with its familiar thump and the grey metal doors slide open. Lily is startled to see a small box – a shoebox in fact – right outside the door to her flat. Her first impression is a bizarre one: she thinks of a hamster, a small creature. It's because the box is so deliberate, so placed-there, the way a child – Matthew – would put something if he wanted her to notice it.

She stares at it, feels for her door key in her pocket. Inside the flat she dumps the bag of washing on the bed, comes back outside the front door to stare at the box. It has a lid, firmly closed. Grey cardboard. She gives it a feeble nudge with her foot. There is no sign of any kind of animal bedding or droppings. She crouches down to knee level and sniffs. The box is from Clarke's. There is a Clarke's on the High Street, she intends to go there at the weekend to get Matthew some shoes. The box smells clean and new; the floor outside the flats does not.

She picks it up and carries it, a little stiffly, into the flat. It feels reasonably light, but not empty, something is definitely inside it. She sets it down on the kitchen table, gingerly, as if there were a kitten inside, hitches herself up on to the counter-top, and stares at the box, swinging her legs. Her heart is ticking like an overwound clock. She has no cigarettes. Outside, the pigeons purr on the ledge of the balcony, aeroplanes draw white scribble over the envelope square of blue sky. In a while she should go out there and hang the washing out. Matthew is at school, not back for another six hours. It might be a bomb, a mistake, not for her, nothing. She should throw it away.

She jumps down from the kitchen counter and flips open the lid.

Inside are two Kit-Kats, two Mars Bars and two bags of salt and vinegar crisps. Walkers. Nothing else. Lily takes each item out, slowly, feeling faintly absurd, examining them for clues. She almost laughs, but she doesn't, a laugh forms but stops short of erupting.

But it is absurd and worse than that: stupid. Her heart is not ticking now, it sinks to the floor like a wet sock. There's no way she can eat any of this – for God's sake, she doesn't know where it's been, or worse, what it means – but she has no idea what to do with it. She puts the lid back on the box. Her temples are aching, now she would like to cry, she would like to fling herself on the bed along with Matthew's T-shirts and underpants and sob herself silly, but she doesn't do that either, that would be ridiculous. She picks up the box again, puts it in one of the empty kitchen cupboards. A shoebox of confec-tionery. Bizarre, bizarre. Who would give that to her, leave it there for her, or for Matthew? And why, what's the point? She decides she is desperate for cigarettes. She grabs her purse and her key and doesn't bother with a coat; she leaves the washing scattered on the bed.

Lily's life is bordered by school picking-up times. Book ends: a nine a.m. start, three thirty finish. As the school is virtually opposite the estate that means leaving the house at 8.55 a.m. and 3.25 p.m., making sure the time spent hanging out with the other parents and child-minders is kept to a minimum. Today, it's twenty-six minutes past three when Lily calls the lift outside her door. Once inside, the lift also stops at the floor just below Lily's and a young woman in a long leather coat steps in, pushing a baby in a buggy. The lift is filled with a strong perfume; something familiar, Lily thinks it's Calvin Klein's CK One, her friend Kate used to wear that.

'Hi,' the woman says. The lift doors shut but the lift doesn't move and both women at once press the button for the ground floor; Lily's finger gets there last. Lily smiles at the baby, she knows this is required of her.

'Hello,' she says, in her voice for babies, a little high-pitched, sing-song. 'All wrapped up in your furry coat. Don't you look sweet?'

The child, a girl of creamy-brown skin and huge eyes, stares unblinkingly at Lily. Lily feels like a fraud.

'She's bloody teething. Dribbling everywhere,' remarks her mother, mopping at the child's spotless face with a tissue. The lift bumps to the ground. Lily holds the *Doors Open* button while the other woman struggles out with the buggy.

'You moved in upstairs didn't you?' the young woman asks.

'Yes. Couple of weeks ago.'

'You on your own?'

'No, I have my son.'

'That's what I mean. You on your own with the boy?'

'Oh. Yes.'

'Me too.'

The young woman seems pleased to have established the link and pushes the buggy alongside Lily, both heading in the direction of the path leading from the estate to Wishley Street. Talk about the kids, Lily is thinking, it's an obvious route to making friends but one which she finds difficult, because she doesn't chiefly think of herself as a mother, it isn't the first thing she finds in common with other women.

'How old's your son?' the young woman breaks in.

'Five. He's at Wishley School.'

'Oh yeah. My niece goes there. Shamilla. I'm picking her up for my sister. Right little madam.'

Lily coughs, already out of small talk. They are standing on the pavement waiting to cross the road towards the school and the number 26 bus is passing in front of them, drowning whatever it is that her neighbour is saying, so that as they cross Lily asks her to repeat it. The woman, who has a round open face, freckles and the longest eyelashes Lily has ever seen, is grinning at her.

'Did you get your present? What was it, a pair of shoes?'

'What do you mean?' Lily wonders if her voice sounds alarmed, she is startled to discover that the other woman knows about the box.

'I saw Josh put a box outside your door. Present for you. Must have a crush on you.'

'Who's Josh?'

'The guy downstairs. Flat number 2. Black guy. He's

married but I ain't seen his wife lately. I think she might of left him. They had a son. It was terrible. He got killed outside the Co-op, mugged or a fight or something. About a year ago.'

'How awful. God . . .'

'Broad daylight. Someone stabbed him.'

Lily walks in silence for a moment. She has never lived close to someone who has had a child murdered. Or any relative murdered, come to that.

'Oh. It was Josh who left me the chocolate? You saw him did you?'

They arrive at the school yard and the woman nods to several of the other mothers, but continues talking to Lily. She laughs at the last question.

'Tell the truth I saw him go up the stairs to your flat. I thought, fuckin' hell, she's a fast worker. But he came straight back down. So I thought I'd have a look. Wondered what he'd been carrying. I saw the box. But I didn't open it, honest.'

'That's okay. I'd have been curious myself,' Lily assures her.

She is wondering at the bit about being a fast mover. The young woman is pretty, with a large mouth skilfully lined in browny-pink lipstick; it occurs to Lily with a jolt of alarm that she may be competing with her. Perhaps she fancies this Josh person, whoever he is?

'Anyway, it was a weird present. A few Kit-Kats and Mars Bars. It's hardly a box of Belgian chocolates, is it?' Lily adds.

An attempt to down-play things, to level the pitch. A well-practised female trick, Lily thinks, even as she is doing it: rubbishing gains to fend off aggression from other women.

To her surprise, however, the other woman doesn't

stick to the rules. 'Oh I don't know. He's a nice guy Josh. Flat number 2 if you want to say thanks to him.'

Lily stares down at the ground, feeling shy. The bell to finish school still hasn't gone and now the walled playground is filling up; huddles of women with pushchairs and straggling toddlers. Also two dads, hands in pockets.

The playground is very different from the village school Matthew used to attend in East Keswick. Lily has worked out a few things. The women who slap and curse, white and black women with their Nike trainers who call their children *little bitch* or *little sod*, are not always the mothers. Sometimes they are the child-minders. The children with names like Charmaine and Chantelle and wearing the most expensive designer outfits – matching coats and hats in Dalmatian print, tiny gold earrings, shiny patent shoes, sometimes with heels – and the babies in the fancy prams stuffed into bright coloured furry envelopes so that they look like hot-water bottles, these seem to belong to the mothers on the dole; she recognises several from her estate. There is the odd black woman with dreadlocks and a child to match and wearing African prints. Their children have names like Adenike, or Tunde. There are a few Asian families who stick together, a couple of them with their faces almost entirely covered so that only their eyes are on show, something Lily saw in Leeds occasionally, but never in the village.

Then there are the children with the plain names. Fred and Frank and Jack and Stan and for the girls names like twenties trollops: Ruby and Daisy, Pearl, Holly, Alice. These are the understated children, they wear many more jumpers than the other sort, and shoes seem to be important; good leather and flat.

The bell sounds with its crazed metallic scream and the waiting parents and toddlers surge forward. It doesn't quite seem the done thing to Lily but she realises she and the woman from her estate haven't exchanged names, so before attempting to tackle the seething corridor she calls over her shoulder, 'I'm Lily by the way. My boy's Matthew.'

'I'm Sherry,' the woman calls back. She doesn't offer her child's name and the girl remains impassive, staring up at Lily from her fur-lined chariot with enormous, wide-awake eyes.

When the toddlers and adults burst forward like a spilled packet of frozen vegetables Lily recognises Mrs Jalil inside the school corridor, gesturing to her, over several heads.

'Could I have a word, Mrs Waite?'

The teacher motions Lily into the book room, just off the corridor. Matthew is trundling his way towards the coat-peg with his name on, keen to get home. Lily tells him she won't be a minute, and he sits with a plonk on top of his lunch-box, biting the toggle on his coat.

Mrs Jalil is slightly out of breath. A tiny moustache of sweat is visible on her upper lip and her large brown eyes dart anxiously between corridor, children and the books surrounding them.

'I am rather worried about Matthew,' Mrs Jalil dives in, with her strong London accent and her lilting, up-and-down tones.

Lily is searching for something sensible to say, but the teacher folds her arms across her large bosom and hurries on.

'He's been here nearly three weeks now and he just isn't settling at all. He only wants to sit in the book corner and talk to himself. He brings in these cards about fish and sea-creatures. He's very keen on fish and sea-creatures, isn't he? All he seems to want to do is play with them or talk about them and he isn't really mixing with the other children, in fact, he is often quite mean, terribly mean to the other children. Several times a day I must send him out of the classroom for something. Mostly for biting. He seems obsessed with biting. I've come across that before, but usually in a child much younger. I mean, he bites things, but mostly he bites people, other children. Not even hard, particularly. But hard enough.'

Mrs Jalil is quite a talker, she hasn't stopped for breath.

'I know he is a clever boy, I can tell that sometimes, from when I talk to him, his vocabulary is quite amazing and he tries really hard, you know, trying out new words he isn't sure of, but in his work he shows no sign of ability. He won't write. I can't get him to read. Mrs Waite, I've never come across a child so—'

Lily doesn't want to hear the end of this sentence. Her cheeks are burning, her bottom lip folded beneath her teeth. The hubbub outside is dying down, as most of the parents take their offspring home. The sudden quiet is unnerving; Lily lowers her voice, but the voice that comes out sounds false, unduly dramatic.

'I'm not sure if Ms Brightman passed on our – notes to you. Matthew has recently lost his father. I know he is quite – troubled. We had a fire at our home. We lost – the house was burned – it's a difficult time for him – for both of us—'

Mrs Jalil is blinking rapidly. She pushes a strand of straight hair behind one ear and smooths down the long sleeves of her dress. 'Oh,' she says in a curious, high-pitched way.

Lily holds her breath, waiting for something more. The silence is stuffy, stuffed, uncomfortable; the books feel ready to topple down on them in a room which is hardly a library, more a store room. Mrs Jalil says nothing. Her big eyes widen behind her glasses and instead of blinking hard, she is staring at Lily. Then Lily is aware suddenly of Matthew in the doorway, very small and dark, in a blistering rage, with the hood of his coat pulled down over his face.

'Well, I'll talk to Matthew about the cards, and the fish books,' Lily promises, turning around a little, smiling aimlessly at Matthew, knocking *Big Bear Little Bear* from the shelves with her bag. 'I'll make sure he doesn't sneak any cards into school tomorrow. I'll have a word with him about the biting and everything.'

She speaks as if Matthew is not in the room, standing right between them, staring hard, smouldering. Lily smiles and smiles.

'Well thanks Mrs Jalil,' she says. 'See you tomorrow. I'll talk to him. I'll try harder.'

Josh takes the stairs up to the girl's flat, not the lift. It's not that he's trying to be sneaky, there's no particular reason, he just takes the stairs. The wooden door is unpainted and she's the only one in the entire block not to have a metal security-door in front of it. He wonders whether to mention that to her, how she would take it. She might think he was trying to scare her. He knocks once, knuckles drumming a hollow rap. He puts his ear to the door. Then he realises she has a bell, so he presses hard, jamming his finger on the bell until she opens it, only a crack.

He can see one arm, some blonde hair, one bare foot

with wide, flat toes, a particularly bare foot, somehow, like a child's. He swallows hard.

'All right?' Josh says, and nods to her. Neighbourly.

'Yes thank you,' the girl says, cautiously, in her strange accent. He grins. It might be a nervous grin, maybe not. And then the boy has run down the corridor, pulled the door further open, is blinking his huge grey-blue eyes at Josh.

'What does *he* want?' the child says.

She rushes to cover for her boy's bad mouth.

'Matthew, don't be cheeky! He's our neighbour. He's just – visiting—'

Now she is forced to invite Josh in. He sees it at the same moment she opens her mouth to say, 'Um, would you like to come in?', her need to overcompensate, to squash any suggestion that his being black has anything to do with it. Comes in handy sometimes. He continues smiling to himself, gives the boy a playful tweak on the nose. Although her feet are bare, the rest of her is well covered. A thick wool sweater, down to her knees practically, and long dark leggings. She has a cigarette in one hand and draws on it as she walks down the corridor in front of him, motions him into the kitchen.

'Can I get you anything? Cup of tea? Cigarette?'

'You have a beer?'

'No, I'm sorry.'

Her eyes stray to a lone bottle of wine by the kitchen window. It's clear she's not going to mention that. She leans against the cooker, Josh pulls out a chair at her kitchen table and sits on it the wrong way round, so that he faces her, his legs jutting out on either side like the big folded legs of an insect.

'What's your name?' the boy says, standing very close to Josh, staring at his hat.

'Josh. What's yours?'

'Your hat looks like a sock. Why do you have so much hair in there?'

'Matthew!' The girl sounds nervous, like she would like to control the conversation, have it travel somewhere less personal. Josh laughs, both to show he's not offended and because he's amused, genuinely, by her discomfort.

'That's my locks, them. You want to see?'

He takes off the woolly hat and spidery hair tumbles out. The child widens his eyes, stands a little closer, as if he would like to touch.

'You get the sweets then?' Josh asks, suddenly, smiling at the girl.

Her expression is startled. He thinks she is about to say she didn't know they were from him, but then she smiles for the first time, showing all her teeth. Before she can say anything the child interrupts, his tone accusing.

'What sweets?'

'Here, Matthew. I was saving these for you.'

She opens a cupboard and hands Matthew a Kit-Kat from the shoebox inside it, closing the cupboard quickly as if she doesn't want Josh to see.

'Thank you,' she says quietly.

'You knew they were from me?'

'The girl downstairs told me. Sherry.'

'You know Sherry?'

'A little. I mean, we just met.'

An awkward silence. The girl draws noisily on her cigarette, Josh watches her, Matthew unwraps his chocolate bar.

'So what's your mum's name?' Josh asks Matthew, realising that he still doesn't know it.

'Lily,' the boy says, his mouth full of chocolate.

'Well, Lily, I will have a cigarette, if you're still offering,' Josh says, his eyes fixed on Lily's mouth, a small O shape, blowing smoke.

She offers him the packet. Her hand is shaking, but her voice is controlled: 'Go ahead. Help yourself.'

He accepts a cigarette and she places the ashtray (an empty household matchbox) on the kitchen table.

'You settling in okay?' Josh asks, conversationally.

Truth is, he thought it would be easier than this. He figured her for the chatty type, a bit lonely, keen for company. You're getting rusty, old man, for true, he says to himself. He was never one to be lost for words.

'What do you do? You on your own? You working?'

'I'm – I don't do anything much at the moment. I suppose I'll sign on the dole . . .'

Josh sighs, without meaning to. Something slumps in him. What the fuck's he doing here? He'd better get to the point and quickly, before he loses it all together.

'Is your mum smart then, Matthew?' he asks the boy, resurrecting his playful tone with some effort.

'Yes,' the child answers. 'My mum's a brainbox. She's a librarian.'

'That right?'

'I *was* a librarian. I worked in Boston Spa Lending library – it's a really a library that lends to other libraries. Have you heard of it?'

'Boston. In Lincolnshire?'

'No, Yorkshire.'

'No.'

Josh lights his cigarette. He takes time over this. Then he reaches into his back pocket, unfolds a piece of paper. He coughs, several times, and Lily goes to fetch him a glass of water. He gets a waft of her when she comes back, she smells smoky of course, but beneath that he can still smell clean hair, her newly-bathed skin, baby talc, something like that. He doesn't know what it is but she smells encouraging, like a fresh sheet of paper.

'I have a letter,' Josh states, looking up at Lily. 'I need new glasses. I don't have them as yet. Maybe you can read it for me?'

Lily glances uncertainly at the blue airmail paper, thin as tissue from many creasings. The child, Matthew, has picked up his Gameboy and the funny little beepings that pass for a tune fill the long pause between Josh and Lily.

Finally, Lily says awkwardly, 'It looks a bit personal.'

'It is personal. That's why I ask *you* to read it.'

He keeps his eyes on Lily's, his hand rests calmly on the letter, like a leaf that just fell there. Lily stares into his pale palm, creased with its map of dark lines. She pictures his palm like the letter, folding and unfolding many times. Josh is wondering how it got to feel so sad in here, so quickly. One simple request, man. That's all. This flat is too still, too empty. Thank fuck for Matthew, sitting high on the counter-top, banging his shoes against the kitchen cupboards in time with his Gameboy, his little tongue darting rhythmically at the corner of his mouth.

'Okay, then.' Lily pulls up a second kitchen chair, sits down beside Josh. She glances up at Matthew.

'You want me to read it now?'

'That would be the general idea . . .'

My Dear Landy,

Hoping this letter finds you well and looking after yourself. I have been to see Mark and the kids and everybody is doing fine. It is good to see everyone and have some comfort. Lord knows, I had little of that this last year. Landy I have to tell you. I don't know when I will be coming back to London. For a long time I didn't have my head screwed on to my body. Now I have. Don't feel bad Landy. I keep my ticket open.

Your loving wife, Daphine.

Josh is staring down at the table, nodding. He glances up in surprise at the lines 'your loving wife Daphine'.

'That all she say?'

'Yes.'

'What date she have?'

'September 2nd.'

'A month ago,' he says, bitterly.

Matthew, increasingly annoyed at not being the centre of attention, is singing 'Return of the Mac' at the top of his voice. Josh doesn't appear to hear him. He raises his eyes from the table, stares instead at the letter.

'What address she give?'

'It's just a post office, Portland, Jamaica. That's all. You haven't written back to her, then?'

Josh wonders if she's testing him, or if she really hasn't got it yet.

'No,' he answers, giving her the benefit of the doubt.

'I'm hungry!' Matthew squawks, jumping down from the counter-top. The pale blue cupboard, newly painted by the council, is now zig-zagged with black scuff-marks from his shoes.

'I should go.' Josh stands up. He puts his hat back on, stuffing the locks into the knitted circle and he takes care to stand tall, to pull his shoulders back. But the hand he holds out to Lily for the letter is trembling. He folds it back into the pocket of his jeans. 'Thank you Lily. Be seing you, Matthew. Be a good boy now, for your mother.'

Lily follows him down the corridor to the front door. She is thinking: I love the way he says Matthew. Like a sneeze. She, too, is noticing the smell of him, something familiar, something exotic. When he took off his hat, she smelled warm hair, a kind of oil. His mood has altered, his disappointment is palpable and he makes no attempt to disguise it.

'Any time you need me to read something, if I'm around, that's fine. Just ask,' Lily offers boldly, feeling responsible somehow, taking on the disappointment as, in some odd way, her fault.

He runs a glance over her body, grins at her. But even Lily can tell, he's playing a part, it's a role he can choose if he wants to; his heart isn't in it. She closes the door carefully behind him, chases Matthew down the corridor towards the bedroom.

'Did you see his hair, did you see his hair!' Matthew yells.

She knows she should admonish him, but she is silent, gently helping her son into his pyjamas, wishing she had one last cigarette so she could go smoke it out on the balcony. She would like to stand there, staring over at the tops of cars, at the bracelet of lights from the city, at the blinking tower she's suddenly remembered the name of. Canary Wharf. Another bird. How fitting. This far up, that's all you can see, all you can think of. Birds and aeroplanes and other people's lives.

Alan is *dead handsome*. Lily's exact words to her girlfriend, Sue, in the pub in the village the first night she sees him. Dark, tall, broad shoulders; strong nose, big chin, everything in the right proportion. Sue agrees, they put their heads together, one blonde and the other brown, they always make a stir in this pub, where the customers are mostly darts players and old men drinking stout. Two glasses of Pernod and lemonade wobble perilously on their tiny mats between them. Lily shrieks as Sue whispers *What about the uniform?*

Alan takes a shine to Lily, that's clear enough. Sits down at the table, puts his beer between the two tottering glasses of Pernod and lemonade, squeezes his big legs onto the seat between them, nearly upsetting all three of the drinks. He's there with others from the Station on a charity push for St James's Hospital: the two girls cram fifty pences into his plastic shaker but he doesn't move on, keeps smiling at Lily, staring at her, bringing the conversation around so that he can address a remark particularly to her.

Talking about the Fire Service, how he always wanted to be a fireman, that kind of thing. His eyes glittering when he talks of his work. Lily notices that he isn't really part of the crowd – his mates from the Station are at the bar, all in their jackets with the red lettering *West Yorkshire Fire and Rescue Service* on one side, downing lager and joking with the landlord.

Alan, she is thinking, did something strange. He stood in the middle of the pub like a lost child and then zoomed in on her, on their table. She is flattered: no one has ever given her such clear and unequivocal proof of their interest before. She has just begun an English Lit degree at Leeds University, but the course is giving her some difficulty. All that reading doesn't seem to have prepared her for the main part of her course: talking. Talking in groups, with other people looking at her, her heart sputtering, her face in flames.

She is glad to be living at home, able to escape into the cool green afternoon after each stuffy seminar. Bob says living at home is a better idea; cheaper, and safer. It's a good few years since the Yorkshire Ripper was on the loose round here, but people remember things like that for a long time. Bob does. When the police were trying to catch the Ripper, they played his voice over the tannoy system in the arcade. The weird mix of menace and chumminess floated out over the shoppers, nudging at their regular concerns, their search for shoes and cheap meat, their desire not to know, to remain oblivious. *I am going to strike again. You can be sure of it.*

No, Bob doesn't forget stuff like that, and he makes sure that Lily doesn't either. She sips at her Pernod, laughing at Alan's jokes, picking up on Sue's winks and suppressed giggles, her friend's unspoken approval of Alan, something that matters a lot to Lily right now. Alan smells good, he is clean-shaven and shiny and skilled at teasing the two girls, at making them twitter and screech excitedly, in spite of themselves, their heads bobbing, glasses tinkling, peanuts scattering the table.

Underneath her giddiness Lily is listening with a more attentive, careful part of herself and this Lily is also warming to Alan, to how safe he makes her feel. No, more precisely, she feels *chosen*. As if she really was floating out of control, twirling along a fast river and he came by and plucked her, making decision impossible, protest useless. Surrender delicious.

She gives him her phone number, scribbled on an empty packet of his menthol cigarettes – *Dead sophisticated*, Sue says, being a non-smoker herself. They arrange to meet at the pictures in Leeds.

He says more, more about the Fire Service. He is twenty-one, this is all he ever wanted to be. 'I always loved fires,' Alan says.

Lily isn't listening. She is staring at his eyes, the deep

blue, the wide dark pupils that seem rarely to blink, she can see flames at the bottom, tiny capering lights reflected from the coal fire in the corner of the pub. She is picturing him rescuing people, climbing up to blazing windows, shouldering pyjama'd children, wrapping blankets around shivering women.

She is staring up at him: she feels like an onlooker from the street beneath his ladder. Alan deals in real things, in flames and danger and choking, evil-smelling smoke. This is his attraction for Lily, at least at first. He couldn't be more different than Bob and Brenda with their safe lives, their horror of anything smoky or dirty, anything wild and crackling, anything not easily controlled.

For Valentine's Day, the first one they have together, Alan gets one of his mates from the Station to ring Lily up for a laugh, pretend to be doing a 'nationwide survey' into women's underwear, to ask for her size, what kind of thing Madam likes; teddies or stockings or what. Lily is not fooled for a moment; the voice at the end of the phone with the strong Yorkshire accent bubbles with repressed laughter and no well-informed market researcher would ask *And what cup-size is that, Madam, Double D?* but she plays along, gives her size, she looks forward to seeing what Alan might choose for her.

That night, for the first time, they have somewhere to be on their own together; Alan's sister in Thorp Arch needs a babysitter, so they have her house to themselves. Lily, now in the second term of her degree, has been attending fewer and fewer seminars; she has started to have terrible migraines every Monday morning, is constantly trying a new prescription or aromatherapy, yoga, changing her diet, but nothing works. Tonight her head is bad, not a migraine, but bad enough. Brenda says migraine is hereditary, encouraging her daughter to stay home, not to read so much, it's bad for her eyes.

Now Alan rubs her shoulders for her, she sits at his feet letting the heat from his fingers soak into the tightness at the base of her neck, the knotted muscles. Then he whispers for her to go try on what he bought for her, so she goes into the bathroom with the packet and shyly, very shyly, steps back into the room wearing a robe, untied, over the purple and black lace bra and 'panties' from Debenham's. *Panties* is what Alan calls them, Lily twitches slightly at the sound of it, there's something silly or false about the word, something that makes her uncomfortable. But she says nothing. While Alan's nephews sleep peacefully upstairs, Lily drinks the Thunderbird Alan has poured for her, stands in front of him, lets the robe slip, feeling faintly ludicrous, a tiny girl in someone else's costume, but she hears from the catch in Alan's voice, the slight clogging in his throat as he mutters '*Wow, look at you . . .*', as he runs a finger from her navel to the black ribbon at the front of the shiny purple material, that this isn't how Alan sees her, no, not at all.

And maybe it's that night or maybe one of several that week, when Lily and Alan babysit three nights on the trot, and Alan's sister – a single parent – can't believe her luck, that Matthew is conceived; a Valentine baby which despite the shock, despite the dread of telling Bob and Brenda, is as Lily says to Alan at the time, *The most wonderful present, the best Valentine present, he could ever have given her*.

As it turns out, Brenda and Bob are not shocked, not too badly, not really. Bob declares Alan 'a good lad, the right sort, he'll take care of our lass'. Brenda starts thinking of the wedding invitations, hiring the village hall, putting together a wedding list from the Argos catalogue. For a couple who have lost two babies already, two before Lily that is, babies are precious, not to be sneezed at. There's no question for them, none whatsoever, that their daughter should drop out of university, get married and keep their grandchild.

For Lily, briefly, sex with Alan is a novelty; like a new secret present, all hers. Hidden somewhere, one that she can open and re-open and put away and open again and no one else suspect the pleasure it gives her. Alan is the attentive, gentle sort; he likes to rub oil on her stomach, chase ice-cream around her nipples with his tongue. He lavishes attention and praise on her until her head reels with it; how lovely her body is, how slim, her full hips, her perfect bottom, et cetera. However, it is short lived. Soon morning sickness kicks in and Lily can't bear to be touched, much less played about with. That and anxiety about Alan's job consume Lily for a time. The migraines, astonishingly, disappear completely.

In the dole office, Lily recognises the young man behind the plastic screen, the one she has queued for an hour to see, as the one from the flat opposite hers, the Turkish one with the motorbike. She smiles hopefully at him, reading his name from his shirt. *Mehmet Sulyman*. At least he has a job then. His parents, young enough both of them, don't appear to work, instead hover endlessly at the slightly open door or the window. If Lily nods or says hello the door closes gently again; every time Lily glances up from the entrance to Bridge House they scuttle back behind curtains like slipping shadows.

She's been here nearly an hour in the over-warm atmosphere, which crackles with boredom and frustration. Lily sits upright on her uncomfortable chair, a booklet on her lap, trying not to let her eyes wander to the women with their restless, Coke-drinking toddlers, or the group of dark-eyed men who huddle sullenly around the Turkish translator at one side of the room. Finally, a nasal voice calls her number through the speaker, Mehmet disappears from the screen and emerges from a side door. He motions her to follow him to a small partitioned cubicle, with a desk and two metal chairs. She sits on the seat she is shown, slaps the booklet she just filled out on the desk in front of her.

'It's a bit long, this "form" isn't it? More like a book,' Lily comments, conversationally. Mehmet sits opposite her, slowly turning pages. His dark head is bowed as he regards her answers silently.

'Here,' he says, pointing. 'What are you doing in an effort to search for work?'

His tone of voice is formal, not accusing exactly, but *firm*, Lily thinks. Determined. The accent surprisingly East End. She has heard the parents murmuring together as she passed them, coming out of the lift, talking in their own language. It didn't occur to her that they might have been here in London for some time.

'Well you know,' Lily answers, playing for time. 'Looking at adverts in the paper. That sort of thing.'

He nods, pushes the booklet at her. 'You must write this down.'

She accepts the pen he offers, dutifully writes 'looking at ads in papers', glances up ready to smile again, to remark on how silly it all is, to write down something obvious like that. Mehmet's brown eyes are serious, calm. Measuring.

'I have a child,' Lily says, pushing the form back at him.

He stamps the form, puts it in an envelope.

'Take this to Room 12. You'll find it closes at three thirty, so best to go now.'

Placing both hands on his desk, Lily stands up, leans forward a little.

'It's hard to find work when you have to fit in with school hours. Childcare – I'd have to earn so much just to cover it. The hours would have to be long, travelling across London, for a really decent job, I'd never *see* my child.'

His eyes widen, ever so slightly.

'Yes, Ms – Waite. We have Family Credit to help those working with children. When you find work, you can ask for the form. Room 12.'

A silence simmers between them, humming with Lily's protest, her anger. But there is something in Mehmet's expression which stops it spilling over. And anyway, she is eager to be out of there, glad to discover that as a parent it seems she doesn't have to visit the DSS that often, she can take her Income Support book to the post office. What she can't do is choose times when there are not queues, when there are not many others, just like her. Always standing behind someone else, someone who is angrily tapping their foot or their pen; or someone who has forgotten their ID and who seems to be growing in size, inflating themselves like a puffer-fish, as they prepare to yell at the counter-assistant.

One time she sees Sherry in there, with another woman, another child in a buggy. Lily nods, shyly. *It's like a club*, Lily thinks, *and now I belong to it*. The phrase has formed before she can snuff it. Such a short while ago, she had no idea. No idea at all, about women like

Sherry, about places like that. How hard they can make you. Mehmet with his intense fierce eyes, bloody determined to hold on tight, to remain firmly on the other side of the dirty plastic screen.

Night-times are still the dodgy times. Lily fights with sleep, resisting it, flipping herself from one side of the bed to the other until she feels like a tossed pancake. She has her counting, she has her list, she's up to number four thousand two hundred and sixty now, she's remembering even things stored in the loft; her wedding dress for example. Lily kept meaning to advertise it in the small ads in the *East Keswick Advertiser*. Hardly worn, size 8, full train, but then the years went by and the style of the dress – empire line – went out of fashion, but it wasn't sentimentality that made her keep it. Rolling over again in bed. Thinking, remembering, panicking. Alan. *Alan does not exist any more*. Lily tries saying it, under her breath, but out loud to see if the words can convince her. I've been through a fire. I was in a fire. *I've lost everything*.

Matthew turns in his sleep, startling her with a little animal snuffling sound. Lily thinks, I want to name this thing, this huge gap that has opened up inside me, around me, a weird space that wasn't there before. She can feel it, taste it, she can almost see it, and she knows she could fall into it, even has already, briefly, but then someone raised her up, pulled her out again, or else she pulled herself out, she isn't quite sure. All she knows is that surely there has to be a way to name it, write it down, make sense of it. Otherwise, the feeling will keep pushing at her, pressing on her. It will steal her away in sleep and carry her son to the bottom of a terrifying well, a slimy green well in a dank cave. She has to survive this feeling, find a way to control it, label it, understand.

Lily leans over the side of the bed, picks up her notepad again, her pen. She sits up, pulling the T-shirt she is wearing until it is tucked firmly underneath her thighs. Keep busy, do things, she says to herself. But what kind of things? She turns this over in her mind. This terrible freedom. An enormous freedom, exhilarating at first, she has longed to feel this way. But now she has it, it is also sickening. Like being strapped to a big wheel then suspended at the highest point, about to swoop down, but dangling there at the tipover moment, dangling there, suspended.

Do whatever comes up, she tries telling herself. Look around – look at what other people do. *Go with the flow*. She writes this down. An Alan phrase, a little too hippyish for Bob's liking. She underlines this and then after a pause, a pause in which she looks around the bedroom, stares at the walls, the window, carries on with the list. *Wedding Photo Album. Baby Photo Album. Christening blanket. Diaphragm, brand new, still in its packaging*. Her eyes are bright, but no tears threaten. The cave closes up again. That crisis has passed.

Three for a Girl

As a small child living with Brenda and Bob Lily worked hard, exceptionally hard, to persuade herself that she did exist. Really exist, in her own right. Live, breathe, move, independently of her parents. Not that Brenda and Bob did anything wrong. Not that they were cruel parents. Bob, on the contrary, with his huge bulky stomach, weighing on the belt of his trousers, was what other men call a 'gentle giant' or 'salt of the earth', or if they had lived down here, in London, at the time, maybe a 'diamond geezer'.

Privately, Bob thought that after Brenda's second miscarriage they should give up on this baby lark. He was scared. He remembered waiting outside St James's Hospital and making a pact with God that if He spared Brenda this time, he, Bob would never put her in the pudding club again. He did intend to stick to his part in that deal. Not that he could keep his hands off Brenda, with her lovely big hips (the phrase 'child-bearing' came to mind, and then was quickly quashed) and her scent of flour and warm baking and the funny little startled movements she made sometimes, when he put his hands around her waist from behind, lifted her hair up and kissed her neck. He tried his best. He persuaded Brenda to have an IUD fitted because he didn't want to lose her, and French Letters always made him think of the Navy and were wrong, all wrong, for making love to his wife.

Well, somehow or other, Brenda did get pregnant and he never knew if she did it to defy him (which didn't seem much like Brenda) or if it was a genuine mistake, one of those women's things; that little piece of metal tying some tube or other, his daughter managing miraculously to slither past it, or something else about Brenda's body that he didn't understand.

One way or another, along came Lily. Such a tiny baby. Tiny, pink, a little glow of silver-blonde fluff around her head for hair, like a dandelion clock. Hard to believe this precious, minuscule child was really the fruit of his loins and his image of Lily, somehow navigating that wire in her mother's womb, made him picture a little fish, steel-coloured. Her eyes too, a silver-grey, put him in mind of steel, he worked briefly in a steelworks as a lad, that colour is very particular; it's not what people think. It's neither grey nor silver, it has its own colour: steel.

Bob and Brenda were very, very careful with Lily. Those were the years before Brenda's sickness was really bad, but all the same, Brenda stayed home a lot. Bob fixed a fireguard around the gas fire, he fixed a stairguard on the stairs, child-proof locks on everything. Those years he fondly remembers never being without a drill in his hand, a new project, some other adaptation of the house, to make it safe for Lily, to keep Brenda and Lily safe inside.

They never gave Lily a hard time about getting pregnant. They stood by her, they stood up for her if anyone from the village made a comment, shotgun wedding, any cheeky remarks like that. If anything, they were delighted, they understood her need for a child better than they understood her desire to go to college, to stuff her head full of books, to give herself migraines. How well they looked after her. No parent could have done better, tried harder.

And now this. After all his care, all Alan's care, Lily's home and husband gone up in smoke and she's moved down South with the boy, without a by-your-leave.

This morning, Saturday, Lily is oddly cheerful, despite her lack of sleep. She pads to the kitchen in her bare feet and puts the kettle on to boil, grateful for a few moments to herself while Matthew is still curled tight as a ball of string, a humped shape inside his sleeping bag. She can hear the pigeons purring on the balcony; in the hall she gathers a bunch of letters from the floor, none of which are for her. Two look like circulars: she throws these in the bin. But one is for a Ms L Stanley, and is addressed to flat number 1. The postman has delivered it by mistake. Lily is curious about this letter.

For a start, she knows that number 1, the flat opposite Josh's, is vacant, boarded up, and has been since her arrival. She lights her first morning cigarette, sits on the chair Josh planted himself on last night, puts her feet up on the counter-top – with some difficulty, her legs being on the short side. Still, the position she's sitting in gives her pleasure. She imagines Josh smiling at her, his eyes resting on her slim bare legs. Her T-shirt wrinkles up to her thighs. The letter contains a credit card renewal. Ms Louisa Stanley is urged to sign it right away.

Lily smokes her cigarette and the kettle steams to boiling point. The pigeons on the balcony are cooing a soft, persistent purr, a plane trails across the sky in her grimy kitchen window like a streak of white crayon, and from the flat below she can hear grunts and bed squeaks and the unmistakable sound of Sherry making love.

Making love. Being fucked is what Lily thinks at first, but that isn't a phrase Lily would use. It's unsettling, hearing such sounds. Apart from once, in a hotel, Lily can't remember ever being this close to someone else's intimate life before. She feels embarrassed, sneaky, an odd little tickling in the roof of her mouth. Perhaps she should go into the living room? But she stays where she is, legs up, now dunking a teabag into a cup. The squeaks of the bed-springs are pretty vigorous and they're going on for a long time, longer than Lily would expect. She herself would have come by now. Alan always took care to please Lily, he was attentive, the sort of man women's magazines call a good lover, considerate, putting Lily's needs first. Sometimes it bothered her. Once Matthew was born, she was preoccupied by the constant demands of a toddler and it irritated her, ever so slightly, Alan's constant attention.

She remembers him now, sneaking up behind her while she was doing the washing-up, putting his mouth close to her ear, whispering how lovely she looks, his hands under her breasts as if they needed support, as if they couldn't sit on her ribcage all by themselves. Lily would be gently batting him off, saying *Sssshhh what about Matthew, behave yourself* . . . It never occurred to

Lily then, but it does now, how rarely she actually looked at Alan in bed. How she kept her eyes closed, making love. How she blanked him out, made the experience she was having into another one, one which probably involved other people, people like Sherry, or people in sexy magazines. At any rate, not herself.

The grunts and squeaks now give way to Sherry's moaning, and Lily can even make out the words if she puts her ear to the kitchen floor, low and rhythmic. Sherry is repeating over and over *Yeah. Yeah. That's it. Yeah. Oh. Yeah.* How predictable, Lily thinks, straightening up, pulling her T-shirt down, running her hands along her hips. She stands at the window but she can still hear Sherry, a little more vehement now. *Oh yeah*, Sherry says. For God's sake. You take your bloody time don't you? Lily mutters, to herself. She sips hungrily at her tea and then shrieks a little, scalding her tongue.

Come – on – yeah – yeah! . . . Sherry continues, the gaps between the words increasing. Lily is wondering what position she is in. Her voice doesn't sound at all muffled, in fact it suddenly sounds freer and closer. She could even be standing up. Although how would anyone have sex standing up? Lily conjures up another image, startling in its intensity. *That's not something she ever wanted Alan to do to her*. Then Sherry's voice takes a shift, a downturn; it's different and it's suddenly horrible, there's a long silence and then a shriek that doesn't sound right at all. It sounds like a blast of air was punched out of her. The sounds are muffled and indistinct but Sherry's voice isn't and she is making this ugly whimpering sound and saying *No, no, that's hurting* and there are other noises, thuds and crashes and a male voice, Lily can't make out the words, but the tone, the tone is unmistakable. Lily gives in to an instant temptation to put her hands over her ears. Her heartbeat accelerates and her mouth is dry and the images that flash in front of her are nightmares, they are green and murky and can scarcely form themselves. She releases her hands from her ears, crouches down, flattens one ear to the cold kitchen floor. She can't be sure, they could just be playing, a bit of S and M or something, what does she, Lily, know about things like that?

She jumps up. She bites her nails. She paces the room. She goes to light a third cigarette. Other people's lives. None of her business. You should never get involved. This is how people who live on top of each other manage to get along. They close their ears. It's not like a village. There people are too nosy, won't mind their own business, no matter what. She'll have to learn the rules, learn to tune out; like turning a dial on a radio station, losing the connection, driving into a tunnel.

But it isn't true about back home, about living in a village. The more she lives here, the more she knows that. Once, when she was about ten or eleven, she heard a fight at the bus-stop right outside their front door. Brenda was home with her, the curtains drawn, baked potatoes cooking in the oven, in the warm smoky kitchen. Lily was at her bedroom window, ran downstairs to tell her mother. *I can hear fighting, I can see them from the window upstairs, it's a man and a woman and he's pushing her . . .* Lily tweaked the curtain of the living-room window, looked into the darkness. The couple were two dim figures, their voices clashing in the cold night, their argument taking place some yards from the only streetlight. Behind them were unlit corn fields, a track snaking towards the farmer's house. Brenda stood behind Lily, angrily shook the curtain closed, waved her hands to scoot her daughter into the kitchen as if she were a mouse.

'Leave it. They'll sort it out. Lovers' tiff. No need for us to get involved . . .' She turned her back to her daughter, bent to the oven with her gloves on, gloves that looked like two large fishes swallowing up her arms.

Lily felt a viscous stab of anger, of hatred and shame and then a creeping, curling fear trickling from her neck to her toes, seeping from her mother's body towards her own. Brenda was afraid. She was always afraid. Afraid of everything. She wouldn't get involved if her life depended on it. *Don't get involved. Keep ye'sen cheerful lass.* Between Brenda and Bob, Lily was steered through life as though it was an endless (yes, definitely endless) Disneyland labyrinth and the trick was, never to brush up against the walls.

Matthew wanders sleepily into the kitchen to find Lily frozen in indecision, standing on the spot which she imagines is right above Sherry's bedroom, still listening.

'I'm hungry,' Matthew begins, his tone plaintive. Lily makes no response, her head cocked, then shakes her head involuntarily, puts a finger to her mouth. Nothing. She can't hear a thing. All sounds from downstairs – frightening or otherwise – seem to have subsided.

She tips some Coco-Pops into a bowl, slides the bowl towards Matthew, gliding around the kitchen silently, as if she were on ice-skates. When Matthew asks for milk, he asks three times before she hears him.

Monday afternoon Lily sees Sherry's sister at the school, picking up her daughter Shamilla. She has Sherry's baby with her, beautifully turned out in shiny patent shoes and a red and leopard-print fur hat. The sister resembles

Sherry only she's larger, slightly engorged, as if this is how Sherry might look like if she wasn't whippet-thin. As if the sister is the plum and Sherry the prune. Lily, with great effort, prepares to say hello to the woman, even phrases in her mind a casual question, How's Sherry? Before she can do this, the woman strides over to her, plants herself only a few inches from Lily's surprised face.

'You're Matthew's mum, aint you?'

'Yes—'

'Well, my Shamilla says your son bit her today. He's always biting her. You'd better tell him to keep his fuckin' teeth to himself or he'll have me to deal with.'

The woman is wearing a shiny black blouson jacket, opened, and beneath it a yellow T-shirt with a hint of cleavage. Lily finds herself mesmerised by the cleavage, realising it's the last place she should be staring but unable to raise her eyes to meet the other woman's. Lily knows her face is blushing a deep, flaming red. Her hand flies up to her cheeks, as if she could keep the colour down by the coldness in her fingers.

'Oh, I'm sorry, I – yes, I will tell him – I—'

Lily fixes a smile on her face and directs it at Shamilla. *Keep y'sen cheerful lass.*

'Is Matthew in your class? I'll tell him off for you, I know he's naughty but he's new you know, he's having trouble making friends.'

'He's a fuckin' mad boy,' Sherry's sister snaps angrily. 'Your son's a fuckin' racist. And I wonder where he gets it from?'

Other parents are bustling past them, there is a hum around them, a bristling energy-field. Somehow Lily knows the word 'racist' has created an extra frisson, put Sherry's sister instantly in the right. Sherry and her sister are white, Lily is confused and wants to say, I don't know what you mean. Panic is rising in Lily, she feels as though a mob is bubbling up; she's sure Shamilla isn't the only child Matthew has hurt and that other parents would like to see him (or her) get what they deserve. Staring wildly at Shamilla, floundering for something to say, then turning to Sherry's baby, Lily realises for the first time that both little girls could be sisters rather than cousins. They are – now she's thinking about it – the exact same shade of milky-brown and finally it dawns: they must both have black fathers.

'I'm sorry,' Lily mutters, 'if Matthew has been making – racist remarks I'll – I'll seriously tell him off – I really, yes that's terrible—'

Matthew has run on ahead, providing Lily with the perfect excuse to hurry away, still red in the face, yelling after him as ferociously as she dare, '*Matthew, get yourself over here!*' There is a fine line between appeasing Sherry's sister and drawing further attention to herself, so her voice is a little lower than she is capable of. She breaks into a trot to catch Matthew up at the point where he is waiting with the other kids and the lollipop man, ready to cross the road. Lily grips his skinny arm, digging her fingers into the wool of his duffle coat, to try to take a proper hold.

She has never been madder at him in her life, never felt this desire to hurt her own child before.

'What have you been doing?'

'Get off me! You're hurting my arm.'

'Get over this road. You've got some explaining to do.'

Lily is only barely under control, the anger is boiling up, about to spill. She marches Matthew towards the entrance of Bridge House. A council worker astride a lawn mower, a cheeky one who usually yells 'Hey

Gorgeous' to Lily in the mornings, watches them with a laconic expression, the mower's engine drowning whatever it is he is saying. Lily can guess and longs to give him a fuck off sign with her fingers. To her annoyance she sees that other people are waiting for the lift: the Turkish couple from the flat opposite hers. Well, luckily she has learned they don't expect her to say anything to them. Lily stabs at the lift button. She practically drags Matthew inside. The doors close in the metal box and the unmistakable smell of old urine rises up.

The lift drones up to the top floor. The elderly couple stand in silence, their dark eyes fixed to the floor, Lily and Matthew pinned to the other side, the puddle of urine between them all. Lily can hardly contain herself and the moment the lift doors burst open she turns to Matthew, spluttering 'What have you been doing to Shamilla?'

'Nothing.'

'Matthew! I just had the most embarrassing encounter with her terrifying mother, who happens to be Sherry's sister. So you'd better tell me the truth!'

'I just called her one name and she told on me.'

'One name! One name! What did you call her?'

Matthew pulls the hood on his duffle coat, trying to obscure his face.

'I only said what the other kids say. She's horrible. She's always whining. I hate her.'

'What did you call Shamilla, Matthew?' Lily's voice rises to a shriek, she struggles to find her key, forces it into the lock, then turns with a spin towards her son.

Matthew mutters, 'I called her a Paki.'

'What?'

'A Paki, a Paki – I called her a Paki and she is!'

'And you bit her, you bit her, what is it with this biting thing?'

They are standing just inside their own flat. The couple opposite have shuffled inside their own door, Lily doesn't care if they can hear her or not, she feels helpless, helpless and furious, in fact wild with rage, with terror or shame, or guilt, or dread . . . she doesn't know what, what she is wild with, only that she would like to stamp this child out, stamp him into some kind of shape, stamp understanding into him, stamp something or somebody. She bites at her bottom lip so hard that blood springs up, a bead of sour rust under her tongue.

'Get in here.'

Matthew moves with exaggerated slowness, brushing against her as he moves along their hallway. His bottom lip trembles but he doesn't lower his gaze.

'Look,' Lily says, crouching to his level, trying to keep the desperation from her voice. 'I know your Dad isn't here. You know he would whack you for this, don't you? But I'm not going to do that.'

She takes several deep breaths, working at keeping her heart from leaping into her mouth, stoppering the words. She tries to push Alan from her mind, it was a mistake to invoke him. She tries again.

'You know Paki is a bad thing to say, don't you? It was the worst thing back home you could ever call a child, and I know you know that. It's a bad word here, too.'

'Why?' Matthew asks, his tone defiant.

'Well, it means someone comes from Pakistan and—'

'But why is that bad?'

'Well, it's like swearing and Shamilla doesn't come from Pakistan so it isn't even accurate . . .' Lily is floundering. Her mood is easing and now her logic doesn't sound too convincing to her. He thinks Paki means: horrible, bad person, he knows it's a term of abuse, he knows he shouldn't use it. But he doesn't mean it the way adults hear it. He's five years old, for God's sake. He's not a member of the British National Party.

'Everyone is as good as each other. If you call people names to do with where they come from, that's stupid, isn't it?' Lily says, taking off her coat.

'They call *me* names.'

'What? What do they call you?'

'They call me Geordie.'

Lily sniffs, makes a noise that sounds something like hmph.

'Well, you're not a Geordie are you, so that's equally stupid. It's just because you have a different accent from other children. Look, I don't want to hear ever again that you called anyone a Paki or any other racist name, do you understand me?'

'What other kinds of racist names are there?' Matthew asks, eyes wide.

Lily hesitates. She stares at Matthew for a moment.

'Look, you know what I mean. No name calling of any kind, but especially not to do with the colour of people's skin or where they come from.'

No name calling of any kind. Is that what racism amounts to, mentioning where people come from or their skin colour? Lily feels she just failed a test, and at the same time issued a ludicrous decree. She knows full well that the entire conversation of little boys is peppered with phrases like 'worm breath' or 'willy-head'. She sighs, her anger spent, and now instead her body is filled with a deep depression, a sweeping hopelessness.

Mrs Jalil's worried expression floats up into Lily's head, the teacher with her arms folded across her heavy bust, saying 'Mrs Waite, I've never come across a child so . . .' Lily did her bit, she tried talking to Matthew about the sea-creatures, about the biting. He listened in silence, his little moon-face blank, his eyes dutifully fixed on his mother's but closed, utterly closed to her.

What would Alan do, she wonders. Truth is, they never agreed. Slap first, ask questions later, that was Alan's approach. The way he was raised. Once or twice, she stuck up for Matthew, protested. He's too small for that. That's not how children learn. She tries to flush this image, this memory. *You're on your own now, girl.* But it's Bob's voice she hears, so is she? She leaves Matthew in the living room in front of the TV, *Bodger and Badger* making comforting, goofy companions for him. He's lonely, Lily thinks, and it's as if someone is holding her heart and squeezing it, pinching nails into it.

Her mind flicks terrible possibilities in front of her, a long ticker-tape, full of prison mug-shots, late-night calls from police stations: *Maybe I'm raising a racist, a thug, a future gang member? What do I know about boys, about raising a boy, a young man, on my own?* She goes to lie on her bed, needing to be away from Matthew and with nowhere else to go. Tears stream into the pillow but she doesn't feel relieved. The shame, the memory of Shamilla's mother keeps looming up for her and each time it does, her heartbeat quickens again, a voice in her head drums: *I can't do it, I can't do it on my own.* And then, suddenly, knowing that it is not Matthew she is angry with, not really.

Thinking, *Alan, you bastard, where are you?*

Then it's five p.m. and the sky is splitting into pink streaks like a mouth ulcer, the sour yellow lights of the estate snap on automatically and there's cooking to do and washing-up and putting-away and a small boy asleep in front of the TV, who has to be fed and bathed and scrubbed and teeth-brushed and kissed and eventually put to bed.

It's not what I imagined. The sentence forms in her head, not the idea, but the words and alongside, a picture. A little girl at a table, a big pine table, in a room with light streaming in, like melted butter. On the table a plain glass vase, something square and modern, duck-egg blue, holding flowers, irises or arum lilies, the kind of flowers Brenda associates with funerals, but Lily knows are sophisticated, they populate *Elle Decoration* magazines. The girl at this table is crayoning, her head down, her tongue peeping between her lips, her hand colouring a sky blue, a house red, a tree green. The mother is sipping coffee, wearing light trousers in a sandstone colour and a fluid material, and her toes are tanned and stretch luxuriously in front of her in open-toed sandals. The child even has a name. Rose. Something sweet and old-fashioned, something small too, that would go well with Lily; another flower.

Lily wonders about this picture, wonders where it originates. So easy to take care of, the little girl called Rose. Such small needs. It would be just as Brenda pictured things. A fair daughter with shiny hair to plait and limbs to dress; a beautiful child other mothers would admire, a child always sunny, always playful, always sparkling. In Lily's version the child wears dungarees, not dresses, Rose might be small but she has energy, more than sparkling, she sparks. Still, in essence, the child is the same. Lily had no idea, until this moment, that this is who she expected, who she conjured up, when she was pregnant, a sweet little girl child just like herself, just like her own mother did; at any rate, not Matthew, not him at all.

Later that evening someone raps loudly on the door. Lily wonders why whoever it is doesn't use the doorbell, she knows it works. The wooden knocking is insistent, like a quickened heartbeat. Matthew is in bed. Lily is wide awake, sitting in the living room on the one thin sofa, the colour of a cereal box, reading a book called *Taming the Dragon in Your Child* and nursing a cup of tea. She stands close to the closed front door, whispering.

'Who is it?'

'It's Joshua.'

His voice – like his knocking – is booming, has no respect for the hour or the likelihood of a child sleeping. Lily finds this a good sign: he's not creeping around. She is aware of the Turkish couple in the flat opposite. Lately, the man has at last begun to say hello to her, but the woman hasn't so much as nodded. Sometimes in the mornings near the entrance-way she sees Mehmet noisily starting up his motorbike, but it is hard to tell what his expression might be behind his black full-face helmet. After their encounter in the dole office, Lily doesn't expect him to be smiling. In any case, if the Sulyman family are listening right now, Lily is thinking, unable to drop the habit of considering herself watched or disapproved of, at least they can know that Josh is calling on her with no furtiveness, no sneaking around.

She darts into her bedroom to fetch a jumper long enough to wear over the T-shirt. The flat is centrally heated, over-warm in fact, and too many clothes make Lily's skin feel overcooked, like bread rising. She rushes back to the front door, to prevent Josh knocking again, in case he wakes Matthew.

'Just a second!'

She opens the door a crack, peers round it.

'Why don't you use the bell?' she asks.

He smiles. 'Add a little variety, you know.'

She is struck again by how tall he is. In the hallway his height and darkness are exaggerated; his beard jutting, the shock of hair uncontrolled by a hat (locks flying, that's how he described it to Matthew, which Lily agrees describes it perfectly).

'Brought you something. Is the boy awake?'

Lily hears it as 'sometin'. She notes that his expression is direct, candid. Eyebrows raised slightly, eyes smiling.

'No, Matthew's in bed.' She opens the door a touch further. She doesn't say 'come in', but it's clear that's what she means. He steps over the threshhold on to the bare concrete floor.

'The council didn't give you no carpet yet?'

'I'd rather do it myself. When I get the money, you know.'

The corridor is narrow: it's impossible to stand around in it. Lily walks towards the kitchen knowing that he'll follow, conscious of him behind her, conscious that she is steering him away from the living room, where the sofa will be warm, the cushions imprinted with her elbow, the book laid open; all with a look of disturbed intimacy. Josh thumps a tall Tupperware jug down on the kitchen counter-top and takes off the lid. He does this with a flourish, quickly, with one hand, and Lily smiles, she can't resist smiling.

'Guinness Punch. You had that?'

Lily peers in at the jug, at a milky-brown liquid, and shakes her head.

'You have some glasses?'

Now it is Josh who is smiling, a big wide smile, as if

they have a shared secret, a shared joke. Lily, flustered, turns her back to fetch two mugs from a kitchen cupboard, taking care not to stretch up. The sweater reaches halfway down her thighs. Beneath it she is wearing cotton underwear. Her legs are naked. Josh pours a generous amount of the creamy drink into each mug and hands one to Lily.

'Put some flesh on your bones.'

There is nowhere comfortable to sit in the kitchen. Josh pulls out the wooden chair again and sits heavily on it, this time the right way round. He is a little too close for Lily's comfort, she untucks another chair from the table and sits opposite him, staring into her mug. The kitchen also seems suddenly naked, and Lily feels exposed, as if the flat itself is exposing her. The painted concrete floor, icy under bare feet, the toneless manilla walls, the bare bulb dangling over them, as if they are being interrogated. The kitchen is clean, the floor swept, the surfaces wiped with bleach, and bleach is what it smells of; not cooking or spices or anything homely. Behind Lily's head one bare window, metal-framed, holds its square of night sky. Seated, like this, even the lights of the London tower blocks and houses are absent from view.

She has a sudden desire to explain to Josh, to explain that she has nothing, that every time she turns around to fetch an item she took for granted – a garlic press, a cheese grater, a linen dish-towel, she has to add it mentally to her list of missing things and that these thoughts jab at her like angry fingers; she wants to forget, but she can't. Then there is the endless budgeting: can I afford to replace that? is there a jumble sale I can go to, could I get Brenda to send me one of those? A whole lifetime of things is missing for Lily, her two suitcases gaping, unzipped now beneath the bed and everything she has in the world rattling round this in this flat, like peas in a drum.

'What's in this?' Lily asks politely, breaking a silence. 'It tastes good; sweet, creamy and with a definite kick.'

'Guinness. Eggs. Sweet-milk, you know that? We drink a lot of that in Jamaica. And nutmeg. Fresh. I make it last night and keep it in the fridge. It's better if it mix up good.'

Lily glances shyly at Josh's hands around the mug, noticing the short nails. She finds his hands reassuring, male, square-fingered and large. They remind her, she realises with a bubble of surprise, of Bob's hands.

'So. What happen to your husband?'

Lily wonders if she gasps out loud. Inwardly she does. She takes a hasty swig of Guinness Punch, feels it slip down her throat in one large glob. She thinks Josh could hear her swallow, hear her stomach rumble, hear the blood racing in her veins.

'He – was a fireman, with the Fire Service in Yorkshire, where we lived. Where I come from. A place called East Keswick.'

This is not what she meant to say.

'Where is he now? You left him?'

'Not exactly . . .'

'But. You finish your marriage, huh?'

'Yes.'

Talking, speaking to somebody so new, so different – Lily doesn't let the word 'black' form in her head, but it hovers around anyway, afraid to land, wheeling like a bat – in this situation, late at night, Lily feels giddy, even a bit demented. She feels as though she has been pedalling since the fire, gathering speed. All the effort involved, the newness of the last few weeks, leaving her home town, her parents, leaving everything, then negotiating so many new situations. Life has been rolling and rolling and now in this one moment, newness is gathering into one spot, like a road flying so fast beneath her that it appears to be standing still; and on this road Lily is at last freewheeling, exhilarated, hair streaming behind her, arms and legs waving madly.

Josh stands up, and Lily's mood plummets. But he only moved to take her cup, refill their drinks, ask her did she want a next one? He sits back down again, the chair scraping. He is looking at her very hard. He runs his tongue over his lips.

'I thought you might write me a letter. A reply to my wife.'

'Yes. Yes, that would be fine. Do you mean right now?'

'No. I don't mean right now . . .'

'Oh.'

Lily thinks for a moment and then asks: 'When do you get your new glasses?'

'Huh? Oh my eye-glasses. Yeah.'

There is a pause. They both sip the Guinness Punch at the same moment, put the cups down in unison, two light taps on the table. 'I don't give a fuck about no reading and writing. I don't need that shit.'

'You don't read or write?'

'What do you think?'

'Well, I did wonder, if that was the reason . . . How do you get by then?'

'Oh I get by. Daphine, my wife, she fill out form and thing. When Daphine by her family I mess with little girls like you, don't I?'

Messing. Little girls. Lily thinks these comments over.

'I'm sorry if I've annoyed you. I – I'm only curious. And – I'm not so little. How old do you think I am?'

He finishes his Guinness Punch, goes to stand by the window, without answering, his back to her, throws her question back.

'How old you think *I* am?'

'I don't know,' Lily says, too shy to hazard a guess.

'I'm thirty-eight. Been here since I was eighteen.' He seems restless now, he takes his jacket off and puts it on the back of the chair, he drinks the last of the Guinness Punch from the jug without offering any to her, strides back to the window, turns around, stares at her. Lily wonders if things are not going as he planned, wonders what she can do to help him get them back on track. She is surprised by her own assessment of the situation, by her calm (albeit a little heady, with the hastily-drunk punch swirling around inside her) readiness, willing him to get on with it.

'Lily, are you afraid of me?'

This is not what she expected him to say. She wonders what her face is doing, tries to compose it differently. She puts her elbows on the table in a nonchalant pose, but they tremble too much so she lowers them again.

'No,' Lily replies.

'You have a cigarette?'

She leaves the room to fetch them, she has a new packet of Benson and Hedges near the bed. When she steps back into the kitchen he is waiting at the door, he seems to have recovered, his arms spring around her waist and he turns her face to his to kiss her, the wiry beard tickling her mouth.

His mouth is dry and his hair brushes her face. Lily thinks of trees, of twigs and branches, and notices, before she closes her eyes, that the moon has appeared in the envelope of kitchen sky, sliding from behind a cloud.

Lily, in six years of married life, and despite Alan's entreaties, has never made love in a kitchen. *Don't be daft*, she used to say. *The baby will hear.* She is struggling not to remember, but remembering presses at her anyway, the words string themselves to each other and insist on being heard. *It was never like this. Kissing Alan never felt like this.*

Lily is astonished by many things about Josh and one of them is how candidly he undresses in front of her, every last thing, expecting her to do the same. She would like to switch the light off. She would rather Josh couldn't see her face when she is looking at his body. She is astonished too, at how ready her body is, despite the lack of build-up, like it was waiting, anticipating, knew something she didn't, all along. She would rather things could last a little longer and be less hasty and urgent and that there were fewer cooker-knobs sticking in her back. She is astonished again when Josh pauses with no embarrassment to produce a condom from a jacket pocket: she would rather not have known how sure was his estimation of her.

Mostly she wishes she could keep certain distracting images from her mind, because in her nervous giddiness, they are in danger of making her giggle. Milk pans boiling over. Dumplings bubbling in hot fat. A half lemon grinding and squirming on a squeezer, squirting juice. And then one image; startling, precise, perfect. A plum, hard and slightly unripe, deep pink, dimpled in the centre, with a neat seam.

'You ever been with a black guy?' Josh asks, thrusting the words at her, his voice husky in her ear.

'No!' Lily gasps, feeling her spine buckle, spasms chasing along it, her head rattle the top of the grill-pan, the weight of Josh welding her repeatedly to the cooker, his hairless chest slapping gently against hers. Lily thinks that, *seriously* and *no exaggerating*, she would like this moment to last for ever (or at least, say, ten minutes longer), but of course, she has no intention of saying so. That would be impolite. His climax is short, nothing more than a spasm. He pulls away from her, kisses her on the cheek. Recognising the kiss as a seal, as a finishing touch, Lily's body aches in disappointment; newly opened, seeping heat like, she thinks (unable to stop herself), an open oven door.

Josh goes to the bathroom to get rid of the condom, comes back, immediately begins dressing, pulling on boxer shorts, a white T-shirt. He looks at Lily as if he is about to say something, thinks better of it. The packet of cigarettes is still unopened on the kitchen table in front of them, so Josh takes out two, lights them both with the gas cooker, hands one to Lily. She feels she hasn't even exhaled yet.

'You have a good body. When you have your child young, your body spring back like piece of elastic. My wife is the same. She's big but she's strong, you know, firm.'

Now Lily is astonished that he can introduce his wife into the conversation – compare their bodies, even – so easily, at this precise moment. She understands quickly that this is to be the tenor of things. Casual. That although Lily has never in her life been more surprised by her own behaviour, couldn't be more surprised, in fact, if she had just opened a window and flung herself out, she should by no means let Josh know this. He'll think she's dumb. Naïve.

She offers him a cup of chamomile tea, and when the kettle has boiled, they take their cups into the living room. This room is cosy, a little less Spartan than the kitchen. The boiler, hidden in an airing cupboard in the alcove, emits heat and there is a gas fire which, it being early October, Lily doesn't light. They sit together on the cardboard-coloured sofa in T-shirts and underwear, more comfortable now but still wary; smoking, drinking and staring at the unlit gas fire as if it were something more romantic, intermittently batting the odd sleepy sentence back and forth. The conversation is late-night, circular, chit-chatty. Lily does not ask about Josh's son. Josh does not ask Lily why she moved in with no removal van, no furniture.

Josh picks up one of Matthew's drawings that litter the floor, all of them drawings of fish.

'That one look like red snapper. You had that?'

'No.'

'I'll make it for you one time. It's good.'

Josh stands up, yawning, goes to the kitchen to fetch his jeans and his jacket, pick up the empty jug of punch. He seems reluctant to leave but Matthew's drawings have made an intrusion.

'What about that letter you wanted me to write?' Lily asks, following him out to the corridor.

'Bit late now.' He yawns again, stretching up. They stand a little way apart, saying nothing. Lily follows him again, down the corridor to the front door.

'I'll bring you the paper for write me the letter a next time.'

'Yes,' replies Lily, acknowledging his assumption that there will be another time.

He smiles at her, whispering: 'Your son sleep like a log.'

'Yes.'

'Goodnight then Lily. Mind the bugs don't bite.'

'Yes.'

He doesn't move to kiss her. Lily hesitates, then closes the door behind him with a soft thud.

When she returns to the kitchen to get a glass of water she finds two crisp, clean twenty pound notes on the counter-top. The notes are placed neatly, in a prominent position. They look to Lily like an envelope propped on a mantelpiece, with her name on it.

Picking up the notes, Lily folds them carefully, stares at them. Forty pounds. Suddenly, forty pounds feels like a great deal of money. Shoes for Matthew. A new duvet. She stands in the kitchen, her glass of water untouched, staring at the notes for a long time. She wonders if she should feel insulted. She wants to giggle. To her amazement, the money makes her smile suddenly, the phrase that springs up from nowhere is *Have your cake and eat it too*. She doesn't let herself consider what Bob would make of this, knowing that it's hardly the way Bob would look at things, he's not likely to see the fact of Josh paying her as a *bonus*. That's what she finds funny. Her own response. She can't stop grinning. She finds her purse, slips the notes neatly inside. The brand new purse, with no old photographs, no used bus tickets. Only one credit card, and that one not even hers.

Lily lies in her bed, at the edge of sleep but she is unable to fall over the edge, slip into the delicious stupor her body demands. She lies on her back, staring at the ceiling in the semi-dark, listening to Matthew breathing, tracing a hairline crack in the wall beside her bed with her finger.

She tries writing her list, but quickly abandons it, dissatisfied. Josh's arms. Beautifully defined, muscled. He has only light body hair, on his legs, low on his stomach. The feel of his skin, silky; she can still smell his skin and because of the Guinness Punch she associates him with nutmeg, healthy but spicy. She grins to herself, in the darkness. He looks great for – what, nearly forty.

His dreadlocks are threaded with grey at the roots but his stomach is neat and hard, his navel one of those flat, folded navels, nothing untidily scrunched up or sticking out. And remembering his skin, daring herself to picture again his skin, she decides it has a polished quality, that the nearest colour she can come up with, and even that is inadequate, is the colour of a rich, glossy brown conker. These thoughts make her uncomfortable, she feels guilty about her own fascination but there's no denying it. When Josh is up close it is impossible not to take in the tiniest of details: how dark the pores are around his nose, how his skin colour – now that she is seeing it properly for the first time – is not uniform, any more than hers is, how he is paler and darker in different places, how some of him is pink, which she has to admit is something she never thought of before, it surprises her.

Something kicks inside her, that's how she thinks of the feeling, a *kicking* feeling (like Matthew did once, inside her) when she pictures Josh. She experiments running the film again, the film of Josh making love to her, and each time, the kick. She never had this feeling with Alan. That is the painful part, the shock. Six years of married life. Alan always gentle, always coaxing, a sex life she would have said was good, fair enough, *satisfying* or whatever those other words are, the ones she is supposed to use. But she never before felt anything like this.

And it's nothing she could name, make sense of. It isn't about orgasms, orgasms are two-a-penny to Lily, she thinks that's a problem of her mother's generation, not hers. This feeling is about something else. It's completely new. She thinks of Matthew, learning the names of his beloved fish, how he has moved these days from the fish in aquariums to sea-fish, from Yellowfin

Groupers to Atlantic Tripletails, from Rainbow Fish to Bermuda Chub, how it is the names he loves, sounding them out loud; practising them. One time, around age three, he came crying to her that his leg had gone fizzy and it wouldn't work properly and Lily, laughing, had reassured him it was a common thing, perfectly normal, called 'pins and needles', and that it would go away soon. Matthew loved the phrase, he danced around chanting it, instantly understanding the image, and obviously reassured that his feeling had a name, which meant that other people experienced it.

The sleeping bag rustles noisily as she churns around in bed, aware that her restlessness is disturbing Matthew, who also fights with his sleeping bag, periodically kicking and thrashing. We need proper sheets, pillowcases, duvets, Lily says to herself, making an effort to move on, to turn her mind to practical things. She remembers the credit card which arrived at the flat by mistake, the card meant for Ms L Stanley.

Yesterday she signed it, just for fun, for an experiment. She used her own writing, but holding the pen more sloppily, allowing the 'e' to become a loop, the 'a' to whirl to a spiral. Ms L Stanley. It looked good. And she could easily repeat it. She wonders how accurate handwriting analysis is these days. Could anyone tell, by comparing her writing with this disguised signature (from such a small example after all, and where even the pen grip is different from her own), that it was actually she, Lily Waite, who signed it?

Four for a Boy

Bob refers to himself as a Barnardo's Boy, he's not ashamed to mention that he was left outside the orphanage at the age of six weeks, with no note, no nothing except the grey blanket he was wrapped in. He never knew his parents, but he's sure they were good folks, they had their reasons. Maybe his mum was a young lass, his dad a bit feckless. They had no one else to turn to, that's how it was back then.

He did all right in the orphanage. Naturally enough he was keen to leave, quick as he could, which was age fifteen, in his case, when he ran away to join the Navy. Well, that didn't really suit him – too much like hard work, he laughs, his big belly shifting a little, rising and falling like Santa Claus. That's when he came back to our Taddy, to John Smith's Brewery to be exact, and that's where he's been ever since, give or take a brief stint at the steelworks when he fell out with the new foreman.

'Just as well I were took back when I came to me

senses, as that were the year I met our Brenda.' Brenda was working at Rowntree's sweet factory, he had an invitation from one of his mates to the Christmas dance, that's how he met her. He knew right away Brenda was the lass for him. He likes to tell Lily what a looker her mum was, but he withholds other things about Brenda that drew him. She was fragile, like blown glass. She needed protecting, she needed him, Bob, to do the job. And Brenda would not be going anywhere, she was one woman who wouldn't be straying.

Bob has two regrets about the orphanage and he mentions them just once to his daughter, in keeping with his motto, to 'keep y'sen cheerful'. One is that there was a lad there, another lad, just a year younger than him and called, funnily enough, young Bobby. Young Bobby didn't get to leave when Bob did, he never joined the Navy, in fact Bob never saw him again because, despite promises, he never did visit the orphanage after he left. One time he thought about it, he thought, I'll invite young Bobby to me wedding, but when he rang the orphanage they told him the lad died of diphtheria the year that Bob left. They grew up together like brothers, young Bobby and Bob, our Bob, big Bob as he has since become.

The other regret isn't so much of a regret, more an observation, a wry comment on himself, given with a chuckle. What he remembers most vividly about the orphanage is meal-times. A big dining room, a bit like school dinners, nothing too shocking, I mean, don't picture a scene out of one of your books, Charles Dickens or something. This was decent, regular food, shepherd's pie, Lancashire hotpot, veg, potatoes, but small portions, no extras. And Bob, always having Hollow Legs, as he referred to them, felt constantly anxious. He remembers the feeling twice a day, before each meal-time, his stomach groaning and his heart pounding with anxiety, a voice drumming in his head: will there be enough for me, will there be enough?

He hated to be greedy, he knew the other boys were hungry too, but if ever there was a chance, he secured the biggest portion. If he spied an unattended potato, he'd advance on it with devastating speed and agility, spike it with his fork and install it on his plate, quickly camouflaging it with gravy, before an enemy boy could inform on him.

'Been making up for it ever since,' Bob says. That's what his story is leading up to: an explanation for why he is 'a bit of a tub' as he calls it; 'well built' in his wife's words, 'Fatty Arbuckle' in Lily's. 'That were before you mind, before your mother and you. Now I've got everything a man could want; food on the table, food in the cupboards, a good wife, and the grandest daughter a man could wish for. You're all the world to me, lass, and don't you ever forget it.'

This afternoon at picking-up time Matthew has a letter which he thrusts at her. He doesn't say hello and Lily watches hungrily as other children run to parents, grin, fling arms around them, a flurry of smiles and hugs. She opens the letter.

Dear Mrs Waite,

Matthew has been excluded from school for four days. He has been biting other children, repeatedly ignoring reprimands from teachers, he refuses to talk in class or discuss his behaviour. Please bring him into school next Monday morning and arrange to speak to

*me – Ms Brightman – about Matthew's acceptance
back into school.*

Yours, Ms Brightman (Headteacher)

Lily reads the letter twice. Included with it is a booklet
entitled: *Fixed Term Exclusions in Primary Schools: Some
Notes for Parents.* Matthew's head bobs beside her. 'Can I
have some sweets?' he asks, as they wait to cross the road.

'Matthew, do you know what's in this letter?'

'No. Can I have some crisps?' He is tugging on
her arm. They are in the middle of the road and
Matthew makes a dash over it, in the direction of the
newsagent's.

'Matthew!! Come back here!'

Other parents leaving the school are staring at them.
Lily has a desire to yell *What are you fucking looking at?*
and she would, she almost would, except that she has
never said 'fucking' out loud, directed it at anyone in her
life, and the words can't quite get past her lips. She
catches up with Matthew at the newsagent's, grabs his
arm, tugging on a mitten which starts to unravel from his
coat, still attached to the string she recently sewed on it.

'No, you are not – having crisps! We're going home.
You're in – big – trouble!'

Her voice comes out in gulps, she's breathless with
the effort of holding on to him, now she has his skinny
little arm, rather than the mitten. He spins around and
kicks her.

'Ow!! You little sod!'

There is a second when they stand stock still, staring
at each other with exactly the same shocked expression.

Then Matthew bursts out: 'You called me a name!
You called me a name! You said it's wrong to call people
names!'

'You kicked me!' Lily yells right back, in exactly the same tone.

She tightens her grip, a combination of dragging and marching finally wrenching Matthew from the shop and towards the Flanders Estate. All the way there, his feet continue to strike at her in a fury, until her shins sting; she feels his small form in her grasp, a raging thing, something unleashed at her. She is saying *'Matthew, Matthew, calm down,'* but no one is listening, least of all her. Tears spring to her eyes; she is struggling to point Matthew towards the lift, while other people, a couple of grinning children, pass by in a blur.

It's only when Matthew manages to swing his head towards her arm and she sees his teeth bared, the glint of white and red, that she lets go of him, fully expecting him to whirl around anyway, his mouth stretched, ready to sink his teeth into her as if she were an apple. Instead he runs towards the stairs, she hears him pounding up one flight after another, while Lily waits, panting, crying, for the lift to arrive at the ground floor. Inside the metal box of the lift she composes herself a little, steadies herself in readiness for a 'calm but firm' approach, like the one in the book on taming the dragon in your child. She wipes her eyes with the back of her coatsleeve.

The lift doors slide open and there is Matthew, not eager for another round, as she expected, but dumbfounded, staring at the door to their flat, which is open, floating on its hinge like a flap of skin on a cut. It takes Lily several seconds to understand. She stares at the door, the debris of shredded wood around it, the broken lock, the dark empty corridor to their flat exposed for everyone to see. Her mind feels clogged, she can't put the simple information together; when she went out she locked the door, now she is back, the door is open, the lock is broken. Someone has been in her home.

'God, we've been burgled . . .' Lily is only dimly aware of Matthew, his eyes huge and silent, his small heart thumping heavily, nestling against her arm. They stand there for many seconds, transfixed, as if staring at the door could make the facts add up differently, offer an alternative explanation. Matthew breaks the moment, making a slight move, as if to step into the flat, and Lily shoots out her arm, to prevent him.

'No, don't go in! Someone might be there.'

Matthew obediently stands still, all defiance spent, staring at Lily, waiting for directions, what to do next. Even in the fog of her own swirling thoughts, Lily is aware of him, waiting, expecting something of her. For her to be the adult, the parent. To know what to do.

'Come on,' she says, a whisper, her voice surprisingly calm. 'Let's go down the stairs, not the lift. We shouldn't go in, just now. We'll go find Josh. He'll help us.'

She steers Matthew towards the stairwell, once descending they speed up, they're almost running. They arrive at Josh's flat breathless, Lily feels the sweat dampening her palms. She rings his bell, willing him to be home. When Josh comes to the door, unlocks the metal security grid, he is sleepy and disorientated. It's three forty-five on a weekday: he should be at work. Who could be ringing his doorbell – checking him – who knows he is here? Bewildered, two thoughts surge to the surface with equal power, equal irrationality. One is: it is Daphine, home; home to stay. Two, it's the police. It's about Neville, he's alive, they made a mistake.

Standing in his flapping shirt in the doorway, he sees that it is neither. It's just this girl, the white girl from upstairs; it's just Lily fluttering around like a ghost, with her dark shadow of a son hovering behind her. He tucks his shirt in, tries to tuck away his thoughts of Daphine and Neville, such damn foolishness.

'What happen?' he asks her.

'Someone's been in the flat – I've been burgled—'

'How you know that?'

'The door, the lock's all kicked in and smashed up. Can you – would you – come upstairs? I don't want to go in on my own. I don't know if someone is still in there.'

Josh rubs at his beard with one hand, nodding sleepily, trying to take in what she is saying. Guilt tweaks at him: he should have mentioned the security-door, pointed out to her that everyone else in this block has one. He registers the thought that someone might still be in her flat and tries to remember if he heard the lift go lately. But he was sleeping heavily, a sleep so deep and dreamless he is still having trouble coming up to the surface.

'Somebody in there?'

Now his voice sounds alarmed, he is conscious of his mouth being dry, of the tongue sticking to the roof of his mouth like a stamp to a letter.

'I don't know,' Lily says, her tone exasperated. 'But would you mind coming upstairs with us?'

Josh's feet are bare, dusty floor tiles beneath his toes. Slowly, without answering the girl, he goes to fetch socks, shoes, deliberately selecting the steel-cap boots he wears for work. He's in no rush. His heart beating fast. He would like to say no to this white girl, he doesn't even know why he isn't saying no. Just because he did give her one, once, that doesn't mean he owes her any little thing. His heart is thumping. Why do women expect men to do this thing, this being brave thing? That guy in there, might have a knife. He's thinking about Neville and she can't know about that but maybe Sherry told her something.

The three of them take the stairs, five flights. He walks behind Lily and the child, not fast. They emerge from the sludge-brown stairway to the landing outside Lily's flat. The door is just as she said, mashed up, and she stands there looking from the door to Josh and the child hasn't said a word, he stands like he's dumbstruck and Josh can see that the pair of them seem truly to expect him to go in there.

'The thing is, Lily, don't feel no way, but I don't think I can go in there . . .'

'What? What do you mean?'

She's scrabbling in her pockets for a cigarette and then lighting one and tugging on it without offering Josh a smoke and her skinny wrist, her twitchy line of a mouth, they make Josh feel sorry for her. Her eyes big in her head like a doe or a scared wild rabbit. He leans against the tiles. The three of them stare at the open door.

'He must have run by now,' Josh suggests.

'I suppose so,' Lily concedes.

'You call the police then?'

'No.'

'Go on, girl,' Josh murmurs, giving Lily the merest push. 'Leave the boy here with me.'

She hesitates, draws deeply on the cigarette and then steps gingerly over the threshold, the door thudding against the wall behind it. He understands her plan: to make as much noise as possible, to alert anyone hiding in there to her presence. Josh tries to breathe, closes his eyes against the pictures of Neville which won't stop flashing like a flicking card. Neville running, Neville, with his ghetto blaster, head to one side, arguing, Neville falling, slipping against a wall, against the bright shiny shop window. With an effort, a huge effort, Josh puts Neville out of his thoughts, puts instead an arm around Matthew's shoulders, tries a squeeze he hopes will reassure the child. The boy is silent, still as an owl in a tree; watchful.

In a short while Lily comes back and the three of them breathe out, slump their shoulders.

'Bloody TV's gone,' the girl says, bitterly. She grinds her cigarette under her foot in the hallway like she might want to grind a piece of Josh's head.

He steps towards her, touches her elbow.

'You can claim for the TV. On your insurance.'

The girl sniffs. She slumps against the door, like she's defeated, like somebody just punched her.

'I'm still in the middle of a bloody great battle with the insurance company. Over my last house. We had a fire. I had a visit from the loss adjuster to see if – if it was deliberate.' She looks at the child but she doesn't lower her voice. 'If I did it myself.'

Josh doesn't know what to say. He's wide awake now; the flick-book pictures of Neville, the frightened heart-beat, they've subsided. He watches her expression, the way she folds her bottom lip beneath her teeth like a child. The feeling he had about her that other time, when he saw her chase the boy across the estate, the feeling that prompted him to take her the box of sweets, whatever that feeling is, drawing him to Lily, he feels it again right now and strongly, in a rush, like oxygen filling his lungs.

They were in a fire. That explains a few things.

'I could come around later,' he suggests. 'Bring you some wine. Fix your door for you. Cheer you up . . .'

'I'll get the council to fix the door. But the rest. Yes please. Come round later.'

She does her best to smile, ushering the child into the flat. As an afterthought, she calls over her shoulder – 'thank you' – but Josh is in the lift now, the doors are gliding shut, there's no time for him to say it's all right or better still, I'm sorry girl. Take care of yourself.

So, later that night, Josh does come upstairs and Matthew is asleep and the girl leads him into the living room, fully dressed this time in jeans and a tight black T-shirt. Her small mouth is darkened with lipstick and her cropped hair looks different too, like maybe she washed it and can't get it to sit flat. Josh smiles to himself; she reminds him of a fluffy baby chick, but he senses she wouldn't like that, so he's not about to tell her. He has cooked her some fish, good and peppery, and brings it up in a covered dish; it's the red snapper he mentioned, he bought it fresh this morning from Ridley Road. His dad worked as a fisherman, briefly, before he left Jamaica, and red snapper was a Friday night treat when Josh was a pic'nee, around the same age her son is now.

In another dish he has rice and peas with coconut. Lily fetches cutlery from the kitchen, and he watches as she digs in hungrily, takes the first forkful to her mouth, then splutters, her grey eyes glittering with tears. He can't help laughing.

'Jamaican food too hot for you, huh?'

'Wow,' is all she says.

He asks her if she phoned the police. Where the TV used to be there's an obvious gap, the sofa and one chair directed towards it so that they can't avoid the foolishness of staring at an empty space.

'Oh the police. They were here for about ten minutes, took some notes. They don't exactly sound optimistic about finding who did it. They thought it was probably kids. I gather it's an occupational hazard of living in London, being burgled.'

'It didn't happen where you come from?'

'I've never been burgled before, no.'

He has brought beer, too, cans of Red Stripe that he had planned to drink by himself, stealing the day off work to lie in bed and drink. That's what he was doing this afternoon, when Lily came by his flat. Now he has other ideas for how to make use of his day, how to soak up a few hours.

'Why did you move here?' Josh asks.

'The council rehoused me, after the fire. I mean, I could have been rehoused in Yorkshire, near my parents, near my old house, but, I don't know. I wanted to come to London. I wanted to get away. Make a fresh start. These are Hard To Lets round here. It took a while but the council wants to fill empty properties. At least in theory.'

She sips her beer. He thinks: she wants to escape the memories. Like Daphine, going to Jamaica, as if Neville is not going to follow. But he knows different. He doesn't want to push her, but he can't help his curiosity, makes one last attempt. 'I thought you said your husband was a fireman?'

'He is – was.'

'Seem funny, you having a fire. You didn't have no smoke alarm?'

'The battery was finished. I kept meaning to replace it.'

Lily stands up, holds out her hand for his empty plate. She doesn't look him in the eyes, walks towards the kitchen.

'Your husband rescue you?'

Her back is towards him. Her voice is very quiet and she doesn't turn around.

'No,' she says, letting the door swing behind her.

When she re-enters the room her expression is different, smiling, she brings him a fresh can of beer from the fridge and sits down again beside him. 'Thank you. That was a lovely dinner.'

'You didn't get burnt then,' Josh says, softly.

Lily turns her bright smile on him. 'No. Totally unscathed. We just lost our belongings.'

She snaps open her can of beer. A noisy snap. A silence. Josh stares at her a moment longer, willing her to look up at him. She stares into the beer can like the secret is in there; the husband, the house, whatever. When he realises she is not about to look up, he drinks from his own beer, pulls a folded airmail letter from the back pocket of his jeans.

'I have a next letter from Daphine.'

He hands it to Lily, who finally raises her eyes. She unfolds the letter slowly, begins reading.

Dear Landy,

Hope this letter finds you well. I've been to visit every-one – Mark, the kids, Sophie, Stephanie, Maxine. Everybody asks after you. They are all wondering when you're coming to visit Portie or when I'm going back to London. They ask about Neville but I can't tell them much Landy. Sometimes I think maybe if we did talk about Neville things might be easier between us. But it feels like that boy is still tied to my apron strings. I can't believe he was even full grown. I still can't believe we lost him. All those years, all that

work, that grey rain, living in London. I don't know
what it was all for.

Landy forgive me for this letter. I do hope you
been getting to work on time, not playing too many
card games with Winston and Laverne, and I hope
you're eating good.

Your loving wife, Daphine.

Now a longer, bigger kind of silence. Lily folds the letter, hands it back to him inside its envelope, as if she's sorry she ever looked at it. Josh closes his eyes, trying to make the room, Lily, disappear. Eyes closed, he feels how drunk he is. He feels himself sinking, feels his ability to bob to the surface deserting him. The girl's voice drags him back, her hand on his arm.

'Do you want me to write back to her?'

'No. It's fine.'

He stares at Lily's mouth, the lipstick licked off now, the bottom lip folded under. He remembers last time, the feel of her skinny ribcage beneath his hands. He thinks of her as something tough, something like him, the feel of her is like a wicker basket, and just as springy, just as impenetrable.

He strokes her face with one finger, tracing the worried lines around the mouth.

'I don't feel like writing to Daphine just now. I feel like being with you.'

He sees the leap, the light dart in her eyes. She's shy but she doesn't try to hide it. She edges a little closer to him on the sofa.

'You want some ganja?' Josh asks, remembering her nervousness last time and seeing her reach for her cigarettes.

Her expression is surprised, but she says yes. Pulling a cushion from the sofa, he flings it on the floor and pats it. 'Why don't you lie on here?'

He rolls the joint for them, sprinkling in it the last of the grass that Winston brought him. Lily obediently puts her head on the cushion and grins at him. 'Skinny girl,' he mutters, into her hair; the girl responds with a small moan, as if he'd said he loved her. They smoke the ganja and then he is running his hands over her skin inside the T-shirt, peeling back the lace of her bra.

'The boy's asleep?' he asks. She nods. Josh kisses her; tastes fish. 'You like this?'

'Yes.'

'Close your eyes.'

'I want to keep them open.'

Josh knows that last time he was too quick and he doesn't want Lily to think he doesn't know how to satisfy a woman. The girl is kind of tight, she's not relaxed but she is certainly keen. She allows him to lift her, to suggest a few things to her, she sits up on him when he asks her, she bends her body different ways for him. She's willing but to Josh she is like a virgin, this little blonde bendy thing; he can't believe she was ever married. Josh takes more care this time, he tries not to lose himself in her, but that, in the end, is the point, and finally the drink and the spliff and the not-thinking about Daphine and Neville catch up with him and he is plunging into her anyway, plunging and diving and never wanting to come up for air.

He is shocked then, when, afterwards, already dressing, the girl says: I need thirty quid. Do you have thirty quid? She sits in her jeans leaning forward slightly, doing up her bra.

'You need thirty quid?' Josh says, recovering himself.

'I've spent my Income Support. I have a book, the next date is Monday. I could pay you back then, if that's okay—'

It's one thing to give, another to be asked. Josh wonders if he insulted her. He holds out a cigarette to her, but he is mad suddenly, he wants to call her a silly white girl, *white* is what he wants to call her and to say it bodily, spitefully. Instead he feels in his jeans pocket for his wallet, takes out two crinkled notes, dirty notes, this time. Exactly the kind Lily might expect a police mechanic to handle, that is, if she knows what he does for a living.

She stands up, nods her thanks for the money. They walk to the front door in silence.

'The emergency team at the council fix your door then,' Josh remarks, pausing before opening it. 'You should get an iron door, like everyone else. For security.'

'I will,' Lily answers.

He pictures his own flat, the unmade bed, the closed windows, the fridge now emptied of beer.

'Not scared to stay here on your own, after the burglary?' he asks.

'No,' the girl answers firmly, surprising him. She opens the door for him. Then she surprises him again with the boldness of her question.

'Neville – is, was that your son?'

'If you know, why ask?'

'Sherry said—'

'I don't want to talk about him.'

'Okay. I'm sorry.'

It's the first time she has kissed him, spontaneously, on the mouth. She does it shyly, standing on tiptoes and with her lips closed; a dry kiss, merely a brush. Josh suddenly has a powerful longing to be kissed by

Daphine: Lily's kiss is like a leaf, like something falling, scarcely passing his mouth on the way down.

The memories which stay on the surface are always the bad ones, like sour bits in milk. All the times Josh did things wrong; shouted at the boy, had no time for him, slippered him that one time when Neville didn't come home straight from school and gave Daphine a bad scare. That slippering moment, the once, just the once he raised his hand to the boy and only because, he thought briefly, that was what fathers were meant to do, what his own father never did: care enough to show the child – he must have been eight, nine at the time – that staying out like that scared Josh and Daphine *bodily*.

Now Josh cannot get his own misdemeanours out of his mind. He struggles to shake them and replay every little thing until Neville's whole life, from start to finish, looks like a happy one; worthwhile. Occasionally he pictures Neville in Jamaica, walking home at night through the banana trees, listening to an owl hoot and him calling back *Who, who? Who there?* Then Josh realises it is himself he is picturing, not Neville; Neville never even visited.

Josh met Daphine in Jamaica, she was on holiday in Portland. She walked into a bar where he was playing cards with his brother Mark, she tells them she thinks Jamaica is so romantic with its beaches and its mountains and it's where her family comes from. He says to her *No your family come from Africa . . .* and Daphine, a year older than him at nineteen, sassy with it, said of course I know that, that's ancient history. He likes her English accent so much, she did a lot of schooling, he never heard a black woman with an accent like that; he thinks he could fall for her, right then and there, and he does.

Sure, he thinks, it's true like his brother says at the time, that he thinks of Daphine as a meal ticket, a British passport. He always did mean to go to London, to seek his father who left Portland in the fifties to work for British Rail and sent no letter, no word, since. Then when the child comes, Neville, Josh gets to loving Daphine more than he meant to and forgetting about his father and to thinking hard about this thing, this difficult thing of staying with your baby-mother and of what being a father really means. Josh has his own theory and he shares it with Daphine and he likes the way she thinks he's brighter than her, despite his lack of learning, and never does nag at him to go back to school. She doesn't have a problem with writing his cheques for him or nothing like that. Daphine thinks his Rastafarianism is not for true because he eats meat, he isn't strict, but she comes to learn that Landy, as she calls him, her Landy, cares about the I and I, he knows his history. Why can't we stick by our baby-mothers, why do all the fathers leave? Josh wonders. It's like Bob sings, the African family is all mash up, the fathers torn from the children.

Landy's father didn't write not one time, he just cared for his own sweet self. Daphine has Spanish blood from some bastard she thinks of as her far-back-centuries grandfather, that's why she thinks the boy Neville so beautiful.

Neville. The child playing on the estate, darting between rusty cars, kicking a ball up against a wall, up against a sign that he finally confesses to Josh reads: *No Ball Games*. Neville climbing on the bins at the bottom of the flats, Neville that one time he got the slipper from Josh for hiding out at his friend Junior's flat, when he should be coming straight home. Neville with his hand over his big brown eyes, trying not to cry, taking the blows from Josh, the blows which Josh tries to knock into him: I'm your father. I love you. Don't scare your mother like that. *Rass, boy don't ever do that to us again. Neville, Neville, Neville.*

Lily listens, frozen in her hallway, as the lift takes Josh downstairs to his own flat. She lied: she is terrified of being on her own in the flat. Before Josh's visit, she'd phoned the police. They arrived in half an hour, in no hurry at all. Cursory, uninterested, asking: So, it's only the TV that's missing, is that right? and Lily is forced to answer yes, yes, she thinks so, but her strongest feeling is that it isn't true, something else is missing.

When they left, she wandered from room to room, trying to take stock. What was touched, what was handled, what else has gone? She has to appear calm, keep a hold of herself in front of Matthew. She watches his worried face and tells him 'We're fine aren't we? Just the TV gone and we can soon get another—'

It's this acting, this holding herself together for Matthew, that keeps her going. After he falls asleep, once she has soothed and reassured him, brought him hot milk, read him a story, after she has spent the evening making love with Josh, telling him she's fine, too. After all that, she's convinced herself. She's coped, even, while not really meaning to cope; just going through the motions, taking care of Matthew. Thinking of the months after the fire, the months before coming here, when she stayed at Bob and Brenda's, how she felt in a permanent fog. There was no reason to cope. Bob and Brenda did everything for her.

In her first term at Leeds University, one of the girls she met – Camilla – told Lily her bedsit had been burgled. Lily remembers being horrified, secretly glad she herself was living at home, where no such thing could happen. But then she also remembers Camilla telling her that the bedsit was covered by her parent's insurance policy and that before the police arrived to talk to her she made a list of things – expensive camera and equipment, Gucci watch, CD player – that she intended to claim for.

'I didn't know you had a Gucci watch,' Lily said.

'I don't, silly. But I have the *receipt* for one. I bought it for someone ages ago. You have to save receipts, you know, then you can claim for things.'

Camilla – to Lily's astonishment – was true to her word and had drawers stuffed with receipts for everything she had ever bought, every purchase ever made. Lily was shocked, she can distinctly remember the feeling. But more than an affront to her honesty, which she has to admit now was scarcely ever put to the test, it struck her as *unfair*. Because Camilla always *had* plenty – of things, of money, of security; she could easily get more.

The real trick – the one Lily is learning now – is how to start from nothing.

It was embarrassing, asking Josh for money. She had bought Matthew shoes with most of the forty pounds, and wishes now she'd saved it, bought food. So much to worry about. Between the burglary and money and Matthew's exclusion, she doesn't know which thing to worry about first and that – oddly – is helping too, it means she is preoccupied. Basic day-to-day stuff, food, money – survival issues. She has to just get on with it.

Then there's the card, the credit card, the one wrongly delivered. Ms L Stanley, Louisa Stanley on the envelope.

Lily has it in her purse. She has been looking at it again, ruminating. The police were so unperturbed, crime in this part of London, or perhaps just on the Flanders Estate, seems to be a run-of-the-mill occurrence. It's only a matter of time before that little slip of plastic burns a hole – as Bob would say – right into Lily's pocket.

After Matthew's exclusion, Lily has to visit the school. She has the word *supplicant* in her head, she knows she has to persuade the school that Matthew will shape up and that his current behaviour is a temporary settling in problem. She has rigged herself up already with a smile so sharp the top half of her head is in danger of falling off.

Lily rakes the comb through Matthew's hair, snaps shut his lunch-box, twists the toggles under his chin.

'I've got my grain,' Matthew tells her, 'like Nannie has her grain, I can't go into school,' and Lily corrects him unsmilingly. 'It's not your grain, its migraine you mean, and that's not what you have.'

Monday morning is windy and stepping on to the street Lily has a sudden melancholy, scattered feeling, as if the children and adults are being blown around like the empty sweet wrappers which flutter at her ankles; as if no one has control over anything, least of all where they are going.

'We have to make more effort.' (Brightly she says this. Cheerfully.) 'This is all we have now. Each other.'

It's true, but she feels guilty for saying it, for rubbing it in.

Matthew refuses to hold her hand, marches slightly in front of her, hands in pockets, yellow and green rucksack like a strange, bright insect, clinging to his back, barging through the doors to school, not looking back to see if she is following.

'Thank you for coming Mrs Waite.'

Today Ms Brightman is dressed in a short grey skirt and a fitted cardigan, in a deep red. She looks business-like and sexy all at once, and Lily has a flash of Ms Brightman's home life, her marriage to a young arts education officer, their house one of those new-built confections by the river, full of windows and light. She doesn't know any of this but there's one thing she's certain of: Ms Brightman doesn't have children.

'As you know, we are increasingly worried about Matthew—'

'Yes.'

'I understand that he has had some difficulty settling in, but we need Matthew to know that we are on his side. Matthew? Do you understand that?'

'He does, I'm sure,' says Lily quickly, when it is clear that Matthew is not about to answer.

'Matthew, I need you to look at me when I'm talking to you.'

Ms Brightman sighs as Matthew, kicking his heels against the back of his chair, stares blankly towards the calendar on the wall, at the smiley faces of children in an African school with their white dresses and their outdoor classroom.

'Well. I have some recommendations, Mrs Waite, but Matthew can run along now to his classroom, as I think you and I should discuss them on our own. And Matthew – no more nonsense, do you hear me? You are a clever boy – a very clever boy – and you aren't doing yourself any favours with this dreadful biting and non-communication. Do you understand me?'

Matthew gets up slowly, lifting each limb as if it were

stuck in treacle. Lily has to resist a desire to slap him, to push him physically out of the room and out of her sight, but instead she says, merrily: 'Come on Matthew. Off you go. I'll see you at three thirty,' and then turns back to the headteacher, a smile ready on her lips.

Ms Brightman's office is tiny and colourful, with children's pictures and plastic box-files competing for space. Everything neat and in its place, as if the office were made of yellow and red Lego blocks. But what Lily really marvels at is how Ms Brightman keeps the rest of London, of this part of London, out. Outside her office, outside Wishley School is greyness, cracked paving stones, dog shit and crisp packets, overflowing bins and police sirens and steel council doors boarding up flats. Wishley School seems to be just that – wishful thinking – with the happy faces on the multicultural calendar and the cheery children's drawings, which right now look pretty sinister to Lily: balloon heads and stick bodies and wide, jagged mouths, open in expressions of sheer terror.

'I think we should begin a Statementing process for Matthew, to enable him to get some extra help,' Ms Brightman announces.

'I – I'm not sure what that is—'

'Well. It's what the law requires, when a child has E and B – sorry, emotional and behavioural – problems.'

She produces a cardboard file, and begins writing. 'Matthew has been excluded. That entitles me to involve the Ed Psych—'

'Sorry?'

'The Educational Psychologist. She can do an assessment on Matthew and we can go on from there. I also suggest you visit the Child and Family Services unit . . .'

Lily looks puzzled, so Ms Brightman painstakingly explains: 'What used to be called Child Guidance – and talk to someone there about Matthew's behavioural difficulties.'

Ms Brightman scribbles something on a yellow Post-It sticker and passes it to Lily.

'That's their number. Or you might want to try Family Therapy. I understand Matthew's father is not around?'

Lily nods, shortly.

'Hm. Here's the number for the Family Therapy Centre.'

Another Post-It sticker, this time red. The pad has five different colours. Lily can't help thinking how much Matthew would like that notepad. He likes every kind of stationery, the more important and business-like the better. Lily's eyes are filling with tears, she feels a strange kind of betrayal, as if they aren't talking about her son at all, as if her desire to smack him of a few moments ago never happened, as if there is something else, and there is: something easily understood, ready to be applied to Matthew, but just out of reach. Beneath anger at Matthew, in fact whenever the anger abates, is an appalling, aching sadness for him. Her picture of Matthew, the tiny flash she has right now, is this: last night, he held out his hands in his sleep and said *Not that, I need that!* as though someone were trying to take a toy from him. Matthew is keeping up his own litany, similar to hers.

She is afraid of Matthew's list. At least her own list can be addressed, she's building up slowly, she has a plan.

'Thank you very much. Well, I – um – I hope I won't have to call in again about Matthew.'

Lily stands up to leave. She wishes she were taller, at least over five foot one, for around the ten millionth time in her life.

'I'll start the Statementing process straight away,' Ms Brightman assures her. 'I wonder if you could close the door on the way out? Bye now, Mrs Waite, thanks again for coming.'

It is as she is obediently closing the door behind her, then padding down the tiled corridor, then glancing at a display of tissue butterflies with *Class 2B: Visit to the Butterfly House* written underneath, that it swells up, the memory Lily has been suppressing for the entire meeting. It must have happened to her in junior school. Bob and Brenda don't know about it, she doesn't remember them ever coming to the school. It involved the headteacher – Mr Royce – and another teacher, a woman with a wool skirt and hair smelling of strong hairspray, whose name floats around her somewhere, just out of Lily's grasp.

This teacher gave off to the ten-year-old Lily a rasping sound; the texture of the woman was stiff, exactly as if the whole of her – skirt, jumper, tights – was doused in hairspray, would chafe to the touch. The two adults stood in the Head's office, blocking the light from the window, until Lily felt smaller than ever, in their shadow. They were talking, the words lost now to obscurity but not the tone: hefty with disapproval, portentous even, predicting all the ways in which Lily would go to the bad, if she carried on like this. It was the only time, the one and only time in her entire schooling, she was lectured like this and Lily was frightened. She felt the weight of their forewarnings soaking into her. Day dreaming. Staring out of the window. Not listening. Compulsive scribbling when the teacher was talking. Switching off.

Lily listened in silence, her grey A-line skirt floating around her skinny spaghetti legs, struggling not to bring to the fore the very thing they are accusing her of: the switching off habit, the ability to tune out. Don't get involved, Brenda says. Keep y'sen cheerful, Bob says. And now this: stop switching off. How hard she has battled to obey their contradictory decrees only she, Lily, can know. But what she can't shake, then or now, is the sense of inevitability, that despite her attempts to please the adults, to fashion herself in their image, someone else, some other little girl – one who is involved and is *not* cheerful – keeps surfacing, and with her comes the feeling of being deeply, utterly wrong. The wrong child. Unwelcome.

As if by magic, the second this thought formed, the word itself came up, Mr Royce droning on: you are developing the *wrong* attitude young lady. So now it was said, done. Everything about Lily was wrong and she must work hard at all times to keep this fact hidden, she does work hard, she worked hard right up until losing Alan in fact and even now she is trying to go back to that habit of work, but something is lost and she can't, the effort needed feels too immense.

Her head is aching, as she closes the huge security door at the front of Matthew's school, aching with the effort of summoning up this old Lily, the childhood one, who saw herself in the light the adults shone on her and understood completely her *wrongness*. She thinks something similar is required for Matthew but she is weary, perhaps she doesn't care enough, she is not like her own parents, without Alan around, she can't be bothered to do it. Instead she keeps picturing Matthew in the Legoland office, staring over Ms Brightman's head at the calendar, chewing on the collar of his sweater, his woolly hair uncombed, making sure his eyes roam the room and land anywhere, anywhere but on the headteacher's face. And Lily has an odd desire to say: it's okay, Matthew, you're bloody difficult, you're not what I expected, but you didn't ask to be here, I'm responsible, I called you up from God knows where, but you're welcome, all right, *come as you are*. Of course Lily knows it would be counter-productive, downright irresponsible of her as a parent, a newly single parent, to say such a thing.

She stands for a moment, blinking in the sharp yellow light of the leafy concrete playground, letting her memories curl up inside her like a sleeping cat. She wants to be a good mother. She doesn't know what's happened to her lately, nothing is the same and this giddy elation that keeps sneaking up on her, the same giddiness she feels whenever she pictures her new apartment, her view of planes and birds, and particularly when she summons up Josh. Well, she definitely needs to work on that giddiness, fight it a little, try harder. She must try to remember what Ms Brightman had to say.

Come as you are. A strange expression. It drifts around in her head. Lingers, like smoke.

Five for Silver

Brenda has a problem – a type of special illness, she tells her daughter, and it's called agoraphobia. It means that she must stay at home, but it has its advantages too, doesn't it, she says, because it means I'm here when you come in from school. I can be waiting with cookies and milk like on the American programmes, like *Bewitched* or *The Partridge Family*. See, every cloud has a silver lining. Depends how you look at things.

Brenda does leave the house sometimes, but only with Bob. The ritual is a bit convoluted but Bob is a good man, he understands. The three of them, Bob pushing the trolley, Brenda throwing in the packets of All-Bran, the Penguin biscuits, Lily reading out the list, doing the family shopping together on a Saturday at Asda. Brenda couldn't possibly leave her daughter in the house on her own, and she couldn't expect Bob to do the shopping on his own when he has worked a long week at the Brewery. Anyway, Bob likes choosing food as much as she does.

He always adds something a little extra, with a wink: a packet of Malted Milk biscuits, or Bird's Instant Whip. He loves to have food in the cupboards, does Bob, so it isn't too much of a chore for him.

The launderette is a bit more tricky, Bob hates to sit in that overheated soapy atmosphere, watching the socks go round. Still, Brenda gets around that eventually, she persuades Bob to buy her an automatic on the Never Never. People in the village are used to seeing Brenda and Bob together, Tweedledee and Tweedledum, never Brenda alone. If they want to see Brenda they visit her at home, they bring her magazines and baked almond tarts as if she is ill. She reminds them constantly, cheerfully but politely that she's not, that she doesn't mind not going out, she's perfectly happy. Sometimes she offers to do a spot of sewing for her friends, line their curtains, fix up the sleeves on Mandy's birthday frock, she doesn't mind at all, she's happy to help. Lily's a good girl, never gives her mother a moment's bother, always home from school on the dot of 3.33 p.m., it takes her three minutes flat to run down the hill to their house.

Once, her daughter did ask her if she's bored, if she's lonely, doesn't she just long to go out, sometimes? Brenda is quick to reassure her. 'I've got everything I want right here at home. You and your Dad. That's enough for anyone, that's plenty, my girl.'

Brenda's hobby, her habit, Bob calls it, teasingly, is shopping from home. She orders every kind of home shopping catalogue. The great heavy books arrive on the doorstep with a smell of shiny new paper and a feeling like opening a Christmas present, only Brenda doesn't open them at first, she saves them; better to take that pleasure later, when Lily is at school, when she can be sure of being undisturbed. After she has listened to

Jimmy Young on the radio, that moment between washing up the plate from her cheese and beetroot sandwich and making a cup of milky coffee, she can feel the itchiness in the roof of her mouth, anticipation sneaking along the hairs on her arms. She reaches into the cupboard, thumps the hefty book on to the kitchen table with a resounding thwack. Sometimes she is still moored there, riveted in the same position, when Lily gets home from school; her hair mussed, a mug of tea cold and scummy on the table beside her, biting at the nib of a pen until blue ink spatters her lower lip. One hand busily filling out the booklet, the order forms.

Then the packages arrive, always as Lily is leaving for school, so that Brenda whips them to one side, stuffs them in the same cupboard, feigns a casual interest. 'I'll look at that later. That might be something for your Dad.' When Lily has gone she dashes upstairs and soon the bedroom is awash with packages, plastic and tissue and coat-hangers strewn on the bed, the dressing table, flopping over the back of a chair. When Brenda twirls around and surveys the room she has to laugh at herself, the scene is one of frenzy; she pictures herself tearing at the wrappings with her teeth, like a wolf.

Brenda is generous with these parcels, once they have been opened. Often what is inside is for Lily or Bob. 'Come in here,' Brenda beckons Lily, home from school, calling from her pink and white bedroom and holding out to Lily something squeaky, still scented with newness, with its arrival from somewhere else, somewhere outside their house. She turns her doll-sized daughter in front of the mirror, smiling and smiling at the sight of her in the whipped-cream fake-fur coat. 'Who's my lovely girl then? Aren't you the pretty one?'

Bob pays for Brenda's habit, but he never complains.

Most of the parcels are returned, anyway, you have fourteen days if they're unworn. Some she keeps without opening them, for future times, times when she's down in the dumps. Things to cheer her up; crisp new pillowcases, brand new socks for Lily, the pleasure of unpeeling them from the packet like two fresh kippers.

Any road, it's not the pleasure of opening or using, that's not it at all. It's the pleasure of dreaming, having, keeping. Only Bob understands this, how things can be such a great comfort, how safe they can make you feel. He understands. He feels the same way about food. Also, something more. Something Bob wouldn't understand. It's the phoning up. The writing of the order forms. The complaining if they get it wrong, send the wrong thing. Brenda enjoys this, too, the interaction, the friendly women's voices on the end of the phone, the comforting picture she has of other women, in villages all over Britain, cups of coffee and a jaffa cake beside them, a pen at the ready, listening to the radio, ordering from catalogues.

Lily is broke, she can't ask Josh again for money, she wonders whether to ask her parents. She dials their number without fully meaning to, she's lying on the sofa, feeling sleepy. It's Bob who answers the phone. 'Hello girl.' As if she was just down the road. As if she never went away.

'Your mother's been worried sick.'

'I didn't say I'd ring every day. I've been busy Dad.'

'How's the lad?'

'He's fine. He's doing okay at school. It's near the flat. It's nice.'

'He likes it then? Settling in?'

'He's fine.'

'That's good.'

'Yes.'

'Well, d'you want a word with your mother? Brenda! Here's our Lily . . .'

'No, Dad, I wanted to talk to you . . .' Fizzing on the line while Bob fetches Brenda.

'Hello love.' Brenda's voice a little breathless.

'Hi, Mum.'

'You didn't give us the number there. Let me get a pen. I've been worried sick—'

'Dad said. It's just I've been busy. Settling in, getting Matthew to school, getting everything sorted—'

'How's the job-hunt going? How's the flat? How's our little lad? We miss him, you know—'

'I'm still looking for work. Everything's fine.'

Brenda's questions come in a volley, one after the other. Lily wonders why her mother bothers, since she never waits to hear the answer. The giddy feeling again.

She gives her mother the telephone number and address, leaving out the 'estate' part and calling it Flanders Road. She thinks it will still get there and she knows that Brenda imagines a terrace; council owned maybe, but maisonettes, each with an individual, envelope-sized garden.

'There's another letter here for you, from the loss adjuster at the insurance company,' Brenda informs her. 'Your father opened it. Just more of the same. Sorry for the delay, they're still making enquiries, that kind of thing. Do you want me to forward it?'

'No cheque then?' Lily asks, without optimism.

'No love. What about the money we lent you? Surely you haven't spent it all yet?'

'Oh, no, it's okay, I'm fine for money,' Lily replies hurriedly. 'Anyhow Mum, I have to go soon . . .'

'And Tommy was asking after you, remember him? Tommy Spottiswood. I met him in the dentist the other day—'

'Mum, I have to go—'

'Okay, love, I've got your number now, so I'll ring again soon. As long as everything's all right? The flat's nice and you have nice neighbours?'

'Yes, Mum, the neighbours are fine.'

'Give Matthew our love, then. Look after yourself . . .'

'Yes, I will. Say bye to Dad for me. Yes. Bye Mum.'

Lily's twelfth birthday party, Brenda has made her a cake, iced pink with twelve candles and twelve roses, handmade by Brenda from icing sugar and a recipe in *Woman's Realm*. She has bought Lily clothes from the catalogue that Lily picked out herself, and a first bra, the smallest possible, size 28aa.

A cosy moment, mother and daughter together in the kitchen, opening packages. Lily would have liked a friend over, more than one perhaps, even to go to the pictures, but Brenda isn't up to that.

Pink and purple flowered paper rustles on the table between them. Lily rests her elbows on the table, amidst crumbs from the cake. A slatted blind allows light into the kitchen in neat stripes. Brenda is licking her fingers, absent-mindedly, pleased that her daughter likes her presents, imagining Lily in the sweet checked A-line skirt she's chosen. She's quite unprepared for the sharpness of Lily's question.

'How did it start, your agoraphobia? Were you always like that?'

'Oh. I don't know,' is Brenda's first startled response, playing for time. Her daughter is staring hard at her, that unnerving line of her mouth set determinedly.

'Was it before you met Dad?'

'Yes, yes it was. I mean I had the same panic attacks as a child. I was quite sickly. I had the smallpox and no one thought I'd pull through. I think they started after that.'

'But you went to school? You even told me you had a job once, when you first met Dad . . .'

'A job of sorts. I worked at Rowntree's. The sweet factory. I used to bring home bags of misshapes, you know the chocolate that comes out wrong. Doesn't look so good, but it tastes fine . . .'

'Well. How did you manage that then, if you were so – ill – every time you went out of the house?'

'My brother worked there too. I was all right if he was around . . .'

'But did it get worse, then? I mean – *I* won't get it will I?'

Brenda relaxes, smiles at her daughter, realising at last the reason for the questioning, glad it's something she understands, easy to reassure.

'Of course not. It's not *genetic*. The worst attack I ever had was on my wedding day. All those people. It was when we stepped out of the church and someone threw rice at us, and a photographer ran up to us. I just keeled over. Straight into Bob's arms.'

Lily ponders this. She has seen wedding photographs and it's true, Brenda does look a touch *green around the gills* as Bob would say, leaning slightly against a much thinner Bob, clutching a tiny posy of flowers. Lily has looked at those photos many times. Perhaps this news of Brenda's worst attack explains the disquiet Lily always feels, staring at the photos.

'Any road. At least I met your Dad. A good man, willing to take care of me. He never gave me a hard time about my – special illness. He's worked hard, your father, for us, you know. Especially when you think of where he came from. I sometimes think' (and here Brenda smiles again, clearly safe in the knowledge that it never crossed Bob's mind), 'I sometimes wonder, why didn't he just marry someone with money, why fall for me, the local drunk's lass, somebody just like him, without a bean? We didn't have much in our house when I was a girl. I can't remember owning a book, having books, like you.'

Allowing the thought to sink in, Lily feels a stab, a twist in her stomach. Not to own a book. She stares at her mother, searches Brenda's face for what this must be like, this not owning a book, but Brenda is smiling brightly, hurrying on:

'No need to look at me like that, lass, those days are over. Look at what we have now . . .'

Brenda sweeps an arm around the small kitchen; the shiny toaster, the brown and cream painted cupboards, the framed pictures of Venice, Rome, Paris. Lily feels a tug – a terrible guilty tug. She loves her mother. She doesn't know why she is sure, so convinced, at twelve years old, that her parents never visited Venice. Or Rome or Paris. The most sorrowful, painful, confusing feeling of all. To streak ahead, like this. To have so much, so many lovely things, for no good reason, to be undeserving.

I'm sorry, Lily thinks. I'm sorry you never got to Venice, you never had a book. Brenda is still smiling, soon she is at the sink, pink rubber-gloves on, washing their plates. Lily sweeps crumbs from the table into the palm of her hand, scattering them over the wrapping paper she finds in the pedal-bin. When she takes her foot from the pedal, the lid flips back down with a resounding plastic snap.

Lily is writing fervidly at a table in a café, writing her list. She's in the West End near Covent Garden, hungry for things. The café is one she guesses is stylish; the decor black and white and minimalist, with metal chairs that Brenda would think are for putting in the garden and a visible, white-tiled kitchen at the back. The lighting reminds Lily of being at the dentist, but the comforting thing is that writing in a notebook is not weird at all; a quick glance around at the young women in their leather coats, the guys in their black jeans, assures her that everyone here is doing it. Lily's heart is racing, her mouth is dry. She feels how she does when she pictures Josh, standing in her kitchen, suddenly naked, his brown eyes smiling at her.

Duvet cover with Winnie the Pooh design, she writes. The writing gets faster and faster, messier and messier. *Bodum cafetière*. She can smell the Guinness Punch Josh made for her, the oil he uses on his hair, the scent of his skin, warm and salty. *Photograph of Matthew in Brenda and Bob's arms, wearing silly Santa hat*. She can feel her body leap, leap towards him as he bends to kiss her mouth. The notebook is full, she flips it closed with a snap and reaches in one of the bags at her feet for another, this one from Muji, with a silver and pink cover.

She breathes in the smell of clean paper, continues writing ferociously. In front of her on the table is a glass of cranberry and orange juice, untouched. The murmur of voices, chinking cutlery, the rain outside drumming, combine to make her feel cosy, invisible; drowned by the noise, like being the only silent one in a demented school dinner-hall, or in the kitchen with Brenda while the old-fashioned washing machine thunders through the spin cycle.

Lily tucks the plastic carrier bags at her feet a little closer around her, resists the temptation to peep in them again. Her heartbeat is so fast she feels giddy, in danger of fainting. Slender new plastic bags, soft to the touch, with their light rustling sound, their shiny good things; stockings in the finest denier, a suede purse like a baby's cheek and at the bottom, wrapped in lemon-coloured tissue paper, a tiny delicious parcel like a pastry, the best thing of all: a night-dress in apricot silk with lace in the palest vanilla, to fit bust size 32–34. ('*How would you like to pay, Madam? Cash or credit?*' '*Credit card, please.*')

Her heart pounding and pounding, her stomach ready to leave her body, but then elation, her heart flying up again, her lungs filling with air. It's so easy. Easier than she could ever have imagined, to cross this strange barrier, to feel it dissolve around her as she does so, not a barrier at all, like walking into fog, once inside, what you saw from outside no longer exists. Simply to hand the card over, to sign it in the practised writing: Ms L Stanley.

Lily sits in the café for a long time, long enough for her heartbeat to return to normal, for a deep, blissful calm to envelop her, an afterglow. She observes the *No Smoking* sign, stares dreamily at the details of the current photography exhibition: *Finding Roger Fenton*. The list keeps up its own momentum, pictures flickering in front of her. Beautiful linen tea-towels. A sage-green angora sweater. A brushed cotton vest-and-knickers-set for sleeping in. *Other women have these things, they have them, have all of them.*

Now a woman slips into the picture, a young woman, she has long hair, neat in a pony-tail down her back, she has a child with her and she is lightly scented. She is in her home, which has many windows and polished wooden floorboards suffused with light, with warmth and goodness. She herself is good: slender and pale as an ivory paper-knife. The cup she is drinking from is good too, good quality bone china, fine and pale, hand-painted in duck-egg blue, laced at the edge with a narrow cream stripe. The coffee is good coffee, expensive, Colombian, freshly ground on a neat little machine she keeps in the kitchen by the juicer and the three bone-china containers, one labelled Coffee, one Tea, one Sugar.

Lily brushes a bag with her foot, feels the touch of glossy paper. Glossy, shiny. Alongside the woman there's the child, a boy, dressed in a waistcoat, velvet trousers, from Angel Darling, an exclusive catalogue for children. He's laughing of course: his happy face fresh as a brown egg, dusted with freckles. *Fulsome*, Lily thinks, then stifles it. It's just a word, like *supplicant*, she didn't ask for it, she's no idea how it landed in her head like this, from nowhere, almost with a splash. She doesn't want it, it's a stupid word. She reaches forward, drains her glass of juice finally, in one gulp. Too much. Her stomach tilts, a little. Maybe it's all too much.

The roofs of the cars are speckled with leaves. A dog sniffs around the metal bins, two skinny boys who ought to be in school are playing with a shopping trolley, pushing each other for noisy, shrieking rides around the one beaten-up tree. Lily hopes to catch a glimpse of Josh. She's standing at the bedroom window, smoking, watching the young lad who works as a cleaner for the council, wheeling his cart with brushes and mops, chatting to Sherry, her hair whisked up in a blonde whirl, looking from this angle like a peak on a mashed potato.

Lily's shy, she could go downstairs and knock on the door to number 2. It's a weekday, Josh should be at work, but she didn't see him leave this morning. She's noticed how his routine seems all over the place just lately, she can't rely on seeing him. She even wonders if he's avoiding her. Tired of staring out over the front, Lily goes to smoke a cigarette on the balcony at the other side of the flat, blowing smoke down towards Wishley School. It must be break-time; she can't see Matthew but she can hear children's voices, the odd squeaky scream. She picks some dead-heads from the geraniums, tosses a few curled-up wood lice over the edge of the wall. She's thinking of the garden in East Keswick, how the weeds will be tangling around everything she planted, how no one will pick a leaf of mint to present to Matthew or show him where the lemon-grass is, how the leaves will mostly have dropped and carpeted the lawn and how no one will be there raking them, stuffing them into bin-bags, and before she can help herself the garden has flames in it, also thick, choking smoke, crushing at her lungs, stabbing at her eyes. There is a sound like distant screaming in the back of her head, there is a child's drawing with a jagged mouth and a fireman and it could be Alan, it could just be a drawing, but whatever it is, it's not welcome.

Lily stubs the cigarette out, grabs her door keys. Outside the flat she takes the stairs, not the lift, two at a time, holding her nose against the smell of bleach, practically running to Josh's flat, before she can change her mind. She finds the iron security-door to number 2 swinging open, rings his bell. There is light in the narrow strip of window above the door and the smell of cooking, of spicy fish. It's a long time before she hears something, she is about to ring again when the door springs open, noisy on its hinge. But it's not Josh, it's another black guy, younger, short hair, stocky in build, and he isn't smiling.

'Yeah?' he asks curtly. Lily tries not to look startled or affronted, but she wishes she could turn tail and run.

'Is – is Josh in? Please.'

The young man picks at one tooth with a fingernail, turns lazily back towards the corridor. Lily notes his body language, his ease. Like he belongs there. As soon as this thought has formed it's impossible to dislodge it. He's at home here and she isn't.

'Yeah. Josh!'

He doesn't say *someone here to see you* and Lily is grateful for that, wondering how he would describe her, not wanting to hear him call her girl, or worse. His accent merely London, no trace of Jamaican. When he turns the smell of smoke and cooking whirls around him. He has Nike trainers, the kind Matthew keeps asking for, with a bubble in the heels.

Josh appears, in no hurry, he has a can in one hand, his shirt undone and flapping. Relaxed. At home. From inside the flat Lily hears laughter, more voices. Again she feels embarrassed, intrusive. She has caught him in a private moment. Hanging out with his buddies. Skiving off work.

'What happen?' Josh says, sleepily.

His expression is quizzical, not unfriendly, but he

doesn't invite her in. She feels foolish. She cannot think what she is doing here.

'Oh nothing. I just thought, if you weren't busy—'

'We're playing a little card game,' Josh replies. 'I have a next friend here.'

He nods his head as if that should be enough.

'Yes, I can see that. Sorry.'

Lily wonders if she is blushing, her face is hotter than normal, the hand with the keys in, rubbing compulsively, like making pastry. It's the first time in Josh's presence that she has felt like this, and she's struggling to work out what 'this' is. Separate, foreign. A stranger, even. She is surprised that this realisation should come now. Sleeping with Josh, making love with Josh, fucking with Josh, it's intimate for God's sake, how can she feel this way?

She is further hurt to note that Josh is making no attempt to smooth things over. There is a wave of something hostile from Josh, either hostile or – she can pinpoint it finally – embarrassed. He likes to come to her, that's all it is; not the other way round. His world is private, she is not permitted there unless he says so. There is a blurry picture at the back of her mind, something that tells her it's more than this, but Lily can't bring this picture forward: like faulty focus on a camera, it remains outside her vision. Why wouldn't he want to protect himself? She has probably shown him up in front of his friend; maybe the friend knows Daphine, suspects something.

She tries to smile, to show him that she really is sorry, jingling her keys. 'Maybe – later?'

'Fine. See you later,' Josh tells her.

He is just about to close the door, he pauses, noticing that she is still rooted to the spot. He puts his face close to the gap between door and wall, and lets a slow smile slide over it. 'Feeling horny, huh? Come check me later.'

He doesn't wait for her reply. The wooden door creaks shut and Lily is left in the narrow space between that and the metal security-door. Trapped, she thinks, in a space like an air-pocket so small, so impossible to bridge.

By 10 p.m. Matthew is sleeping. The sound of the police helicopter drones around the estate – one minute close enough to shine the beam right through Lily's curtain-less living room, the next minute buzzing off in the direction of Canary Wharf. It is a strange evening-sound that replaces the presence of traffic or the council lawnmower from the daytime and which Lily finds oddly comforting, although she knows that most people on the Flanders Estate wouldn't share her view. She has been in London less than two months but already she finds too much quiet oppressive, spooky.

She finishes her cup of tea and slips her feet into some shoes. Glancing in at Matthew, the brown brush of hair above the sleeping bag, her foot knocks against a book, *A Golden Guide to Fishes*, and she picks it up, notes that it belonged to the library at Matthew's last school, is now way overdue. She didn't know he had this book and wonders where he had it hidden. Some of the pages are floating loose, she reads at random something about Lantern Fish with their luminescent organs and then this:

Fishes do not see very well, partly because of their eye-structure and partly because as one goes deeper in

water, the light grows dimmer. Fishes have, however,
a well-developed sense of balance and of taste.

Lily sighs, remembering the aquarium, in their old house, Matthew's pride and joy. No one would clean it out, neither Alan nor Matthew ever considered the work involved; just the buying of the different fish, the little house for the fish to swim in, the plastic mermaid preening on a rock. They wouldn't take heed of the man in the pet shop either, who warned them not to mix certain kinds: Lily was always scooping dead fish from the top with the tea-strainer, flushing them down the toilet while Matthew was at nursery. Finally she put her foot down. 'You never look after them. You don't feed them, you forget about them. All you like to do is decide which one you're buying next, go to the pet shop and choose another and then as soon as it's home you lose interest in it.' She took the tank and all the accessories to the charity shop, having emptied the one remaining dog-eared goldfish into a tiny bowl and that was all, all Matthew had, until it died.

She did this long before the fire, but sometimes, making her list, she forgets this. She pictures the glass tank with flames licking the bottom, the water bubbling to boiling point, the fish hopelessly cooking, Matthew weeping in despair, watching them. This didn't happen, she tells herself firmly. There is no need to feel guilty.

'Do you miss Daddy?' she asked Matthew, a couple of nights ago, in the faintest possible voice, sibilant and feathery. She is sitting on his bed, beside him, about to kiss him good night. The smell of his newly washed hair, of his banana-flavoured toothpaste floats up to her. When he shakes his head, she tries another direction, stating clearly, sitting on the bed beside him: 'I miss Daddy. Do you miss him?'

'No,' Matthew says, this time out loud, totally convincing. Lily sighs, wanting to give up but also wanting not to lose the moment, there's something here that isn't always here, between her and Matthew, late at night, the moon dripping grey light on to Matthew's sleeping bag.

'It's okay if you do. You can tell me you know, it won't make me sad.' Lily's voice soft, her hand on Matthew's woolly hair. For a moment his eyes glitter, like something caught in a net, but not for long, not for more than a second.

'Dad's outahere,' Matthew says, sleepily: his new phrase, learned in the playground, a mixture of London and New York slang. Lily sighs, at the toughness of the language, at all the things Matthew is learning in spite of her, in spite of everything she does or says. While she watches him, his drooping eyelids close, the dark lashes spidery on his cheeks. She watches sleep steal into his face, watching it transform him, knowing exactly the moment it occurs. Lily lifts him slightly, changes his position to turn him on his side. Matthew's body is heavy now, it's as if sleep weighs something, she knows from past experience how hard he is to reawaken in this state. She pictures sleep as a cool, dark boat, bobbing on a black sea at night, with Matthew curled at the bottom. Lily wonders if she ever slept that way herself as a child. Somehow she can't imagine it. She thinks she was always wakeful, vigilant.

Meeting Alan, marrying Alan, sleeping with Alan, she had imagined that things would be different, that sleep would be heavier and deeper, come to her more readily, but now that she thinks of it, it never really happened. There was never a time when Lily bobbed like Thumbelina in a walnut-shell boat on a sea of calm water. There was only the dream of such a thing. Then the fire.

Lily measures time from the fire now; there is only before and after. After the fire, everything was swept away for good. Nothing is the same, the years of her marriage, her childhood, her brief time at university, the library, the early years of motherhood, all seem vague to her, distant, swathed in smoke. She cannot quite catch hold of them but she wants to, she rakes constantly through them, digging up remnants. It is only this life that feels real. This life which would once have seemed extraordinary to her. Single-parenthood. Living on a council estate. Signing on the dole. Using someone else's credit card. Sleeping with someone fifteen years older than her, married, and black. And sometimes being paid for it.

Lily brushes her teeth, and takes her keys from her bag. Matthew will be fine for a short time, surely, an hour at most. It's only downstairs after all. She leaves the landing light on, his bedroom door slightly ajar. She feels guilty, irresponsible, light as a feather. Something like heat prickles around her feet as she heads for the door.

He is lifting off her sweater, she is shivery and hard beneath the wool. Lily closes her eyes because the sensation is too much, heat racing up her skin from thighs to tongue and the smell of him everywhere, of his home and his bed and his sleepiness, seeping out of his pores. He is muttering things to her, words falling into her hair. Desire flares over her skin like colours. She is breathing fast, panting as if she is running, and she *is* running,

running away, something is chasing her. Fire. Smoke in her nostrils and throat, smoke pressing in her lungs, her skin curling with heat, her hair snapping, and the fire chasing, coming closer, threatening to take her, overwhelm her, sweep her up, from toe to head, peeling off layers of her skin like foam on a wave. She can't breathe, she can't think, she is neither living nor dead but she dangles here for seconds, minutes, maybe a life-time, swinging between the two places. Each burns and blazes, each contains flames, each is dangerous.

The girl seems uncomfortable in his flat, though she knows her way around: the layout is identical to her own. She wanders from bedroom to kitchen, touching things. He sees her pause at the photographs stuck on the fridge, the poster of Haile Selassie, the map of Jamaica. He stands behind her, rubbing at his beard with one hand.

'I'm from Portland. There. On the coast. Daphine put the yellow sun sticker there.'

'Is your wife from Portland too?'

'No. Daphine from Brixton.'

The girl is still standing in the kitchen, looking at the map, her back to him. Her voice low, talking to herself, not him.

'It's like you're – a tourist or something. All these Jamaican souvenirs. I mean, I don't have a map of Yorkshire on the wall, postcards of the North York Moors or anything.'

He shrugs. 'Daphine. She buys those things. She met me in Jamaica on her first visit. Her dad come from Portland, too. She hear about it all the time. She hear about the sun, the Blue Mountains, the air so clean you can nearly bite it. She think of it as Heaven. Since we lost Neville, that's where she want to be.'

He didn't mean to mention Neville. He tries to remember what he has already said to the girl about his son. He wonders why she drags it out of him, every time, the last thing he wants to talk about, but being around her for long, it always seems to happen. He opens the fridge, takes out two cans of Red Stripe and hands one to her, along with his packet of cigarettes. Lily pulls out a chair. It's odd to see her in Daphine's kitchen, her blue-white legs on Daphine's willow-pattern chair, but he doesn't feel guilty, not for that, only disorientated. As if the girl might lean forward suddenly with a huge cracking laugh, the way Daphine does sometimes. Or the way she used to.

Josh sips from his can of beer, pulls out the other chair and sits on it the wrong way, the back of the chair between his legs. He watches Lily smoking and the silence between them starts to work on him, he's wrong, he does feel guilty, but not about Daphine, about Lily. He thinks that loneliness glows right on the skin of this woman, it's tugging at him, making him sad for her, it draws him in a way that he can't understand, he's not sure he likes. The girl tears her head away from the map, finally. He sees that she has been puzzled by the symbols Daphine drew on it. It never occurred to him before that Daphine did them for him and they look like something you'd do for a child.

'Why did you never learn to read? Doesn't it bother you?'

'I get by pretty well.'

'Yes, you do seem to. I'm not disputing that. I'm just amazed, that's all. It would be like not being able to speak the language, or something.'

'My dad left. I was five, six, I just start going to school. Then my mum, Rose, got sick and she need me at home to look after her, so I stop going to school. No big deal. I just never did go back, that's all.'

'Where did your dad go?'

'England. Liverpool, I think.'

'Don't you know?'

'No. My mum say one time he's working for British Rail, but I don't know about that. I never see him.'

He takes a long hungry drag on his cigarette, exhales.

'A son need a father,' he says quietly, without meaning to.

He's not answering any question of Lily's, but he feels as though he might be. The words float right out, blown on his cigarette smoke. The girl looks down, traces the pattern in the chair with her finger.

'If I had a pound for every time someone said that to me . . .'

He stares hard at her, at the feathery lines fanning out from the corners of her eyes, he would like to put his hand out and smooth them.

'Sherry did tell me about your son,' Lily says. 'I just didn't know what to say.'

'All those years of working hard. Rain. Cold. So many years. All for what, huh?'

The girl is silent. You could hear a pin drop.

'When the police came to tell me, I think at first, I've lost my job. You know I work for the police, fixing up cars and things. The police coming to my home to tell me something about work, it must be bad. Daphine inside watching the TV, *Blind Date* and Cilla Black and that music going on in the background the whole time.

The officers were ones I know from work, but they acting like I'm a stranger, saying Mr Senior sorry to tell you and it happen just now, this afternoon, broad daylight. Your boy get stabbed, somebody stab him in the shopping arcade, we don't know if he white or black or what it all about, but does your boy have any troubles you know, with drugs and thing like that?'

Josh puts his hand up to his eyes, the lines he wanted to smooth out in Lily's face are under his own, he is rubbing at them, under his eyes, rubbing softly, compulsively, tears streaming over his fingers.

'And I say to them no my boy have no trouble like that, he just in the wrong place at the wrong time. Or else it some foolishness, some silly boys' fight gone wrong, but because he is a black boy they seem to think I can't be right, I can't know the truth, but I do know, I know Neville didn't do nothing at all. His mum home making some nice fish and okra for the evening, we expect him around seven, maybe with some girl, Josie or Maxine, we didn't ever think . . .' Josh puts his head in his hands, refuses to look at Lily.

That skinny girl, what can she know? What can she know about losing a son, a grown son, a boy you work all your life in this stinking shit hole to support?

Josh remembers the worst moment, the moment in the police station, the form that was shoved at him to sign, so that the body could be released. When he couldn't fill it out, Daphine had to come, weeping and cursing him, to fill out the form herself. After years of writing his cheques, of reading his work timetable, she finally told him it was the one detail she couldn't forgive him for: that she had to be the one to identify the body. To see her boy like that. Her darling boy. Daphine told Josh there and then she couldn't stay with him a moment longer.

The girl scrapes her chair closer to his, she puts her arms awkwardly around him. Josh has a feeling like something is snapping in his chest, he feels it breaking at the cage of his ribs, he lets it wash through him, a torrent. He allows himself to be cradled, rocked like a baby in the slender pale arms of this girl, this child he knows is doing her best, this virtual stranger.

Neville is all legs and arms. As if the boy doesn't quite know what to do with his tallness, with all those limbs, towering already over his mother and father, with his good looks, his Spanish cheekbones that come from Daphine's side, not his. But with that grin, that impishness that got Neville out of all kinds of trouble when he was little and now is starting to get him into plenty too, now that he's sixteen. Always a girl giggling in their doorway, asking for Neville, wearing big high shoes and tight leggings and her hair in different kind of plaits.

But he isn't thinking of the girls, of recent years. He's thinking of the time by Neville's school, he and Daphine going to see a play. Neville was eight or nine years old, Wishley School, the one Matthew goes to now. The boy didn't care too much, usually, for his parents to visit his school. Still, for this occasion, he insists. Night and day for two weeks he's on their case. Are you coming on Thursday it's six thirty and did you get your tickets and you won't be late Dad, will you . . . ? So Josh puts on his suit, feeling stiff and stupid, sure the other parents know he hasn't set the toe of his foot in a school for years, for hundreds of years. At least he's happy to see other Jamaican families, other black fathers, but mostly mothers. Daphine fetches him a plastic cup of flat lemonade and he squeezes himself into a tiny plastic chair, just about ready to bust in two under the weight of his thighs. He moves the chair a touch closer to Daphine and it screeches like a wounded dog.

The play is *Joseph and the Amazing Technicolor Dreamcoat*, and Neville is Joseph.

There he is in this bright striped bathrobe with a towel around his head that Josh recognises from the kitchen. The boy is looking nervous, scanning the rows of noisy settling adults and smaller children for his own mum and dad. His eyes can't seem to light on them at first, he folds his bottom lip under his teeth anxiously. Josh attempts a quick wave, to attract Neville's attention; feels self-conscious, puts his hand down. But Daphine stands up, her rose-patterned dress wrinkling over her behind, no shyness for her, yelling in her big voice *Neville! Over here child!* and the boy beams a smile for a moment, then glancing nervously at his music teacher, stands waiting for his cue.

When Neville begins singing, his voice falters. Josh feels an elastic band tighten around his lungs. The room is hushed, embarrassed. Then the child seems to find his way and the notes start climbing, one after the other, they creep around, plucking at the hairs on the back of people's necks. *That child sing like an angel.* Josh hears a murmur snake through the parents packed into the hall. He stares at the music teacher, a wizened elderly white woman, and it's clear to Josh suddenly that her eyes are full of tears, that the whole place is now spellbound. Neville singing, *I close my eyes, draw back the curtain* . . .

It's the rawness in his voice, the little boy effort, the shining determination in Neville's face to get it right, not to waver. Josh finds himself wishing his own mother, Rose, were here to see her grandchild, to hear him. Even the white parents – any parent – could share this simple thing: a heart swelling with pride in your own child, your own pic'nee, your own darling boy.

And Josh can still hear him, hear him every night, even if his head is shoved under the pillow: singing in his eight-year-old voice that doesn't even have a Jamaican accent, doesn't sound anything like Josh's: *I close my eyes* . . . and Josh knows that he does, he does close them, some bastard closed them for good.

The summer when Matthew is eighteen months and walking everywhere, trotting around the garden in his plastic fireman's helmet, Lily begins to feel restless, wonders if she regrets giving up her degree. She sits on the child's swing, her legs sticking out in front of her, watching Matthew squat on the grass, staring at a daisy.

When Alan comes back from his shift late in the afternoon she takes him strawberries – cold and hard from the fridge – and ice-cream and beer and sits beside him on the rug on the grass.

'I've been thinking. I could get a job, that job Sue mentioned, at the library.'

Alan puts a strawberry into his mouth, bites hard.

'What about Matthew?'

'It's just part-time. Matthew could go to Brenda for the mornings, and nursery in the afternoons. I'm sure Brenda would love it.'

'Fine. If you think your mother is up to it.'

Alan's spoon clinks against his bowl. He doesn't look up.

'Don't you need qualifications, that kind of thing?' he asks.

'Oh it's just a clerical job. Sue says it's not like a normal library, it does requisitions for other libraries mostly. I'd need typing, word-processing. Just basic things.'

Alan nods, regarding his wife carefully, her fair hair cut neatly in a bob, her slim legs in dark jeans. Brainy. She always seemed so, at first, he'd forgotten that about her. He used to worry in the beginning that she'd out-grow him, want to talk about books and stuff. That was before he realised where she came from. Before he met B&B that is; Bed and Breakfast. Bob being Breakfast, with all that eating. Brenda constantly taking to her Bed. No more educated than he is, either of them, although Brenda, he thinks, is a bit of a snob, just the same. Her greatest aim in life – it seems to Alan – is not to live in a council house, not to live like her own parents did. Beyond that, not a lot else.

Lily is waiting, watching his face.

He picks up his bowl. 'I prefer my strawberries with Carnation. Is there any?'

'Yes, there's a tin in the cupboard, I'll get it,' Lily is quick to respond.

'No bother. I'll get it.'

He stands up from the rug, his knees creaking. Lily watches him walk along the garden path into the kitchen, flapping at a bee buzzing somewhere around his head. Matthew is squawking noisily, wanting her attention. But she can't unpeel her eyes from Alan, wondering what it is about his stance, the back of his neck, the way he is walking that convinces her he is sad, that her suggestion of getting a job has filled him with dejection, made the afternoon heat turn oppressive and gloomy.

So now Lily has a job, a cleaning job, advertised in the *East London Advertiser*. Four pounds an hour and she can work a few hours in the mornings and still be home easily if the school phones. Which they did this morning. Matthew bit right to the bone on Farid's finger: he has been excluded again. Lily marches him through the school gate, steaming with rage, ranting at the smouldering figure of Matthew for five full minutes. Once in the lift, both of them flattened against the walls to avoid a central puddle of urine, Lily relents, snagged suddenly on that look again in Matthew, the flicker.

She's asking him why he keeps doing this, he knows it's wrong, does he want to be endlessly in trouble with everyone? After all, he knows there are other ways to express his feelings. She feels a little silly using this particular phrase with Matthew. She almost detects an eyebrow faintly arching but suspects she is being paranoid. Can a five-year-old be sardonic? She's made an appointment at Child and Family Services, as Ms Brightman suggested, but there's a waiting list, she hasn't been yet, she's no wiser about anything.

Matthew absorbs both her anger and her concern in silence. This worries Lily more than anything else, she recognises the trait. 'The mango don't fall too far from the tree,' Josh says, one time, and the words catch her like a light slap. She's sure she too, as a child, had a particular silence, an attempt to fend off Brenda and Bob which failed miserably, instead she soaked them up like a sponge, until the two of them are inside her, plumping every pore, with little room for anyone else.

Lily sighs. 'Well Matthew, there's no one to look after you. You'll have to come in to work with me.'

The house in Stoke Newington she is to clean is a fifteen-minute bus ride from Flanders Estate but it feels like another world to Lily. This is more like the London she imagined, before she came here. A row of Victorian terraced houses, the road lined with huge pollarded plane trees, big bay windows and plenty of Volvos parked outside. Scruffy, sure, the doors are mostly stripped wood, unpainted, and the gardens are unkempt, flower-less boxes on window-ledges, not prim and cottagey, the way Brenda would expect them to be.

Lily wonders about the women in these houses. Back home she would be able to picture accurately the kind of person inhabiting most of the houses, the stone cottages, around the trading estate, the red-brick council houses, the farm houses, the vicarage, the pub. Here she is a little more at sea. These homes, Lily decides (based on spurious things; the *Guardian* sticking out of a letterbox, an empty packet of tofu in a dustbin), belong to journalists and social workers, middle-class professional women who married the men they were at university with – who are now arts correspondents and shiatsu practitioners – and had a bundle of brightly coloured, hand-knitted, wholemeal children. She is bloody sure, she thinks, ringing the bell, that those children don't have visits from Ed Syke (she can't picture the Educational Psychologist as a woman, instead he is a comic from the fifties, tall and thin, his jokes never blue), don't have Statements and Exclusions and E and B disorders. And probably they have fathers; kind, involved fathers who come home tired from work but still find time to bath them or read stories to them, to have long discussions late into the night, over a glass of wine, about which Montessori nursery is best, or Lawrence's ear infection. Even the separated fathers, the ones who pick them up at weekends for trips to the theatre, are still kind, with glasses and bicycles.

Good parents, good food, good wine, good children. The more she thinks of good, the more she mutters the word *good*, sotto voce, standing on the doorstep of number 16, Matthew beside her, the more ludicrous, hollow and bell-like it sounds. As if it needs to be hit with something hard to resonate at all. *She comes from a good home. He's a good father. They're good kids.* Sitting in the sunlight, bloody vegetarians, Friends of the Earth, feeding their children organic baby food and sugar-free drinks, it's like religion, it's as if in every tiny household decision they re-state their superiority, the luxury of being good. How would you fare if your life went up in smoke, if it was burned to the ground – everything in the world you had, down to the last toothpick; if you stepped out of the flames penniless, husbandless, hopeless and with sole responsibility for a fatherless child?

She wonders at this anger, so hot, suddenly, so incensed. At one time, Lily knew where she fitted in, or thought she did. She had Brenda and Bob's values, their guidelines for the things people need in life, but she also had their longings, their frustrations. One small girl absorbing centuries of *not-having*, of wanting: is that possible? To soak it deep inside her until she has a terror, their terror, of losing it all again. Until she does just that. She rummages in pockets for her cigarettes; her hands are shaking. When the door is opened with a sudden swing Lily is ready to blurt something, the sentences bursting, over-prepared, like an angry meal for a late lover.

Matthew is picking his nose as the door opens. The dark-haired woman inside stands calmly, politely smiling. The moment rearranges itself for Lily into a more peaceful shape. This must be Josie, the woman Lily spoke to yesterday.

'Hi, I'm Lily – about the cleaning job. This is my son, Matthew. Sorry I had to bring him today. He has a cold.'

The slim woman is tall, in cigarette pants and an egg-shell blue top, fine knit, short sleeves. She has fifties-style pumps and a sleek bob, large dramatic earrings. She gestures for Lily to come inside.

'I haven't got a cold,' Matthew says.

Josie smiles, over his head, at Lily. 'That's okay. I know what it's like. Ruby and Jack are both on a school trip today and they get back early at 2 p.m. so my child-minder, Sharon, can't pick them up and Henry has to do it instead . . . it's a nightmare, isn't it, childcare?'

'Yes,' Lily agrees.

The house smells of fresh coffee, fresh paint and polished wood. The living space Lily is shown into is full of rich colours, blue and red, with masks on two of the walls, wooden floors, a huge (and to Lily's mind, rather strange) rug theatrically displayed on the wall opposite the window. Josie shows her the Hoover, the dustpan and brush, the toilet cleaner, chatting easily at the same time, asking how long Lily has been in London, which school Matthew goes to. This, Lily understands, is an interview, of sorts. Not questioning her ability to do the job; it's assumed that all women know how to clean. Just finding out if Lily is suitable, is she trustworthy. Lily can't help wondering about Josie's basis for assessing this. It seems to be based on Lily's – appearance? Accent? Her use of the words environmentally friendly? The fact that she worked in a library, comes from a village in Yorkshire, has an A level in English literature?

These facts established, Josie seems happy enough, and in a short time too. Matthew is sitting on the sofa, chubby fingers picking at the fringes of a large rust cover, which Josie calls a 'throw' (as in 'and give the throw a quick shake, if you will', causing Lily some moments of confusion, which she covers up well). Lily and Matthew watch as Josie spins around, in a whirl of perfume, searching for keys, a bottle of Evian from the fridge, the suit she wants to take to the dry cleaner's.

'Now, I have to pop out for a while. I have my keys here so just close the door on the way out, if you will. Henry will be back around 1 p.m. for his lunch, I don't think he's teaching this afternoon, but I expect you'll be finished by then? It won't matter if the Chubb lock isn't on, just for that short time.'

Lily is about to mention her recent burglary, but stops herself, the dark shadow of Matthew looming into her vision. She has been having a hard time persuading him that they're safe since the break-in. Security-doors cost four hundred pounds to install, so there's no chance of that for a while. The police have phoned her once: no news and that seems to be the end of it as far as they are concerned. She hopes they are similarly cavalier about Louisa Stanley's credit card disappearance. Thinking that the card may well have been reported missing by now, Lily has chopped it up with kitchen scissors so she won't be tempted to use it again. Luck runs out, sometimes, she tells herself.

Lily has been musing, lately, that another thing she misses in London is light. Walking around Josie's house she revises this observation, noticing how abundant the light is, how it makes the kitchen breezy and clean; the study glow with a rich ochre warmth. Light isn't absent in London, then, but like many things, not something everyone has in equal measure. Lily's flat is dark, and Josh's dark too, in a different, subdued, green-gold way. The estate itself is dark. Any light that falls is either grey (daytime) or a mouldy yellow (evening). She thinks of the phrase *good light* but it isn't one she's heard, she can't get incensed about that. (Although now that she is flicking through Josie's copy of *Elle Decoration* she can see that a constant refrain is the importance of good lighting.)

Josie has left, in a waft of Dolce Vita (Christian Dior; Lily saw the bottle in her bathroom) so Lily puts a *Postman Pat* video on for Matthew and goes into the kitchen to have a cigarette. She flips through the letters on Josie's kitchen table; credit card statements (Josie's credit limit is very high, and she's almost reached it), a card from a man called Tim in Barcelona, neutral enough but signed 'love and kisses', a letter from her surgery stating that Josie's recent smear test result was fine and promotional stuff for a private healthcare plan, addressed to Henry.

Lily fills the kettle, helps herself to a generous scoop of Colombian coffee and sets the Italian coffee maker on the stove. She opens the fridge; Josie doesn't seem to cook much but there is an impressive range of Marks and Spencer's prepared salads and stuffed vine-leaves, chicken in lemon and tarragon, various microwavable Thai dishes. There isn't much Lily could snack on without it being too apparent; she finds a bowl of delicious olives steeped in something garlicky and pops a couple into her mouth. She studies the door of the closed fridge; a picture of Daddy to wish him a *Happy Father's Day Love Ruby aged 6*, a fridge magnet of Vancouver in the shape of a maple leaf, a leaflet about the Buddhist Centre in Bethnal Green.

In a cupboard above the cooker Lily finds children's lollipops in a party bag – probably Jack and Ruby aren't allowed sugar – so she takes one to Matthew, who accepts it silently, without unsticking his gaze from the TV.

Josie's washing machine, which has been humming all this time, whirs to a final spin and a shuddering halt and Lily opens the door, begins taking out the clothes. Henry wears Y-fronts, the instant turn-off kind, size medium. This Lily finds reassuring: *I bet my sex life is better than hers*. Josie's underwear is predictably black, expensive, and understated. Her bra size is 32A. The children's clothes are from Gap and Hennes; not designer exactly, but nothing cheap and they all look scarcely worn.

Lily bundles the lot into the tumbler dryer, after selecting a pair of Jack's socks for Matthew. *Next Preppy*. They won't be missed, and Matthew has been wearing the same pair for a week. Next time, she'll bring a bag of her own washing; that will save on launderette bills. She washes up and wipes the kitchen surfaces, selects the prettiest cup, a hand-painted enormous coffee bowl, something arty from one of the shops on Church Street, and pours herself a good strong coffee, adding a generous splash of single cream from the fridge. Lily opens the french windows on to the garden, takes her coffee cup outside. It's late October, definitely autumn now and the lawn is strewn with leaves from a large, overhanging cherry tree.

A drizzly rain is starting: a good job she didn't try to hang the washing out. Lily sits in a swing from the tree, notes the child's bike lying on the path, just about the right size for Matthew. She sips at the dark coffee and a mood – something like contentment – creeps over her.

The warm rain sprinkles her hair, she thinks how elegant her feet look in Josie's black ballet pumps, how pleasant it is to have fallen cherry pips everywhere, as if an extraordinarily rich, bumper season has only just ended. This is how she pictured things. Brenda's picture of things. On the train here from Leeds, glimpses of London gardens through unwashed glass: intimate, inviting, with their assortment of abandoned children's toys, the ghosts of late-afternoon parties outdoors with tree lanterns and barbecues and good-looking husbands with incomes; slender wives with spotless kitchens, cleaned by somebody else. *Life can't be a bowl of cherries all the time you know*. Bob's phrase.

But Brenda remained faithful to *her* picture, over the years. Never ate the cherries, Lily thinks, therefore she was never left with just the pips. All the things women want; a nice home, a good husband, lovely children, shiny and bright, like fat cherries in a blue china bowl. Lily had all that and she *was* happy with Alan, wasn't she? And Lily had work, too: more than Brenda had, a place outside the home, at least for a while. Lily can tell from their phone conversations, how fuzzy is Brenda's version of that. Outside. Brenda has two versions of London; one an ugly, concrete, crime-ridden place (*The Bill*); the other: friendly, terraced houses, Victorian squares (*EastEnders*) and of the two, she has naturally enough selected the latter.

Lily is busy thinking this when there is a noise in the house. She hears the flush of the downstairs toilet and a door banging. It takes Lily a moment to run along the path and in through the french windows and then Henry is standing there, briefcase in hand, looking slightly bewildered.

'I'm Lily.' Lily offers her hand. 'Your new cleaner.'

The man glances from Matthew to Lily, shakes her hand briefly, has that faintly annoyed look of someone arriving home, expecting to be alone. The top button of his trousers is undone.

'I'm *nearly* done . . .' Lily says, although she has hardly started. Matthew has glanced up once, and returned to the TV. He is sitting around five inches away from it, his shoulders huddled. Beside him on the floor is the lolly wrapper and the balled-up pair of socks Lily selected for him.

Henry's hand is at his forehead, compulsively stroking his receding hairline, as if checking it hasn't receded any further in the few minutes he's been standing there. He seems an enormous man to Lily, but it might be the suit and the briefcase and the proper shoes, brogues with heels, creating this impression. She realises he is studying the shoes she's wearing, so she smiles her best Lily smile, turns on the charm she hasn't had to call on in a year and explains: 'I just popped Josie's shoes on to go in the garden for a minute. To see if I should hang the washing out. But it's starting to rain.'

Too late she thinks that explanation sounds lame. Why wouldn't she wear her own boots in the garden? But Henry is smiling back at her. When he smiles, she can see what Josie might have seen in him, once. Before the paunch. Lily wonders if one of the ways Brenda failed with her is this: Lily rates her own sexual feelings too highly. It strikes her suddenly, like a cool breeze gusting up under her skirt, like wind lifting a gauzy veil from her face, that she never – even deep in the mists of her marriage, even perhaps on her wedding night – believed Alan was the last man she would ever sleep with. If she'd thought that, she'd have believed her life was over.

Looking around Josie's home, looking at Josie's

husband, Lily realises she knows nothing, nothing at all about what it takes to go backwards, to go back to being the kind of woman she was, the kind that Brenda wants her to be.

Lily carefully steps out of the ballet pumps, picks up a duster and the Mr Sheen, cheerfully suggests she'll *just finish up here*, then rushes around the living room at breakneck speed, shortly afterwards disappearing into the bathroom to give it a thorough going over. Sweat has broken out in dark patches under her T-shirt by the time she reappears in the kitchen, where Henry is drinking a coffee. Lily puts on her DMs and both of them stare awkwardly through the glass doors to the living room, where Matthew's figure is hunched at the TV.

'Well, we'd better get going. Come on Matthew.' She steps over to the TV to turn the video off, but Matthew yells at her, slaps her hand in fury and picks up the remote control himself, presses the On button.

Lily snatches it right back and presses Off, saying as firmly as she dare, with Henry standing right behind them, 'Matthew, that's naughty. Come on, now, it's time to go.'

She sees that Matthew is about to go for the remote control again, so she lifts her hand high up out of reach, but it's like someone holding a stick in front of a dog, Matthew leaps up, reaches for the control, then finding himself frustrated, sinks his teeth into her forearm. Lily does her best not to scream, tears spring into her eyes and her heart is pounding as she grabs at Matthew's head with her other hand, tries to tug him away from her. It's a ridiculous silent tussle, but Matthew is strong, he hangs on and in the end Henry has to step in, he peels Matthew – kicking and screaming – away from her, and Matthew has blood in his mouth, he takes a little fleck of

Lily's skin with him. He spits at her and tiny red blobs scatter.

Lily is red in the face, she can't escape quick enough, refusing Henry's concerned remarks and the plaster and Dettol he holds out to her. She dabs at her arm with a tissue and gathers her things together hurriedly and it's only when they are in the street that she lets the tears flow, gives in to the urge to hold her arm, to rub compulsively at the throbbing place.

Lily notices Matthew sneak a worried look at her tears and then glance away again, and this gives her hope, gives her an idea. He follows her to the bus-stop, then up the stairs on the 106 bus and squeezes himself next to the window. His dark hair is falling over one eye, the collar of his coat turned up, the string and the toggle at his chin damp and chewed. He stares out of the window, starts visibly when a branch overhanging the road suddenly belts the roof of the bus directly above him.

'Matthew. Look at me,' Lily says gently. Matthew stares out of the window, fixes his eyes on an old shoe decorating the top of a bus shelter. The sky blank, a grey sheet, either cloudless or one big cloud, it's hard to tell.

'I know you don't like it here much,' Lily begins quietly, addressing the back of Matthew's head. She is thinking of his bedroom in East Keswick, his Tamagochi, his red and blue trike, his Pog collection. Each item carefully listed, noted by Lily. She would like him to know that. She knows he has lost things too.

'I do like it here!' he yells, to her surprise.

The bus is mired in traffic, unmoving, the doors hissing like the lid of a steaming pan whenever they open. Under their seat a bottle rolls noisily, threatening either to smash or bounce right down the stairs but then doing neither. Like us, Lily thinks. We seem to be forever colliding, forever rolling dramatically to our separate corners. Smashing up against each other. Coming back to the same wobbly place and then not being able to stay there for more than a moment.

She turns her mind to punishments, some suitable discipline for Matthew. Alan said there should always be consequences. *Each action has an equal and opposite reaction.* Or was that something else?

'You know it's wrong to bite, don't you?'

Matthew says nothing, but he holds her gaze. His eyes dart to her arm for a moment then back to her face again, quickly. She thinks she sees something there, something flit over his expression, like the other night. His eyes glittering. Then dulling again, his whole face closing up.

'For biting me I'm afraid there won't be any sweets, Matthew, for a week. Do you understand? That's the *consequence* of your behaviour . . .'

Lily pronounces consequence carefully, she knows he'll take this in, knows how much he relishes new words. Yesterday he told her confidently that you must not call people half castes like Nannie does, Mrs Jalil says it's wrong, you have to say *Missed Race* because that's what they're called now.

'Do you understand me Matthew? It's wrong to bite people. I know you know that. It has to stop.'

Sometimes in Lily the oddest feeling surfaces when she looks closely at her son. The same feeling she gets in an aircraft, looking down at a new country laid out beneath her: from a distance plain and flat as a table cloth with place settings but as you get closer more and more mysterious, more and more detailed, complicated, foreign; amazing. A whole country. His bottom lip juts out a fraction of a centimetre and his lip is trembling, almost indiscernible, except to someone who is looking as hard as Lily is. Knowing she has his full attention, that he is listening no matter how much he is also trying to shrug her off, she makes one last venture, puts her face very close to his.

'Matthew. No matter what you do to me, no matter how mean or naughty you are to me *I am not going to leave you*. Do you understand this?'

Now she has his full attention. She has him fragile in her hand like the skin of a poppy caught by the wind, like a tiny silver fish out of water, twitching. She holds him a second longer, then puts him back. She takes care to make her voice firm, the truth as hard as a bead.

'I'm your Mum. I'm staying. I'm doing my best and you can count on me. But you could make things a little easier for us. You could try *your* best too you know.'

Lily enunciates every word, watching each fall and hit their target. Luminescence, the pupils widening, something brimming in his face. She knows she got through.

Lily leans back against her seat, exhausted. She's no idea what she's doing with this single parent thing, she's been chucked here, she's improvising. One minute she's swimming, the next treading water, the next sinking under. There's not much to go on, but she thinks it's probably quite ordinary, probably only this. Don't ham it up. And don't imagine that Matthew wants the same things she wanted as a child.

Especially since she hasn't any longer the faintest idea what those things might be.

Six for Gold

The waiting room of Child and Family Services is lit by a fluorescent strip. Lily stares at the dirt trapped inside the lamp, then at various fading posters, cheap photocopies. *Are you worried about your drinking? Are you a woman who has been experiencing violence within your home?* Child Guidance, it was called, in Brenda and Bob's day. For problem families. Brenda would shudder if she knew Lily was here. All Bob worked for, to get away from. One tiny step and Lily is back, it seems, at square one.

There is another woman in the corner, flicking through a copy of *Hello!* magazine. She looks young enough still to be at school but a baby sleeps beside her in a padded cotton sleepsuit, zipped snugly up to its neck. The words *Your Mum* are scribbled about the walls, in pink biro. Lily recognises this graffiti as a London thing, a new term of abuse, Matthew came home with it one day but she was quick to catch on, snuff it out. She understands it as a half sentence, an implication. Your

Mum's so fat her belt is the size of the Equator. Your Mum's so fat she needs an Underground train to take her shopping. *Your Mum*. Lily has seen it everywhere. She supposes it's the modern equivalent of My Dad's bigger than Your Dad. She wonders if kids ever say that these days.

'Mrs Waite? Would you like to follow us?'

Two women have agreed to see her: the Educational Psychologist, Tanya Mathers, and the Psychiatric Social Worker, Suzanna James. They stand at the doorway of the waiting room, introducing themselves and indicating an office down a corridor that Lily is to follow them towards. Both are smiling. Tanya is plump, pale-skinned and freckly, a red-head, with a long, straggly scarf, Indian-style in purple and green, hanging from her neck; the other woman is slim, black, wears a suit in oatmeal, dark tights and flat shoes.

Lily is shown into the office, offered a seat. Suzanna apologises for the noisy traffic, hopes they will all be able to hear each other, but explains they have to keep the window open, as the central heating is set way too high, can't be switched down, the building has a problem with the heating just now.

It is easier than Lily imagined, talking to these women about Matthew. She tells them about the biting, the difficulties in school, the fire, his father. She knows they have other information from his school in Yorkshire, they have been doing their homework, that's why setting up this meeting has taken a while.

'It must be very difficult for you, being suddenly thrown into a new life like this, and having sole responsibility for Matthew in the way you describe . . .' Tanya suggests gently.

She has a rural accent Lily can't place; Dorset

perhaps. The other woman is a little younger and smarter, perhaps she exudes a hint of disapproval? Lily can't decide yet, but she is willing, she is certainly willing, to hear what they have to say.

'I am at my wit's end sometimes with him . . .' Lily agrees, eagerly, glad to have the occasion to say so, to admit it.

'And I wonder if you feel angry at all?' Tanya suggests.

'Angry?' Lily's tone is suspicious.

It is Suzanna who replies, leaning forward a little, as she makes the point.

'I think it's perfectly natural to feel angry – at these times – angry at your husband perhaps, or . . . even at Matthew himself . . .'

'No, no I wouldn't say I felt *angry*,' Lily answers carefully. A double-decker bus rumbles by outside and Lily is newly aware of petrol fumes, of the smog of London seeping into the room.

Tanya, the Educational Psychologist, takes over, attempts to smooth things. 'I think what Suzanna is saying is that in our work with children, Mrs Waite, we do find that many parents, well, of course all parents at times, *over-identify* with their children, and if we are to help you and Matthew we might need to establish whether you yourself would like or need our help, or whether there is some way that we can work with you and Matthew together . . .'

'I don't understand,' Lily responds, her voice rising. 'I thought I was here to talk about Matthew, not me? About his troubles at school? About his biting . . .'

'Yes, yes indeed,' Tanya replies, quietly. 'His anger. His obvious rage at the changes taking place in his life . . .'

'But I had to move! You don't understand, after the fire, there were plenty of reasons, I couldn't stay at my parents' for ever, I was going mad . . .'

Tanya pushes her fringe away from her eyes, is quick to nod. 'I do understand Mrs Waite. We're not here to judge you or to question decisions which I'm sure you made for good reasons. But if we are to help Matthew, I think we need to look at the ways in which his behaviour seems to be demonstrating anger, frustration or at the very least *confusion* about his new life circumstances, including the loss of his father.'

Tears leap into Lily's eyes but she bites down hard on her bottom lip, waits a moment until she has composed herself, before speaking.

'I know I said I was at my wit's end, sometimes, but that's normal, isn't it? Any single parent, any parent, would feel that sometimes?' She waits until both women acknowledge this, then carries on: 'In the main, I'm doing fine, looking after Matthew on my own. I like it. Of course, I didn't straight away, admittedly, I hated it at first. But now I'm doing fine. Matthew's good at home, most of the time. I've talked to him about his Dad. He needs some help at school, that's all. That's why I'm here.'

The last two sentences come out slowly, Lily's tone – although she struggles to prevent it – unmistakably sharp. Suzanna and Tanya exchange glances, minuscule glances, but Lily notices them. Suzanna coughs, crosses her legs.

'Of course, of course. It was Matthew's headteacher, wasn't it, who recommended Child and Family Services? Well let's run through some of the options with you and then Tanya can explain what Statementing is and how that might help Matthew . . .'

The afternoon rolls on. The too-hot office and the

grey winter air outside fill Lily's lungs with gloom and petrol and an even firmer determination to persist on her own, a dread of coming here again, sitting in the waiting room, staring at a poster: *Are you a parent, unable to cope with your own child?*

Mrs Jalil is worried about the children who are not reading or writing, the children like Matthew. For a project entitled 'A Letter to a Famous Person' she allows the ones who have difficulty to dictate to her, she'll type it straight on to the computer.

> *Dear Dad,*
>
> *Hello Dad. Have you finished Doom yet on Sega Megadrive? Will you buy me a piranha fish and a new tank?*
>
> *Love, your son, Matthew Waite.*

My Dad is a fireman. My Dad plays football for Leeds United, Miss. He can do back heelers and he buyed me a piranha fish. My Dad can do Doom on the Sega Megadrive. He can shoot geese with his special geese gun when they do that nasty geesy poop, the green stuff at Vicky Park. My Dad came to my school and he said all teachers are stupid and he said Mrs Chakrabatti went to a party did a little farty blew up the party.

My Dad's going to buy me a Sony Playstation and a Black-winged Hatchet Fish and four Tamagochis and a Blue Emperor and a Neon Tetra when he makes lots of money by scoring for Leeds United.

It's Matthew's sixth birthday, a rainy Saturday afternoon

and Lily has invited ten children to a Pool Party at Kinder Hall Leisure Centre. Sherry is in the water with her, the two women shivering in their swimsuits; Lily's flesh blanched like an almond in her navy one-piece, Sherry tanned in a silver and black bikini, a tiny bird tattoo on her left shoulder-blade. Josh told her something recently about Sherry that Lily is having trouble believing, although it explains a lot. He said Sherry turns a trick now and then. That she's on the game. That he thought Lily was a friend of hers, in the beginning, seeing them talking together. That's why he left her the money.

('Why did you think I left you money?' 'Well, just because I needed it.' 'Yeah. That too.')

Lily is somehow sure it couldn't be true; Sherry is so ordinary. Anyway, Lily is wary of the other woman after the incident with the sister. She didn't exactly *ask* Sherry to help out, but she did feel obliged to invite her daughter, Charmaine, the only child in Flanders Estate that Lily knows by name. Of course in Matthew's view the child is too young and, worse, a girl, so he is currently engaged in ramming her from his battleship: a giant float, shaped like a flattened frog.

'What time is it?' Sherry asks Lily, holding Charmaine by extended arms as if she were a metal detector and swirling her gingerly around in the water, her eyes on Matthew. He picks up Sherry's warning expression, propels his boat in the other direction, towards the steps.

Lily glances at the clock at the other end of the building, trying again to make out the hands from beneath a mass of swirling plastic foliage.

'It must be about half two,' she guesses. 'I told everyone two o'clock on the invitations.'

The food – eleven plates of chicken nuggets and chips, eleven drinks of Coke, *Lion King* paper plates – is the responsibility of the pool's manager, and that's what you pay for. Use of the children's pool exclusively for one hour, two members of leisure staff in their white sweat-suits to act as lifeguards, and food and drink, cups, plates and napkins, provided by the Leisure Centre café. When Matthew begged for a party, Lily quaked at the thought of ten little boys tearing through their tiny flat, scattering crisps and spilling drinks, and ten sets of parents silently observing the lack of wallpaper, curtains and proper furniture. Seventy-five pounds seemed a small price to pay to avoid humiliation. She and Matthew wrote the invitations together, Lily guessing at the spelling of the names; Ashok, Vijay, Tyrone, Dotun, Junior, Tunde, Mehmet, Kye, Emanse, Bolar? Bolar? How on earth do you spell that? It begins with G, Matthew insists. And when she looks at the name the next morning above the boy's coat-peg, so it does. Gbolagh. How ordinary things quickly become, for Matthew. Once, Lily commented to Josh that there had only been one girl in her whole secondary school who was black, Pamela Dickinson, and how Lily didn't like her, the girl was a bully and a nuisance, always picking fights.

'One black girl in the entire school?'

'It was only a small school, our local comp.'

'That girl must have thought she was in hell,' Josh said, with feeling.

Anyway, here it is now quarter to three and there's no sign of Gbolagh or Kye, and Lily is beginning to wonder if any of the children actually received their invitations. She swims over to Matthew, her knees gently knocking at the bottom of the shallow children's pool.

'You did hand out the invitations, didn't you Matthew? I mean, did you give them out personally, or did you put them in your friends' work-trays or something?'

'I gave them of course,' Matthew replies, unperturbed. He is lying on his stomach, on his frog float, tapping at the water with one dangling foot. Lily swims back to Sherry.

'We'll give it – what, another half-hour?'

Sherry nods. 'Perhaps they didn't take the invites home. Forgot to tell their mums. Kids do that.'

Lily links her arms round the silver bars edging the pool, stretches her legs out in front of her, tightening her stomach muscles. She studiously watches her toes in front of her, avoiding the doorway to the changing rooms, but she is still expecting a gaggle of little boys to appear at any moment, like a burst packet of colourful sweets, red and blue in their swimtrunks, noisy and excited.

At three thirty a lifeguard crouches at the pool side, dangling keys, to say he's sorry ladies, but he's afraid that he'll have to ask them to get out now, he has another Pool Party booked for four.

'Maybe some mix-up with the dates on your invites, eh girls?' He is grinning at Sherry, at the small breasts bobbing in their wet black lycra, and Sherry smiles back, absently, without opening her mouth. Her hair is scooped up in a series of clips and she must, Lily observes, be wearing waterproof mascara. A Caesarean scar like a pink zip on her stomach.

Matthew thrashes the water with his hands, soaking Lily's hair.

'But nobody is here yet! My friends aren't here! I haven't got any presents . . .'

'I know Matthew, but it's half three. It looks like they – I think your friends are probably – their mums couldn't bring them and they – aren't coming . . .'

Lily knows there was no mix-up with the dates, or the times, she wrote the invitations herself, carefully. She watches Sherry by the pool side, enfolding her daughter in an oversized gown, prodding the toddler towards the changing room. Charmaine is like a chick in front of a hen, obediently running, easily rounded up. Now, to Matthew, splashing up an angry froth, one small boy in a marble-blue pool. Empty except for mother and son at opposite corners.

Lily takes a deep breath, dives under the water. She emerges with a gasp on Matthew's side of the pool, spitting water like a sperm whale and he does at least laugh, Lily manages to make him laugh.

'Sit on my back,' she tells him. He clambers his slippery legs over Lily's back, and she takes another breath, as her body sinks under with the weight of Matthew on top of her. The pool is so shallow her belly practically scrapes the bottom. She swims breast-stroke all the way to the steps, by which time Matthew has admitted defeat, he knows they aren't coming, they won't come now, he won't get a Power Rangers action figure and he doesn't think his Dad is going to turn up either, although he thought he glimpsed him, just then, in the big pool, by the diving board.

'Look at that man, Mum. He has black swimming shorts with a white stripe, just like Dad's!'

Lily says nothing. Water clogs her ears. Perhaps she didn't hear him.

Here is Lily, Wednesday, on a bus passing St Paul's,

heading for Regent Street to go shopping. Matthew is back at school, Ms Brightman gave them both a clipped lecture this morning with references to all the usual mysterious Statements and Special Needs Co-ordinators. Ed Syke's name came up, as usual. Lily's face is taut as elastic in a smile ready to *ping* at any minute. She escapes quickly.

It's raining again, the bus is practically empty of people but full of the smell of wet wool and wet hair and wet nylon seats. Lily, on the top deck, leans forward to clean the window with the sleeve of her jacket, craning her neck to get a better look at the dome of St Paul's. Through the smeary bus window the scene is smudged, a charcoal sketch, and Lily is surprised at how dirty the cathedral is, how a hairnet of scaffolding fences the dome, how the pale sky offers the plainest, most vacant of backdrops.

Postcards of Trafalgar Square, Buckingham Palace and red buses, the sort of thing she pictured before she got here. It didn't occur to her they didn't show London in the rain or grey like it mostly is, but a sunny London for tourists in open-top buses and boats on the Thames for people from Yorkshire villages. This rainy London is better to Lily, less prettified – the very thing she wanted to escape – but also less foreign. It's rainy England, after all, the same clotted milk sky she used to stare at through the school window. She likes to look through the windows at the offices and see people snuggled in their work places or the poor sod under his *Evening Standard* umbrella at Liverpool Street Station. The pounding of rain on the roof of the bus, the hiss of the air-brakes or the bus doors opening and the colours: every shade of grey, then splashed with red, traffic lights, the red logo of a City Thameslink station. She suddenly wishes

Brenda would come down, Brenda would like this, for a visit, but then she checks herself, that's ridiculous, Brenda would hate it, she would be terrified.

Isn't this the biggest toy shop in the world, no, maybe not the biggest, but surely the most famous? Lily is hit by the whiff of cellophane, brand new plastic and the dazzle of the blue-white lights, the criss-crossing of her path by excited children and determined adults, stunned as rabbits snared by headlights. By luck rather than design she finds herself surrounded by action figures, the sort of things Matthew drools over; the gold Power Ranger with his motorcycle helmet for a face and his legs that bend at the knees, the pink one – the girl Power Ranger – that of course he would shun, and the Action Man watch with five astonishing features including an SOS bleep, should he need an emergency rescue.

The poignancy of this particular feature does not escape Lily. It snatches at her, fetching up tears. She wonders whether she should mention to Matthew that even if he'd had this watch six months ago, she doubts that the bleep is loud enough for people outside the house to hear it, for fire-fighters to hear it down at the station, for his dad to hear it, for instance, if that's what he is thinking.

It's only a small watch, slim in its cardboard and polythene packet. Fourteen pounds and ninety-nine pence. The Power Rangers figure is bulky, awkward: twenty-two pounds. She has ten pounds with her – she had thought that would be enough to get Matthew a decent birthday present after the seventy-five she blew on the party. As she has already been paid by Josie, nothing more is due for another month, although Josie has mentioned another friend, Isobel, who also needs a cleaner, and has a far bigger house in Islington, so would need Lily to work more hours.

Lily wanders round and round, now retracing her own path, mesmerised by the lighting and the boxes of Sindy dolls and Lego sets, her mouth dry, her heartbeat prickly. She is hungry, she needs a cigarette. The smell of wet wool drifts up from her wrists, the damp sweater beneath the flimsy jacket. She is remembering that she hasn't even replaced the TV that was stolen from her, thinking about the bastard who took it, took even that and the fucking police who seem to think the matter is over, and the home contents insurance that she can't fucking afford and it's all fucking unfair, unfair, and one tiny little Action Man watch for her son's sixth birthday, what could be wrong with that, who could begrudge Matthew that, after everything? Don't they know, for fuck's sake, the child doesn't have a single friend, not one child came to his bloody party, he's lonely for fuck's sake, she's doing her best but she can't do everything; she's broke, she's only one person, she can never make up for everything.

Lily wouldn't describe it as a dream, she doesn't describe it as a dream, hours later, sitting in the assistant manager's office at the back of the store, opposite the young Mr Kramer in his Hugo Boss suit and the young WPC with her opaque tights. She tells the truth. It was not a dream because she has never before felt more alert, more wide awake, more conscious of being alive – feeling her heart beat, the blood flow in her veins, the sweat seep over her palms.

The cramped office is steeped in the scent of rain-soaked plastic, of the street outside, brought in on the damp coats of the officers, police issue, hung up and dripping on the back of the door.

Lily is crying, tears streaming down her face, over

her nose, bouncing on to the soft leather of Mr Kramer's desk top, spreading into tiny dark splashes, little continents, islands in a sea of brown. She pictures Matthew, supine on his stomach, the bones of his shoulders beautiful and pointed, prominent as little wings, dangling one foot from the edge of the frog float. She has no idea what he is thinking, can never get inside his head. Does he know he has nobody, nobody in the world to rely on, except her?

The Action Man watch lies on Mr Kramer's desk top, glowing. The special features, the digital face, the adjustable strap: the only way Lily knows of making Matthew's face beam with pleasure. Mr Kramer pushes a box of tissues towards Lily, glances at his watch.

'We do have a policy, Mrs Waite. There are clear signs everywhere in the store. Shoplifters will be prosecuted. We can't allow – extenuating circumstances – to dictate policy.'

The young WPC says nothing. She holds her hat in her hand, glances at the police raincoats, with their bright green reflective stripes, noticing that now two small puddles have formed beneath them, dark pools on the laminate floor. Her colleague is in the toilet and he has been gone a good ten minutes.

'Oh God!' Lily shrieks suddenly, making the others jump. 'What time is it?'

'It's two fifty-nine,' Mr Kramer replies, with what seems to the WPC like great guesswork.

'I have to pick him up from school. I've no one to pick him up. Could I – I won't get back in time—'

A clear image of Matthew, standing at the school gate, expecting Lily and not finding her there, produces new sobs, a racking wave of sobbing that finally catches the others in its wake, rolls over the room.

Mr Kramer sighs. 'We can allow you to make one phone call. Why not telephone a friend and ask her to pick him up for you?'

He pushes the phone towards Lily, his eyes on the WPC to be sure that this is acceptable procedure

'I don't have anyone's number. I don't know anyone.'

Lily is thinking: who? Who could I ask? Josh? She doesn't even know if he is on the phone, doesn't know his last name, or Sherry's. Their phone numbers are unnecessary – she only has to pop downstairs. Mr Kramer and the WPC exchange glances, both heads turn at the reappearance of the other officer in the doorway.

'What's the problem, Trace?' the officer asks the WPC, as if he expected it to be all sorted by now. The WPC looks pointedly at Mr Kramer before speaking.

'She doesn't have anyone to pick her son up from school. We're suggesting she make a phone call.'

The only number Lily has is Josie's. Josie has kids, usually she has a child-minder, but not every day, she only works part-time. She is the last person Lily would ask, usually, she has a powerful dread of phoning Josie to ask a favour, but more powerful still is the image of Matthew, outside the school gate in the pouring rain, waiting for her. She picks up the cream phone, scented with polish, absurdly distracted for a moment, thinking again about cleaners. Then she dials Josie's number.

'Hello? – Hello, Josie? It's Lily.'

'Oh, hi Lily.'

Some music in the background, classical, piano music. Josie with her head to one side, the sleek bob cut swinging neatly, some dramatic arty earrings. That's what she does, Lily discovered. Makes earrings.

'I'm in a – bit of a tizz—' Lily begins, stress reviving her Yorkshire accent, 'I'm stuck here in town and I can't pick Matthew up and I wondered – is there any way you could pick him up for me?'

A short pause. Josie's voice is even.

'Pick Matthew up? From school? Um – that's, well, which school does he go to again?'

'Wishley School, Wishley Road, near the doctor's surgery, you know?'

'Yes, I know it. The thing is, Lily, that would take me about half an hour in traffic at this time. It's three fifteen now. And I have to pick up Jack and Ruby at half three . . .'

'Oh. I thought you had a child-minder to do that?'

'Yes, I do. Usually. Exactly. So that I don't have to do this. So I can work.'

The implication is clear: if I pay a child-minder to pick up my own kids so that I can use the time saved to work, what would be gained by picking up your kid? But Josie's argument is muddled. Lily is unsure if she is saying no because the time clashes with picking up her own kids, or saying no because she has a child-minder to do that and needs to work. Lily would like to succumb, here and now, put the phone down before desperation blurts into her voice. She doesn't want to lose her job with Josie, or the one with Isobel, Josie's friend; she can hear the young policeman sighing impatiently.

'I wouldn't ask, except that I don't have anyone else in London. I've only been here a couple of months . . .'

'Yes, I'm sorry Lily, I wish I could help, but I do have to go now and – pick up the kids. Ruby has her violin lesson. If I drove to pick up Matthew I'd never be back in time. Couldn't you ring the school and tell them you'll be late?'

'Yes. Okay. I'll do that. See you Friday. I'm sorry to ring you at home . . .'

'Oh no problem. Sorry I couldn't help. Bye Lily.'

Lily presses the handset back in its slot. The three others in the room look at her expectantly. Mr Kramer taps his pen on the leather top of his desk. He has a tiny nick on his neck where he cut himself shaving and he fingers this absently, staring at Lily.

'She can't do it,' Lily says, knowing that they heard every word. 'She says I should ring the school. Is it okay if I make one more call?'

'Maybe you should have thought of this before you went around nicking things?' interjects the WPC, tartly. Her radio is crackling and she crosses her legs in her seat, one shiny black shoe over the other. Mr Kramer clears his throat. He wears a badge, white with gold banding: *Mr P Kramer, Assistant Manager*. He has a slight speech impediment, his 'r' comes out as 'w', and his nails are bitten down to the quick.

Lily searches him for every kind of clue. His hair is spiked slightly, possibly he is wearing some kind of after-shave, his eyes are a mud-coloured grey, his desk is tidy; it is empty except for an Apple Mac, a box of tissues, a pen and pad, the toy watch Lily stole, a phone and some vitamin tablets. He wears a plain watch, leather strap, either old-fashioned or trendy depending on who is wearing it, the expensive suit, a shirt in a dark blue, a few curls of hair visible at the throat. The silence in the room is the oddest kind; squeaky clean, an air-bubble, time standing still in here, while the bustle of the store carries on just outside that door. Lily has stopped crying now, her skin dry and sandy as a hot pebble on a beach, she keeps her wide blue eyes steadily on Mr Kramer's wrist, watching him draw, hearing the squeak of the pen.

Each action has an equal and opposite reaction. Alan's voice in her head. *There are always consequences.*

I am charmed, I can walk through fire. Nothing can touch me.

Lily needs a phrase to live by, she needs to know the rules. The rules have most definitely changed and she has been frameless, floundering. Clearly there *aren't* always consequences. Nothing has happened since the credit card scam. The person who burgled her has got off scot-free.

Do your best. Keep y'sen cheerful. Don't get involved.

Josh did his best, he was a good father, he did all he could. He still lost his son.

Lily's head whirls. She raises her eyes from the pen, to Mr Kramer's young, faintly nervous face. She knows nothing about him, about what kind of person he is. He might vote Tory, keep gun magazines under his bed, there again he might be an environmental activist in his spare time, or send twenty red roses a year to someone he once loved.

She thinks, *I am completely in your power. A total stranger: your decision in this one tiny moment will surely alter the course of the rest of my life.*

Sweat shines now on Lily's forehead, she feels it trickle down the inside of her arms. The credit card looms in front of her eyes, she is struck almost breathless by how serious it all is, feels sure they will somehow find out about that too, feels a deep thumping sickness in her stomach which she remembers from long ago as terror, or shame.

'Well, Mrs Waite. We are wasting rather a lot of time here. My time and yours. I think it is clear to you that we do have a policy here. And the presence of these officers shows you that we do follow through and take seriously our shop-lifting policy . . .'

The two young officers shift uncomfortably, suddenly conscious of the direction of Mr Kramer's thinking.

'So, taking into account what you've told me about you acting – out of character – because of the distress you've been suffering, and the traumatic fire at your home . . .'

Mr Kramer doodles on a notepad with his pen as he speaks, big round circles, and he doesn't look up, aware of the irritated, restless movements of the two police officers.

'I think on this occasion, I can overlook what's happened. If you want to make one short call to the school, then we'll consider the matter closed.'

Lily breathes out. She sees her breath in front of her as if the room were a mirror. She sits very still, expecting a lecture. The WPC scrapes back her chair noisily, practically landing on the toes of her colleague standing behind her. Both officers stand in the doorway, a little uncertain, adjusting their collars, reaching for their coats. Like two big crows, Lily thinks, jerking their heads back and forth on their necks, full of self-importance.

'If you're sure about this, Mr Kramer?' The young woman officer's tone is sarcastic. Mr Kramer nods, shortly.

Never in her life has Lily experienced the police as anything other than polite, helpful, *on her side*. She remembers what Josh described to her, how they came to tell him about his son, the attitude they took, the assumptions. She feels shame now of another kind. The shame of being protected, of not knowing.

'There's state of the art security here, you know,' the WPC remarks, over her shoulder, flicking her eyes over

Lily, from head to toe. Lily wonders if she has kids, too, if that's what's got up her nose. A terrible risk to take, if you have children. Like that woman mountain climber who died leaving a son and a daughter and a husband who claimed her motto was better to live one day as a tiger than a hundred as a sheep, but no one agreed, the media didn't agree: they all pictured the children at bedtimes, asking: where's Mummy? and crying into their pillows. They tasted at nights their own frightened longings, their own fear of abandonment and heaped them on the climber, buried her under them.

Mr Kramer pushes the phone across the desk to Lily, soundlessly, and she dials the school number, the only one in London she knows by heart. Sandra, the school secretary, is shirty with her, especially as her excuse is so lame: 'I got caught up in town.' Sandra says she can keep Matthew, for a little while, but she'll have to be there by four thirty, otherwise she's afraid the school will be obliged to phone social services. That's school policy.

Lily stands up, not entirely sure if she is free to leave. She has a handbag over her shoulder, a jacket she hasn't removed. Rain-spattered jeans. A squashed packet of B&H cigarettes in her back pocket. The Action Man watch lies in its packaging, spanking new and enticing, even now, next to the notepad decorated in inky circles.

'Thank you,' murmurs Lily, without knowing how to say more.

'Goodbye,' replies the young man. Mr P Kramer, Assistant Manager.

She wants to say it. He is making love to her, she is up on all fours, she swings her head beneath him like an animal, like a horse grazing, she wants to say *I love you Josh, I love you* but she doesn't know why she wants to say it, these are new feelings, entirely new, nothing like her feelings in the past, her feelings for Alan. Isn't it just this, this sensation that she never had before; as if she just crawled along a knife edge and it might be pleasure but it could tip over, one slip and it could tip over. It's exquisite, not an orgasm but a long line of orgasms, a tightrope, a blade full of speed, she doesn't know if she is not quite alive or more alive than ever, it's something no one else produced in her. She mustn't say it, she doesn't know what it is she is crawling along, knife or rope, she thinks it's alight, she never did this before. *No one could feel this much pleasure and live*. She is not going to say it, he wouldn't want to hear it.

He rolls away from the girl, on to his back, giving a big sigh. He is laughing. 'I'm getting carpet burns. My knees.'

His knees are rubbed raw, skin scuffed grey next to the red-brown of his thighs. He pats her backside. Lily turns over. She is shining, everything about her glows like silver.

He is sitting up already, reaching for the cigarettes. Once lit, he makes a squeezing motion with his other hand, shows the contractions to Lily.

'You have strong muscles. Your poonani. Sweet like this.'

The girl smiles, she looks mildly astonished. She takes a drag on his cigarette, pulls her shirt on.

'I'll make us some coffee,' she offers.

'No,' Josh tells her. 'I forgot – I brought something.'

In the kitchen, he has a carrier bag. He loves to bring

presents. The girl is a pleasure to give pleasure to; her eyes widen, her face glows and he feels her watching him, hungrily. He is naked except for his blue boxers, taking out two small limes and a bottle of dark rum, then another bottle of Jamaican syrup. He fetches glasses from Lily's shelves, fancy glasses, salts the top of each glass, humming to himself. The smell of limes fills the kitchen. The girl sits on the chair, wearing his big white shirt and her underpants, Josh's beaver hat on her knee. He sees that she is turning over in her hand three small pieces of his hair, three dreadlocks.

'It snap off easy,' Josh explains, handing her a glass. 'My hair dry these days. I need to buy some Vitalis, oil it up good.'

Sipping at the sweet drink he hands her, Lily keeps her eyes on the locks, brings them up to her nose, breathes in. Josh stops humming. *The girl is in love with me*. He feels a short stab, just under his ribcage, the threat of something more. Lily is in love with him. His mind races. Had he reckoned on that? What had he been thinking of?

Josh produces the airmail envelope from the same carrier bag. His hands smell of the limes. He hands her the paper, a little awkward.

'My letter to Daphine. Is that all right? I need to write soon to her.'

Lily finds a pen. Josh chews his nails, fingers his beard, sips his drink, stares out of the window. Outside there is the sudden bang of a premature firework going off. Four days until Bonfire Night. This has been going on for nights, making Josh jump out of his skin every time.

In Lily's kitchen there is only the sound of a pen scratching on paper.

My dear Daphine,

I have received both of your letters. Hope my letter finds you well. Give my love to the kids them and Mark and Maxine and all the rest of the family. Brian at work is writing this for me. All is fine here. Yes I am eating fine. I am keeping well. I am working hard. I am keeping out of trouble.

A long pause. More fireworks. The pen raised in Lily's fingers like the head of a small creature, a salamander.

Well, Daphine I don't have much else to say. I am looking after the house. It is raining in London. I hope you will soon come.

Your loving husband, Landy.

'Landy?' Lily queries.

'It's short for Larkland. Daphine's name for me. White people can't get along with it, so I just tell them to call me Josh.'

Lily folds the airmail letter, goes to write the address, but she hasn't licked the seal yet.

'Why did you say Brian was writing this for you?'

'What do you think?'

She flinches slightly, he sees that his words were sharp and feels guilty. She nods shortly, finishes her drink. But she doesn't give up.

'Don't you ever want to *learn* to read and write? Go to classes, that kind of thing. I mean, you're obviously clever, you would pick it up quickly . . .'

She never leaves this subject. Like a dog with a bone, Josh thinks. It flashes through his mind, pictures of the class he attended a few years back, the years when

Neville was thinking of going to college, when Josh wanted to set a good example. Sure, he learned some things. His name. How to fill out a form with his address on it. *The teacher half his age.* She kept on about dyslexia, half the adults she taught would be called dyslexic now she said, but Josh doesn't know what he thinks about that, whether he believed her, whether he thought she was trying to make them feel better. Most of the class were women. Only two men and both of those Somalian and younger than him. They had a good excuse. They spoke another language.

Then another picture flashes. And this one fudged, hazy. Nothing to do with Neville, but it floods him with the same feelings, the same pain. The school in Jamaica. The dusty road, the long shadows of the banana trees in the afternoon, the walk to school. Day after day waiting for a letter from his father. Rose never mentioned the letters, but Josh knew his mother waited too. At six years old he wanted to be able to read the letter when it came, read it proudly to his mother. And then she died, and the letter never did come. And after that, what was the point?

He could get by. He did get by. And like this girl seems so determined to point out, no one else is meeting any suffering except his own sweet self.

He wonders what expressions have been passing over his face. The girl looks worried.

'Sorry,' she murmurs, under her breath.

Josh is putting on the beaver hat, tucking his hair in, adding six inches to his height. He stands in his shorts, in his big hat, tips the hat to her like a conjurer, to show she is forgiven. Lily puts a hand up, touches his stomach, his tiny flat navel. She touches him as if his skin were silk, gold, something precious. He stares down at the paleness of her hand, the veins on the milky skin.

'I wonder why people never say quite what they think,' she mutters.

He shrugs. 'Daphine and I been married nearly twenty years. She knows what I think.'

He hands her the letter from Daphine with her address on it, or rather the address of the post office in Portland, where Lily is to send the letter.

'Can you post it for me?'

She nods and he plants a kiss on her cheek.

'Goodnight Lily White.'

'It's Waite, you idjut. Lily Waite. Goodnight. Sleep tight.'

Lily is standing in her bedroom, wearing only the long cotton shirt and she is holding the letter to Daphine and listening to her own heartbeat. A faint green light sneaks under the door from the hallway. She has rigged up sage-green velvet curtains, a charity shop purchase, the room is deep and secret, the way she likes it; a forest.

At the bottom of the letter Lily scribbles: *I miss you Daphine. I miss Neville so much. You know long time how I love you.* She thinks 'long time' is how he would say it. The lines fit perfectly just before *Your loving husband. Landy.*

She folds the letter, writes the address in the half light, opening the door slightly to help her read it. *Don't get involved.* Her heartbeat doesn't slow to normal. She licks the envelope. Her heartbeat taps at her ribcage like the rapping of fingers on a ruler.

Her heart starts up again with its tapping when Josh and Lily pass each other the next morning on the estate, Josh on his way to work, Lily returning from dropping Matthew at Wishley School. Not close enough to touch, they smile briefly, and Josh nods his head, once, like a bird, then continues hurrying, lugging his tool box. Maybe it's the sky, the light or the onslaught of winter but suddenly Lily has never seen so much grey in her life; the grey concrete bollards that prevent cars from parking on the pavements, the grey metal grilles on the boarded up windows, the grey satellite dishes clinging to the upper floor flats like barnacles on an abandoned ship. Even the roses in the gardens of a few ground floor flats have withered to a few thorny grey stems on mounds of dried dog shit; the one tree in the centre of the exercise yard – as Lily calls it now – is leafless, pale and skeletal.

Lily reads for the billionth time, as she ducks under the entrance to Bridge House, the sign with the warning, *Liquefied Petroleum Cylinders must not be brought into this building*. She is thinking how old the sign is and pointless; how much rubbish there is that nobody reads any longer and as for Josh, well he never read it once and he's none the poorer for that, in fact you could say that there's a whole host of things Josh has chosen never to trouble himself with and Lily can understand that, she can see exactly why.

She is wondering if what she did was wrong. The phrase taking the law into her own hands pops into her head, which is a joke, isn't it, since she already did that a few times already and as far as she knows there's no law against adding a PS to someone else's letter.

The postman has already been when she reaches the door of her flat and there is a parcel, a large brown Jiffy bag to be exact, propped outside the front door. Lily has a flicker of annoyance at the postman's negligence, leaving it there – doesn't he know she's been burgled once already and she hasn't been here that long – before glancing at the writing on the brown package and stopping perfectly still, frozen in a crouching position, a sudden sculpture of herself. An icy snake shivers down her spine.

It's a bleary scrawl, the kind of writing a drunk might do, or a lazy, indulged professor who doesn't have to bother to make himself decipherable. Which just about sums Alan up. She picks up the package, gingerly, holding it by one corner (it's weighty, it rattles) and unlocks her front door. The snake has slithered down into her bowels and now it curls itself there; the contents turn to liquid. Lily goes to the toilet, comes back, sits down, stares at the Jiffy bag and Alan's writing, reads her own name, curiously accurate. *Mrs Lily Waite*. Alan guesses, rightly, that she has kept the married title but returned to using what she thinks of as her own name, the one she had in school, the one that she herself hears not as a name, but as a description, all one word: Lilyweight, a little more than Featherweight, a little less than Lightweight.

Lily Waite opens the parcel. Lily Waite shakes the contents gently on to the kitchen table. Lily Waite stares at them.

There is no letter, no card, nothing. She makes sure of this first, rummages a little, tips the Jiffy bag to be certain it's emptied, but she's sure, there is no written message from Alan. Instead, there is a small piece of black coal, which has smoked and smudged over everything else. Alan mined this tiny chip of coal himself: his father was a miner in Balby near Doncaster and once took Alan – when he was about nine – with him down the mine. He told Lily this many times, he told Matthew too and the child loved to feel the nugget of rock, to turn it in his hand and have the soot cover everything; he and Alan used to sit on the sofa together, watching TV, taking turns to handle the coal until Lily invariably chirped up with: you're getting that muck everywhere, swooping on whoever was holding it at the time to snatch it and put it away.

There is a leaflet, advertising the charms of *Mother Shipton's Cave* in Knaresborough, a leaflet folded many times and slightly greasy at one corner and now it has been in the Jiffy bag, a little black and sooty too. There is a drawing, Matthew's drawing, one of those painfully sweet children's approximations of a person, in this instance Daddy, wearing his fireman's helmet and holding what is meant to be a hose but which fattens in the centre and undulates and generally looks more like a large serpent or even a dragon, and Alan presumably thought so too, given that Alan, who was sitting at the table with his son at the time the picture was drawn, has added eyes and a tongue to the hose in blue pen.

There is a basketball cap, a Chinese folding wallet, books (*Winnie the Pooh*, *Postman Pat*, *Fireman Sam*), one blue sock, three pine cones (mostly crushed), a balsa-wood aeroplane, still in its packaging, a plastic car, a plastic Simba the Lion King, sandals, baby-sized, blue plastic, several comic papers from bubble-gum wrappers. A photograph, out of focus but she remembers it: Matthew and Alan down at the Station, pretending to shin down the fireman's pole, Matthew in an oversized yellow helmet. A tiny sword, plastic. Also, a box of Mickey Mouse glow-in-the-dark sticking plasters, unopened.

Lily turns each item over, slowly and compulsively. She is crying. The smell of Alan – what is it? Soap? Clean hair? Wool? No, something else: that strange fire-retardant material that lines the inside of his jacket, yes that's it, that's what Alan smells of, even now when he's not working at the fire station any longer. Even now when he has no need of it, of being fire-resistant, his smell flows to her, sneaks into her, his smell is more powerful than a letter, than writing: it carries everything.

Lily needs a cigarette, her hands are trembling. She stumbles to her bedroom to find the packet, lights one, breathes more easily, stops crying. She knows there is something important here, something she is supposed to get, but she is tired, she can't think what it could be. Alan leaves no address for himself. He must have found hers from Brenda and Bob. She checks the envelope. Yes, it's Flanders Street, not Estate, the small deception she visited on Brenda has been passed on. But the parcel found its way here. And now what to do with it?

I never said you were dead. Lily feels accused of something. What was she supposed to do? She has *tried* talking to Matthew. Matthew refuses to be drawn out, closes up like a mussel-shell whenever she mentions his father.

But she wonders about something, something Josh said that sank in with her. How his mother, and later his aunt, never spoke about his dad. How he learned not to ask, but filled in the gaps anyway. *A child makes a father out of the bricks his mother drops about him.* Lego bricks, Lily pictures. She knows that's not what Josh means.

She wonders what is the difference, for a small child, between someone not being around – not existing in the child's world – and being dead? A theoretical, irrelevant difference, surely, since someone *being dead* is hard enough for most adults to grasp. She thinks of Matthew biting, testing. Maybe that's a little too far-fetched.

Lily feels defensive, her logic wobbly. *I never told*

Matthew his father was gone for ever. I didn't know if Alan would ever come around. I didn't want Matthew's hopes to be raised.

It is unclear, even now, whether Alan has 'come around'. What does it mean, exactly, the parcel? Maybe just a way to rid himself of everything to do with his son, to clear the house, pave the way for a new start. Anger flares in Lily, a sudden blaze at this thought.

In the kitchen window three tiny aeroplanes glide across the pallid sky, churning a white ribbon behind them like the spume of a wave.

After a moment, Lily puts the items back in the parcel, not carelessly. She finds a piece of Clingfilm in the kitchen drawer and wraps the coal; places that in last. Then she does her best to re-seal the Jiffy bag (not easy since she has ripped it open hastily and tufts of grey stuffing litter the kitchen floor). She places the package in the highest kitchen cupboard, finishes her cigarette and goes to fetch a warm sweater. She is working today. Ten thirty at Isobel's house, Islington. *Money sweetens labour*, mutters Lily, to chivvy herself along. Another of Alan's phrases. Or was it Bob's? Funny how the two men seemed so different at first, *chalk and cheese*. (Bob's words this time, she's sure of it.)

Harder and harder these days, even to picture Alan. His short, near-black hair, a crew cut. So short it feels tufty and stiff, like the fur of a small animal. And his hands, huge hands, with splaying fingers. The memory is coated with the texture of Alan in his rough wool firejacket. He needed glasses but hadn't got around to the test when she saw him last. Maybe it's that and the hair but all she can think of now is a mole, the velvet coated mole in the *Thumbelina* story, the one the fieldmouse wanted so desperately for the child to marry.

A piece of coal. *A chip off the old block*. A pair of plastic sandals, a toy sword, a Chinese magic wallet, a cap. Isn't there a Greek myth, Perseus, which one is it? Where the journeying son is given certain important objects – a cap to make him invisible, a sword that can't be broken to help him on his way? But it's no good, she can't remember. Which myth it is. Which objects. And most of all, what the hell is the point of it all?

Seven for a Secret
(Never to Be Told)

Alan's counselling starts legitimately enough. He has been off work for three weeks, sleep holding him every morning longer than he wants it to, his back is giving him gyp. Gaynor is a bit of a joke with the lads: an on-site counsellor to go with the microwave, the pool table, the video down at the Station. It tickles them. No one takes her seriously. Of course it's partly because she's a decent-looking woman, smart in her tight skirts with her big breasts, which raise her sweaters so that they don't quite meet the top of her waistband.

Far as he knows, Alan is the first to go to her. His problems are vague, but they're getting worse. If the truth be told he's actually quite alarmed by them, once or twice he's had palpitations, sweat coating his back inside the heavy fire-proof jacket. So bad he thought he might be starting a heart attack; another time he thought he was going to faint clean away. He's not treating Gaynor as a joke at all. He's frightened.

'You see my wife, Lily, and my boy. They've always relied on me. She's not so – strong – I suppose. I've always been the strong one. She needs me to be *together*, like.'

Gaynor crosses and uncrosses her legs at him in the poky box-room the Station manager has provided for an office. Alan is actually only the third fire-fighter to visit her since the job was set up, and his case seems the most genuine. She's trying to suppress her delight, compose her face to an expression of concern.

'Can you say when the insomnia and the – panic attacks started?'

'No, no I can't say as I can.'

'What about that incident you told me about – a few weeks back? That house fire where the two little boys died, the twins. You told me about that in quite a lot of detail, I seem to remember. It struck me as meaning a lot to you.'

Alan runs a large hand nervously through his coarse dark hair. A house in Seacroft. Two boys around the same age as Matthew. Still in their pyjamas. *Casper the Friendly Ghost*, Alan even remembers the design, white on purple. He was the one to go in. It was smoke inhalation, not fire that did it. They looked as if they were sleeping, peaceful like.

'Some of those mattresses,' he tells Gaynor, coughing heartily. 'Stuff they're made of. Lethal.'

'It must be hard for you, an incident like that,' Gaynor says softly. 'A fireman. It's supposed to be your job, isn't it, saving people? It must be very – *painful* when it doesn't work out.'

Gaynor is thinking: what do I know about anything?

I've never seen two dead boys in my life. I can't imagine it. I really *can't imagine it*.

So then she starts on his relationship with Lily and he is even more uncomfortable. Lily is clever, cleverer than him, he doesn't mind that. She was briefly at Leeds University when he first met her, but then she got pregnant and they were married not long after and she never finished her course. She went straight from home to living with him. Her life with that mad mother of hers, Brenda, Lily was glad to give that up, he was sure of it.

When he tries to describe Lily he is self-conscious at first. Here is Gaynor, with her poised bosom, looking like she's about to heave a huge sigh of relief, but then never quite letting it out.

'Lily is frail, small like, even for a woman. But. She has something about her, hard to say what it is. Something you can't help taking note of. Like, like silver foil or something, a tiny piece can make your teeth taste metal all over, make your mouth ting, you can't mistake the fact that you accidentally ate it, along with the chewing gum.'

He laughs. 'What am I trying to say, here, about Lily?' The laugh fades, goes nowhere.

'I rescued her,' Alan mumbles. That's how he thinks of it.

'Rescued her? From her mother?' Gaynor asks.

'More than that,' mutters Alan, uncomfortably, but he can't say what.

'And now you can't rescue anyone? You're a *failed* rescuer, is that it?'

Well, Gaynor is a counsellor, she tells him later, not a bloody psychotherapist. It is her job to listen and to *reflect back* and to help fire-fighters *express their feelings* in a *safe* and *supportive environment*. Absenteeism is causing the Fire Service a whole a lot of worry, the amount of hours fire-fighters take off work for trivial ailments, but as for all this deep stuff, that's outside her scope. Gaynor's training consists of a one year part-time course in counselling and listening skills, taken after her first marriage broke up.

'Not sure you're paid to help out quite like this, though, eh?' Alan asks, several weeks later, round at Gaynor's, his head under the sheets, her nightdress pushed up to her neck. Gaynor concedes that this is outside the normal range of the job and feels a shock-wave of guilt run through her like a seam of gold, like a firework, and shivers.

One time she asks him about his choice of job, about whether he'd always wanted to be a fireman. She means to say fire-fighter, but she finds it difficult to leave behind the word fireman, the childhood name slipping off the tongue more easily.

'I liked to make fires as a lad,' Alan offers, startling her. 'I liked to make them, and then put them out. Sometimes in the fields I'd piss on 'em. You ever done that?' Gaynor shakes her head, mesmerised.

'It stinks. Smells worse than horse piss. Fun though. But that's the kind of thing lads do, that's all. Saving people's lives, that's what being a fire-fighter's all about. That and having a laugh with the lads.'

She can't get him past this, but she knows, she is convinced, something significant happened to Alan that day, the house-fire he attended in Seacroft. He was the first to go in, he was the one who saw the twin boys, who carried them down to his workmates, two brown heads lolling in his arms, who carried the knowledge and the sight of them, the failure, the truth, for the other lads. She pictures Alan, emerging from the house, dark and smoke-covered, like Hades emerging from the under-world, and shivers. Alan, she knows, has seen terrible things. Why choose a job like his unless he wants to do good, to save people?

Well, she, Gaynor, can understand the attraction of *that*. Keeps your mind off your own troubles for a start. Gives you the feeling you can, you know, make things work out, sometimes, have some kind of control over the world. God knows most people have precious little of that. Look at the parents of those twins at Seacroft after all. Their whole world ruined in one short instant. It's hardly surprising that some people, well-meaning people (Gaynor includes herself and Alan in this category), would like to do their best to manage things, things that seem out of control to others. Fire for example. Or feelings.

What Alan needs is a great deal of nurturing, she thinks. Something he's never had. Somebody to show him it's okay to fall apart every now and then; not like that needy wife of his, draining him like a leech. It's clear he isn't ever going to go back to work. He's finished with the Fire Service for good. Gaynor doesn't mind this at all, she assures him he can take as long as he needs to recover, and when he does her dad needs a right-hand man, in his transport business. He'd be glad to see Gaynor married again, glad to give Alan a job.

The only thing Gaynor comes to have some misgivings about is Alan's attitude to his son. Alan refuses to talk about Matthew. After the fire, he visits the boy at Lily's parents, once or twice, spends a couple of days taking Matthew fishing in the River Wharfe. Then he doesn't want to see Matthew at all, says it's too painful. He seems to want something just to seal up, to grow over and never to be unpeeled again. This doesn't fit with Gaynor's version of Alan as a brave man. A good man, a family man. Underneath her version of Alan, the Alan she is attracted to, is another one, a buried one, as if Alan in fact has *always been* the broken person he is now, all along, but shored up by his important role, by being needed, by being the steady hand at the side of his flickering, dizzy wife.

But she shakes this idea, she doesn't allow it to surface properly. Gaynor is five years older than Alan. No spring chicken. And men like Alan. Don't grow on trees. That wife of his, Lily. Doesn't know she's born.

The girl has released something for Josh. Every day he sees his son, it's as though a film runs in his head from waking to sleeping, trying to play every infinitesimal moment of Neville's life, but too quickly, he can't catch the images, only feel them tug at him, as if the boy were still three years old, pulling on his locks, making his head jerk, his eyes sting.

Not that Josh blames Lily. No. He wouldn't miss this for the world. In fact, he wishes it would never stop, this film, this flickering at the back of his eyelids, all day at work the sense of tears threatening, of a grief so great it hums beside him, he is no longer in a half-dead stupor. He has never felt more alive in his life. Every leaf on the road, wet and soggy, every cracked paving stone, he sees as if for the first time: the imprint of a child's trainer on the stairway, the indecipherable red scribble on the tiles near his home – didn't Neville do that? Each a dim memory piling one upon another until the impression is so real he could almost turn and say to Neville: *Rassclat – Arsenal on the telly tonight – you want to watch that?* before remembering.

But remembering doesn't close him down, turn a

screw so tight he can't unwind himself. Instead, remembering cracks him open, it keeps Neville close to him. One minute Josh is doing something, an everyday action like raising his hand to switch on a light, and then it's Neville's skinny wrist he sees; he goes to lock the front door and thinks of something trivial, Neville's set of keys. It's better, he prefers it, he even likes this searing openness. He can sit home and watch TV, he can hear about children dying in Rwanda and feel the same pain for them, for everyone, for the mothers of children in Bosnia, for his Daphine, smouldering in the sunshine of Jamaica. He loves this pain, this pain is better: it flavours his drink and his food, it flows through his dreams and his veins, it keeps his son with him, a living being; a person, a child, a young man.

One time Lily asks him doesn't he care who killed Neville? His answer is slow, he realises the girl doesn't know the full story.

'We know who did it. The boy in jail now. You think that make me happy, another black boy in jail?'

Lily is quiet then and Josh knows she had imagined the usual story: a racist attack, a white youth, as if that is the only possible reason to kill a black boy, because he is black. He is cold to her for a while, he doesn't visit for a few nights, but the child, Matthew, breaks the spell one evening, waving a sparkler under Josh's nose.

'We've got bangers. We've got Bonfire toffee and Roman Candles for a party on the balcony. Are you coming Josh?'

And the girl standing there, her hands deep in the pockets of her jacket, chewing on her lip, fixing him with her big eyes. He feels himself stir whenever he looks at her and he still hasn't worked out why. She isn't his type, even in Jamaica before he met Daphine he never went for blonde tourists, if they were white at all he fancied the brown-haired ones. Girls with skin as transparent as Lily's used to give him the creeps, and on top of that there's her skinniness, her lack of shape; he likes something to sink into, to bury himself in.

No, it's something that was there from the start, something about the way she arrived here. He knew she was keeping secrets. Secrets glittered all around her. He has an odd thought, too, from nowhere: *she's like me*.

'I made some chicken,' Lily says, shyly. 'Jerk chicken. Plaintain. Rice with coconut. I borrowed a Jamaican recipe book from this woman I work for. She says it's really trendy at the moment, Jamaican food.'

Josh stares at her. It's early evening and he realises that fireworks have been whizzing since five o'clock making scribbles over his head in the November sky, but that he hadn't thought about the date, the significance. Bonfire Night. He wonders if the smoky sulphur smell makes Lily nervous, how it is that she can give the boy sparklers. He doesn't mention any of this but his stomach lurches at the mention of the food and other parts of him too. *Lurch* is the word, he feels his whole self lurch towards Lily, he has to pull back, steady himself.

'Maybe I can write a next letter to Daphine. I'll bring up the airmail envelope.'

It is cruel and he watches her face for flickers of dismay but she is preoccupied with Matthew, sliding another sparkler out of the packet.

'See you in an hour,' the girl says. She is saucy, Josh thinks; maybe that's what it is. When she turns her back to him, to walk towards the lift, he's sure she deliberately arches her back, sticks out her behind, ever so slightly, giving her hips an extra swing.

Her flat when he arrives smells good; she has music on – Bob Marley. Josh thinks to himself, that's all she knows about Jamaican music. Still it's a good track, *Small Axe*, and it reminds him of Bob's funeral, 1981, how his brother Mark said half the country was there. This train of thought leads to Daphine again, picturing her drinking Irish Moss in Portie, picturing her – he is aware suddenly – with Mark, smoking, laughing, throwing back her head and laughing wide, in a way that she used to, when Neville was small. He shakes his head, shakes out his locks and the boy, Matthew, comes running, begs to try the hat.

Josh plants the huge felt beaver hat on to Matthew's head and laughs when it sinks down to his chin. Sticking out his hands in front of him like a cartoon character, Matthew stumbles into a wall, deliberately. Then Lily is standing, wiping her hands on a tea-towel, laughing at Matthew and removing the hat for him, placing it carefully on a chair in the kitchen. How pale she is, now, standing in the kitchen doorway; a pale flame, flickering. He can only keep her in his sight for a few seconds before he has to blink, blink, before he is dazzled.

'How does your hair get like that?' Matthew is asking, tugging on Josh's arm, leading him to the balcony. 'Don't you ever wash it?'

Josh laughs, a wicked sound, a blast.

'*Bloodclat*, of course me wash me hair man.' (Laying on the accent, sending himself up.)

He allows the boy to take him out on to the balcony, where fireworks are lined up on top of the window-boxes, stuffed into the earth like flower bulbs. The kitchen window looks out on to the balcony and they can both see Lily, stirring a pan, nodding her head a little to the music from the cassette player:

These are the words of my Master / Telling me that no weak heart shall prosper . . .

'It's like the Bible,' Lily remarks, to herself as much as to Josh.

He stands at the open window, reaching his hand through for the lighter. 'Well, where you think the Rastafarian faith comes from?'

She moves close to the window to talk to him.

'When you say "faith" I hear it as "fate". The Rastafarian fate. I like that. As if your faith is your fate.'

The half-open window is between them and a sheet of black night, scented with sulphur. He looks straight into her eyes, he is thinking about what she just said, thinking how he has lost his faith lately, since Neville, of course. It's hard to believe Jah is still looking out for him, these days. So that idea lodges with him. His faith, his loss of it, has become his fate. *She have me high upon a pedestal sometimes*, he thinks. Maybe he looks at Lily for just a second. Maybe it is a full ten minutes before she smiles a little, tips up the corners of her mouth, hands him a can of Red Stripe, leaning through the kitchen window to do it, her breasts brushing the bottom of the window frame.

'Mum, Josh is lighting a firework. Come out here, come and see!'

A moment's hesitation. Josh watches her. Her hand at the nape of her neck, stroking. She puts the spoon down and follows them out on to the balcony.

Other fireworks are already spattering the tower-block skyline, the screech of a rocket producing an echoing screech from Matthew.

'Did you do this with your son?' Lily ventures.

Josh starts. Why does she seem to want to probe, to

turn the knife? He has the oddest sensation about her. There is something strange in her questions. The feeling he has is this: Lily wants to know what it feels like to lose a son, she literally wants to know if she could feel it, bear it. He is frightened for her. Sweat prickles over him.

'No,' Josh says.

On the grass five floors below them someone is lighting a small bonfire. Children's voices float up. Josh lights each firework in turn and Matthew squeals appreciatively as each rockets from the balcony into the night sky. Smoke rises and yellow flames flicker. Josh watches not the flames, but their reflection in the windows of the pub opposite. *She never seem afraid of fire*, he thinks. You would think she would be afraid of it. Lily smokes a cigarette then goes inside.

Isobel's house is in another league from Josie's, Lily can see that. There is more light, for a start, and huge glass doors downstairs which open on to a manicured city garden (big pots with shrubs, small, curvaceous trees, rattan garden furniture). Tiny ceiling lights blink above her head like little stars when she tries the switch, a long floor of wooden boards glows amber at her feet. This floor is not scuffed with pushchair marks like Josie's but polished a deep amber, rich in natural light from the garden. Standing on the floorboards, Lily feels warm and sunny, convinced that her arms are slender and beautiful, her hair shiny, her slim wrists exquisite, elegant.

In this mood, she makes herself a coffee, grinding the beans first, carefully mopping any spills and choosing Isobel's finest bone china cup, the edges trimmed with gold, taking it into the living room, sits with her feet up on the low glass table. Isobel has left her a note.

Dear Lily,

Josie mentioned that you did some typing for her. I have some admin work – nothing too onerous – in fact I need a part-time assistant and wondered if you would be interested in this? Leave me a note if you are.

Isobel.

Lily pockets the note, pleased. She would certainly be interested. Josie and Isobel are friends, Lily discovers, because their husbands were at journalism school together, and now Josie makes earrings for Isobel, handmade silver leaf and shell shapes, one hundred pounds a time. But the husbands' paths have diverged; Henry teaches at Birkbeck and looks harassed and pot-bellied, and has books with titles like *Ideology and the Imagination*, while Diran, Isobel's husband, works in TV. Lily vaguely remembers seeing him on late-night news discussions, she thinks he might be quite famous, but now she doesn't have the TV she can't confirm her suspicions. There is a photograph of him on the Welsh dresser which Lily examines now, helping herself to a couple of Isobel's cigarettes, the secret stash she keeps in the kitchen drawer, behind the tea-towels. (Lily reckons Isobel has probably told Diran she's given up.)

Yes, Diran is handsome. Lily wouldn't kick him out of bed. He has these swotty glasses and a nice shaped head, a little like a large acorn; short-cropped hair, an imposing forehead. He might be bossy. (Something about the eyebrows.) Lily puts the photograph back on the dresser and sighs enviously. Maybe it isn't so much about race, after all, but about coming from the same background, having the same education. Having similar tastes in books, in films, in kitchen decor. Then she thinks of Josh and knows that isn't true. Both things can tug you at the same time. The pull of difference, the pull of something familiar.

She goes to look in Isobel's fridge. The work Isobel requires of her is pretty light. Sweeping the floors, floating over the glass windows and table with a cloth, hoovering the bedrooms upstairs. It seems that the more money people have, the guiltier they seem to feel, and it always looks to Lily as if Isobel already rushed around with a duster and a can of Mr Sheen before Lily's arrival. Dishes are rinsed before they are put in the dishwasher, the bins always strangely empty. Also, Isobel and Diran don't have kids, although they are trying (according to Josie), so of course their place would be tidier than Josie's. (Actually Lily has discovered that Isobel has contraceptive pills in a tiny make-up bag under the bed, so all that *trying*'s going to waste.)

Today, Lily isn't in the mood to do anything at all. She smokes both the cigarettes, one after the other, wanders upstairs. She sits herself down on Isobel and Diran's huge bed, takes an envelope – Josh's letter to Daphine – out of her back pocket and raids the desk drawer for a stamp. Two stamps in fact, as she can't remember the cost of a letter to Jamaica. Then she lies on the bed, staring at the ceiling. It's high, with a spectacular ceiling rose. She thinks of Diran making love to Isobel and wonders if she's a racist; always thinking of black men in a sexual way. She pictures herself with Josh, his spidery hair tickling at her shoulders, and tears spring into her eyes and she wonders where this feeling comes from, this deep certainty that he isn't hers, she can never have him, it's wrong to even want him.

She tries to picture Josh as a boy with the same neatly tucked belly button that he has now, the same sturdy legs only smaller, the defined curves of his arms, the showing off, the low bow he does, sweeping his hat like a circus ringmaster. She thinks of him now with the grey hair twined into the locks and how the locks snap off, not like her hair would do, not in handfuls or clumps, but neatly, like little twigs.

How hard it is to talk of their differences, of what Lily has learned from Matthew recently to call race, not colour. If she strays into this territory with Josh, the gap between them seems to widen and the words fall into it, the language is all wrong. *I don't have a problem being with a white girl*, Josh says, knowing full well that was not her question. If she pushes him further he shrugs and says what's this race thing you're talking about, this is the nineteen nineties plenty of couples mixed these days, which is true, yes, but that's not all there is to it. His son is important to her in some sticky, prickly way, and she doesn't know why. She knows Josh winces if she asks about Neville but she can't keep off the subject.

Her strongest feeling about Josh is of guilt, the sense of stealing. Of course there is Daphine, Lily hasn't forgotten that. Also, Josh is vulnerable, that was clear enough from the start; Lily sometimes has the sensation of standing next to a brimming cup and she knows this is part of her feelings, and she's guilty about that, too. She places her head on Isobel's pillow, breathing in the scent of Isobel; clean hair, faint medicinal lavender or rosemary and a smell Lily associates with big department stores but couldn't name. Something expensive, perhaps face cream or soap. Lily feels her head fit neatly into the small imprint the other woman recently left (it's Lily's job to plump up the pillows and shake out the duvet but she hasn't done it yet). She stretches out her legs luxuriously and wonders if Isobel ever feels this way: after centuries plundering, must we have love now too?

She wants to rush home and tell Josh something. She wants to grab him by the shoulders and fix on his brown eyes under the corrugated forehead and shriek at him: *You did your best. You loved your son. It's all right. All is not lost.*

She wonders if this is true. She wonders what she thinks is true. She tries for the first time to imagine Alan, out there somewhere, somewhere in Yorkshire where there are stone walls (she guesses, she doesn't know where Alan is right now) and biting winds and endless visitors in walking boots and anoraks with flasks of tea and stupid questions. She closes her eyes on Isobel's extravagant bed and forces herself to imagine Alan missing his son. The little boy he had for five years. Matthew's tiny foot, held in Alan's big hand, clumsy with his attempt to put Leeds United football socks on a new baby. Alan and Matthew in Alan's workshop, both with their tongues sticking out in exactly the same way, heads bent over the model fire engine, paint brushes dipping together at the exact same moment, like a dance, like what it was: something rehearsed. Alan stripped to his pants, washing Matthew's hair in the bath, both of them sopping wet and laughing with some game or other. This scene is framed and Lily realises it's because she was always watching it from just outside the bathroom door, all that maleness, and nakedness; the grown man, the little boy; the tenderness. She felt like an intruder. She has seen Alan cry. She knows how men cry. Alan crumples up, his shoulders cave in on themselves under the clothes, the fireman's jacket, he dissolves like the froth on boiling milk subsiding. He'll never recover. She knows this with absolute certainty, but he didn't give a forwarding address; unlike Josh, she has no way of telling him anything.

The package from Alan says it all. He doesn't want to see his son, he's not prepared to try again; he's done with him, he's trying to slough him off, a dead skin, a former life, a mistake.

Of course men attempt this everywhere, Alan is not extraordinary. All around her on this estate, at Matthew's school, there are boys growing up without fathers, or with the staccato, inconsistent type, who disappear when new girlfriends or new babies come on the scene. Plenty of people, old ones, young ones – her own father for example – are fatherless children and Matthew is not exceptional; his life, his future story is going to include that fact. 'My Dad left when I was five. He kept in touch at first, then he didn't bother.'

Lily sits up again, walks as if through fog to the window, her hand at her mouth, wanting another cigarette. How vociferously we have been protesting, she realises. How hard Matthew and I have worked to refuse the reality, resist our own story as it unfolds. Hard enough to take a match to the page, flutter black debris everywhere, send ashes up into the air like butterflies.

The view from Isobel and Diran's bedroom is of London gardens, other gardens, very like theirs, shrubs in pots and garden furniture, leaves on the grass and neat garden sheds, conservatories, glass and light everywhere. Next to Lily is a picture, something abstract in oils in the autumnal colours Isobel, with her conservative, inoffensive taste, favours. Lily takes it off the wall, turns it around, examines it from all angles and decides Isobel has it hung up wrongly, it looks better sideways. Not that it resembles anything; just that Lily is sure it should be hung that way, she could easily change the wire and screws on the back to reposition it.

Bloody Philistine, Lily thinks to herself, her throat constricting. Does Isobel deserve beautiful things, whatever and whoever she wants? Doesn't she, Lily, deserve the same? Lily fingers the picture at the edges, it has no frame and the paint feels good on the canvas, under her fingers. Lily puts her face close to it, inches out her tongue. Remembering Mr Kramer, Assistant Manager, how close she came to disaster. Matthew at the school gates, waiting. Lily tastes the paint. She tastes gold, green and russet brown and they all taste exactly the same, of nothing at all. *'I want' never gets*, Bob used to say. Lily didn't dare to want, not openly. No, Lily decides, there is nothing wrong with wanting. But it is a risk. You have to be able to bear not-having, you can't let *wanting* have the run of you.

The note from Isobel is in Lily's pocket and she *is* grateful, work is what she needs more than anything. Lily puts the picture carefully back. She walks downstairs, holding her letter from Josh to Daphine in Jamaica. She gathers her keys and her bag. She has probably done a bad thing, writing on Josh's letter. But it's twelve forty-five, the post leaves at one p.m. and there's a postbox at the end of this street. If she hurries, she should be in time and then it will be too late, then it will be irreparable.

Brenda sitting in the car, the engine running, as if she was ready to slip over into the driving seat and speed away, if Bob never came back. Brenda's small grey head in her headscarf, facing front. Lily at the library with Bob, choosing her books in a hurry, both of them nervous, emerging to see the small alert head of her mother in the car, held so still, a tulip on a stalk, you knew she was keeping it there by force of will, you knew she was concentrating.

Some people take no risks, none at all. Risks are good, Lily says to herself. (All risks? I don't know.) Josh takes risks, look at Josh. He's still here, more alive than ever.

Late at night, Lily thinks of the letter to Daphine, winging its way to Jamaica, to a country she's never seen. *Winging*. A strange phrase, suddenly. A letter with wings. Surely it has taken flight now, that letter, no way for Lily to ever reach up and catch hold of it, pull it back down to earth, tear it up, take it back, flutter it in pieces over the ocean, over that green island. Tear it up, scatter it, selfishly, like a child. That way she could have Josh, keep Josh, and every bone in her body, every artery, every cell, wants Josh right now.

She sits up in bed, her usual position, smoking. Matthew asleep in the other bed. Her notebook, the list, is on the table beside her and it's this that she tears up, abandons: page after page littering the bed, a huge snowfall of biro and cheap paper, until tears flow freely, the odd splash smearing the ink, turning a flake of paper to pulp.

Now she knows what she has been missing and there is no point in writing it down. She has it, she has it for the first time in her life and it's not based on need or desperation either, it's based on simple things, on reality. But more than that, Josh has changed her, expanded her, and she can't ever go back, go back to that tiny girl she once was.

I've done the right thing, she tells herself. I've done a good thing. In the long term, for the future. *And it won't always feel like this, that's all I need to remember. It won't always feel like this.*

The night of the fire is like this. Lily and Matthew are in the house in East Keswick, not far from Brenda and Bob's cul-de-sac and Lily's old school, not far from the A1 and the Wetherby Turnpike Hotel – where Lily worked briefly in the evenings, while she was a student. It is two weeks after Alan left to move in with Gaynor. Two weeks in which time stood still. In which Lily virtually stopped. Her heart, she thought, stopped beating but her body went through the motions, taking Matthew to school, making his tea, plonking him in front of the TV but not speaking to him, not responding when he spoke to her. Sometimes she would look at Matthew and realise he must have said something several times, he is staring at her, but she hasn't heard a word, she had no idea he was there.

This evening Alan's voice, his words, *But Lily you never really loved me, I knew that, you just needed me* are rattling around her head. The final insult, after she has phoned and phoned and refused to put the phone down. He is rejecting even this, her brokenness, the evidence of her love for him.

Or Matthew's love for him. Matthew had a bad dream and wet the bed, the washed sheets are humming now in the dryer. Lily sits in the living room with the curtains drawn, smoking. She is drinking whiskey with ice from a plastic Winnie the Pooh tumbler (Alan took most of the glasses; they were a wedding present from his brother) and she has flicked through every channel on the TV and found nothing. Her mood agitates her. She is aware of it through the sludge of the alcohol, without it touching her; it's like swimming in a lake knowing the bottom of the water is rocky or dangerous: it's fine as long as you don't put your feet down. It's not just about Alan. It's not just the shock of being left. It's that everything else crumbles with it, the whole edifice. The idea that she is a grown woman. That she can cope.

She finishes her cigarette, stubs it out viciously, thoroughly. She picks up the phone, puts it down again.

She telephones Brenda.

'Hi Mum.'

'Hello love. How's things? We're just about to go to bed, I were just making a cup of cocoa for your Dad—'

'Mum . . .'

'What, love?'

'I don't suppose . . . I know it's late, but I wondered if you would come over?'

The line crackles. Brenda clears her throat.

'Your Dad's in his pyjamas now.'

'I didn't mean Dad, I meant you.'

'On my own?'

The sentence hangs between them. Lily envisages it as a bird on a telephone line, suddenly swinging upside down under the wire, suspended, pretending to be dead. After some time, Brenda coughs again.

'Well, love, it is a bit late. Why don't you tell me what's wrong? Is it Matthew? Have you heard from Alan and – what's her name?'

'Oh nothing . . . No, it's not that. I don't know what it is. Never mind – I should go to bed, I'll be fine.'

Brenda's agoraphobia, her terrible fear of out there, looms between them, expanding like gas along the telephone line until Lily is nearly breathless with her own daring, with the exhilaration; asking this question of her mother, this enormous question, the test she has never before dared to set. Sometimes, when Alan set off to work, at night, or in the early hours, a terrifying image would come to Lily, of Alan melting like plastic inside his fire-proof suit. Now it has happened to Brenda. Brenda has melted to nothing, shrivelled, disappeared. One puff and Lily could blow her away.

Brenda's voice comes back, recovered, normal. 'I could ask your Dad to call by, in the morning. How's that, love? I've some free-range eggs I picked up for you at Beryl's. I'll send them over.'

'Okay. That's fine. Thanks Mum. No, don't worry. I'm fine, honest, just a bit down you know, but I'll be all right.'

'Fine, I'll send Dad over in the morning.'

'Night Mum.'

Once, around the time Lily is seven, Brenda does a Bad Thing. She tells Lily it is a Bad Thing and she is truly sorry for it and when Lily is a big girl she will understand and maybe she will forgive Brenda for it, but on no account should she tell Bob.

Which part is the Bad Thing Lily is unsure. A weekday morning at around school time, Brenda needs some shopping, so she sends Lily to get it – milk, tea, oranges, aspirin. Lily goes proudly to the corner shop by herself, mingling with her school friends swapping Curly Wurlies for Smarties and calling to her, but confidently ignoring them, knowing her errand, knowing Brenda needs the aspirin and being a highly responsible child. Bob wouldn't be back from the Brewery until early evening and Brenda's headache is bad.

But on the half-mile walk up the hill to the house Lily lingers in the lane, she takes a small detour to the fields at the back of the house, swinging the shopping bag, throwing the ears of corn like darts, singing to herself. When a man – perhaps the farmer – comes striding across the field, she means to run, but he is smiling at her and he asks in a friendly way why she isn't in school.

'I'm looking after my Mum,' says Lily, proudly, tilting her sharp little chin, throwing a corn dart down at the ground, vaguely in his direction.

The man comes closer and stops. He takes out his penis in the swiftest of movements and begins pissing, aiming the arc at her shoes. A few drops of urine splash on the red leather before Lily, for once speechless, turns and runs towards the house.

Lily is frightened but she is also indignant. She arrives home panting, struggling to tell Brenda what happened, certain that her mother will be out there in an instant to shout at him, to get the police or something, to tell him off, because Lily *knows* that can't possibly be right, men shouldn't do such dirty things in front of girls, to girls' shoes.

Brenda's eyes widen and widen, listening to her daughter. Her hand flies up to her hair in an aimless, absent gesture of holding, supporting, patting at the curls, as if she is wearing a wig that's about to slip off.

Filthy! Disgusting! Brenda is saying, but to Lily's surprise she is making no move to go outside. She makes Lily sit up on the kitchen bench, scrubbing at Lily's shoes with Dettol and kitchen paper, throwing each piece of paper away and tearing off a fresh one; in the end Brenda takes the shoes off, her big tears splashing on to the red leather while she begins to scrub them once more.

'They're clean now Mummy,' Lily says.

Lily watches her mother's face attentively, she fixes her eyes on Brenda's, she sees how the place above her mother's eyelids, just under her brows, is heavy, is pressing down on the lids, she watches tears form bright crescents in the bowl of Brenda's eyes before spilling over. Panic spirals up in Lily, from the base of her spine to the tip of her head, as she watches her mother's reaction. This is far, far worse than she anticipated. After all, the shoes are fine, perfectly clean, the man is gone now. She is not sure what Brenda is crying about and given that she, Lily, the *youngest*, is not crying, she starts to feel piqued. Then she feels frightened again, fear soaking into her drip by drip. Privately, Lily resolves never again to let Brenda know about anything bad that happens to her, anything bad she might be feeling. She will take care of her own self, that is the way it will have to be. Safer than risking this; this terrible reaction, Brenda disintegrating in front of her eyes, like toilet paper in water.

Lily peels off her socks, taking them carefully to the linen basket upstairs. She pads back downstairs, barefoot, holding the red leather shoes, T-bar, five punched holes at the front in the shape of a leaf, and places them in the cupboard under the stairs.

Then she steps over to Brenda, sitting at the kitchen table, and pats her hair, copying Brenda's own gesture. 'All fine now,' the child says.

Brenda glances up. 'Don't tell your father,' she snaps, quickly, unexpectedly.

Lily nods. She can make her mother a cup of tea. She is good at that, at making the drink the exact shade of orangey-brown that Brenda likes, at remembering the biscuits, the best ones with the pink icing on top. Now

Brenda is hugging her, tightly, murmuring into Lily's hair *Who's my best girl, my best girl . . .*

And then Brenda tells her it was a Bad Thing and Lily thinks she means what the man did to her but that doesn't make sense, because Brenda didn't do it, did she? So she decides the Bad Thing is that Brenda didn't go out there to sort him out, yes, that seems to be what her mother is saying and she seems to want Lily's forgiveness for this. Just a small thing, not difficult at all, Lily can surely give it. Brenda also says Lily can stay home that day, stay with Brenda, keep her company, and Lily is glad about this. She doesn't want to leave her mother at home in this state.

They watch *Scooby Doo* together and later Brenda bakes bread and plays Snap with her and when Bob comes home Brenda tells him that Lily has a touch of flu, and Lily coughs once or twice to show that she has. Now it's Bob who hugs her tight and says, *Who's my poppet, who's my little treasure* until Lily can hardly breathe, has to make a fuss, scream a lot, before he'll let her go.

Lily pours herself another whiskey, this time minus the ice, musing over the phone call with Brenda. The bottle – Jack Daniels – is nearly empty. Anger is stealing into her, creeping into her blood. She is surprised at herself. The version she had of her own life, how carefully she has protected everyone, everything in it. For the first time in twenty-five years, she is aware of a thundering, powerful anger, another self, rolling along underneath it all, beneath the fragile, *Lilyweight* veneer.

Brenda. Bloody Brenda and her catalogue shopping, her lost babies, her hoarding. *How good they thought they were, at taking care of me. And all along I kept the illusion for them, while I was stronger than both of them, taking care of myself.*

Alan. Bloody Alan. You think you're so smart with your bloody new woman and all her bloody nurturing skills. All those nights worrying about you going out there, dreading you melting like plastic inside your jacket, in the heat, at the coal-face, saving people. Fact is, Alan, *you needed me; you used me* to make yourself feel strong and capable, Mr Nice Guy without all the difficult feelings like *fear* and *dread* and *vulnerability*, just like Brenda and Bob used me . . . but what they used her for, she is too drunk to remember.

She smokes her last cigarette, flicks it over to the wastepaper basket. She read something terrible yesterday; a mother in America who drowned herself and her kids, weighting their pockets with stones. Imagine the little duffle coats, Marks and Spencer's, gathering the stones from the garden, choosing the biggest; dirt on your hands, stuffing their pockets. The same duffle coat you sewed gloves on to last winter, labels in the collar for school. Matthew churns the bed in the room above, talking in his sleep, his usual troubled dreaming.

Downing the last of the whiskey in a huge gulp, she kicks at the wastepaper basket. She is not deadened by drink, not switched off, not at all. She is giddy, exhilarated, rocking herself a little in the armchair. Alan melting in his fireman's outfit. A marshmallow on a stick, dangled in a flame, Brownie Camp. Lily always held the marshmallows too close, or a moment too long, until they blackened and shrank. They were never edible. When no one was looking she threw them away.

It isn't Alan who rescues Lily and Matthew from the fire.

He isn't on duty that night. He's stopped going into work for good, on Gaynor's advice, but he hasn't got round to telling Lily yet. Instead it's a bunch of men she doesn't know, a different watch, as Alan's Station was at another job.

She is told the details later, by Brenda and Bob. The fire starts downstairs, in the wastepaper basket, smoke soon belching from an open window in the living room, oxygen fanning the flames. A neighbour calls the Fire Brigade, but neither Lily nor Matthew wake, the two of them upstairs in bed together, Matthew sleeping with her, his own bed being wet.

Lily remembers some things. The oddest kind of light, blue light, flashing on the ceiling. This is not flame, as she blurrily wonders later, it is the light from the fire engine, reflected from the grass below.

Waking up drunk to a voice at the window. It isn't even surprising that there is a ladder at the window, that a gentle voice is murmuring to her, *Pass me the boy, is your boy there, love?* So she does this, does as she is told, floating around the room in her white nightdress, passing Matthew to the man at the window. Matthew who is usually so heavy; suddenly light. She remembers the story, the *Thumbelina* story with the beautiful blue and white swallow who carries the tiny girl away, carries her off to a warm country and she is glad, glad this is how it ends. Stepping out of the window airily, the nightdress flutters at her feet. There are shadowy figures, an engine, on the grass below.

Matthew, too, takes in the familiar chemical smell, feels himself passed to someone in a thick wool jacket and believing himself secure at last in the returning arms of his father, does not fully wake.

Eight for a Wish

Daphine smooths the creases on her new camel-coloured dress, straightens it over her knees; pats her hair with a wet finger, trying to press it into place. She's sitting on a wobbly wooden bench, in this tiny church, a cool draft sneaking along her arms, the smell of ackee and salt fish still on her hands from the meal she cooked last night. She hasn't come in here to talk to the Lord, particularly. Just to escape from Mark and the kids for a while, to clear her head.

To think about her job. How many months since she worked there, at the council. First she took compassionate leave. Then she was off sick for a while. Then coming here, to Jamaica: must be nearly a year in total. And her boss said that he couldn't hold her job open any longer for her, but that he thought there would always be a place for her in the housing department. That is, if she wants one.

And does she? Does she want to go back to England

at all? Sighing noisily, Daphine heaves her handbag on to her lap, snaps it open, reaches for the letter from Landy, carefully folded. Opens it again. Smooths it flat across her camel-cotton knee. She stares once more at the neat slender handwriting, the crossed 't's and the dotted 'i's. Brian didn't write that letter, that's for sure.

In twenty years of married life, never a birthday card from Landy, never a Valentine, a love note, never has she seen his *own* handwriting, how it would look. She doesn't care, *she doesn't care*. He has got someone to write this letter for him and the idea that he thought he needed to, that he thought she didn't know; *that* gives her pain.

Words, black scrawls on blue paper, symbols, scratchy patterns like the claw-prints of birds on the beach. She's sorry for giving him a hard time over those police matters, Neville's papers. What does it matter to her, now, after all, the words? *You know long time how I love you.*

Landy only has to stretch out his arm in the night, cradle her neck like the sea cradling an island. *Of course I know, you damn fool, of course.* His body speaks everything Daphine needs to hear. The Lord knows it always has.

Waking from a deep sleep, Lily realises a noisy fight is happening downstairs in Sherry's flat. Nothing sexy this time, all Lily can hear is thumping – of furniture turning over, maybe of Sherry's head banging against a wall. Listening, her heart stomping, to the sickening sounds of the baby screaming and Sherry yelling *Don't touch her don't touch her* and then more screaming and a male voice and Lily has to jump out of bed, reach for her gown, stand in the kitchen to see if she can make out the words, but she can't; only the venom, the tenor, the violence.

So close, like standing on a skin of paper, this kitchen floor. How clearly Lily can hear, can picture. Sherry with her slim body, her bird tattoo, the Caesarean zip on her stomach, tactfully quiet at Matthew's swimming party. Sherry and her dusting of freckles, her big eyes, her pink, lipsticked mouth, proudly walking the baby, *You on your own with the kid? Me too*. Sherry never mentioning her sister's verbal attack on Lily in the playground, making it clear she still wants to be friends. Sherry smiling about Josh, in the beginning, asking *What was your present then? A pair of shoes?*

Lily's heart is pounding at her ribcage, trying to escape her body, she can't listen a moment longer. *Don't get involved*. She's reaching for the telephone anyway, dialling. *Which service do you require, Fire, Ambulance, Police?* and not knowing which to say, almost saying 'Fire' and now tears streaming down her face, rocking herself, picturing Sherry curled in a corner somewhere, or already face down in a pool of blood, Lily saying to herself *She won't thank me for this, she won't thank me* and then waiting, jumping out of her skin when the call comes back from Scotland Yard, confirming her number and assuring her a police car is on its way and asking, *Is an ambulance required?* and Lily saying, almost screaming *I think someone is being murdered* because that's what she pictures, she is much too close to this, she can see much, much more than she wants to: the ugly stuff, the messy stuff, men in Sherry's flat, their thick hairy wrists, the sweatmarks on their T-shirts, their lazy eyes. The baby too, engulfed in choking smoke, in a kitchen full of flames, Sherry running to her, reaching out arms for the child, struggling for breath. *Don't get involved . . .*

Lily hears the siren of a police car, the lift engaging, men's voices and the crackle of radios in the stairwell. She gingerly opens her front door at the same time as Mr Sulyman in the flat opposite opens his. Their eyes meet briefly before he closes it again.

Not daring to bend over the stairwell, shivering in her dressing gown, bare feet on the dirty floor, Lily hears doors closing to Sherry's flat, the lift engaging again, without seeing what has happened, or who went into the lift. Silence. Tears dry to salt on her face, her heartbeat calm now. She goes to the front window to watch as an ambulance pulls with difficulty into the estate, negotiating the bollards with painful slowness.

Later, a long time later, the uniformed men emerge from the entrance-way to the building, walking towards the ambulance, carrying a stretcher. On it a green bag, like a sleeping bag, lit by the amber overhead light. The bulk of one of the men blocks Lily's view, she can't see Sherry's head, her face.

A group of people are standing around. Mehmet, newly arrived on his motorbike. Lily looks for Josh but he is not among the small crowd. Lights show in many of the windows of the estate, and Lily can see figures standing in them, feel the interest glow momentarily; flicker, fade away again as curtains drop back, figures disappear, the doors to the police car slam shut, the ambulance pulls away.

What happened to Sherry's child, to the man, Lily didn't see. Smoke cleared, that's how it seemed, a cloud of smoke pulled away like a screen and what Lily sees is not Sherry, but herself, lying on a stretcher covered in green, no flames at all, but like something dredged up from the bottom of the sea.

Others did it for me, Lily is thinking. Perfect

strangers. Caught hold of the thread of me, held tight while I dangled on the end of it, while I twirled a little; while I made no attempt whatsoever to either hang on tight, or fall.

At Christmas Lily takes Matthew to East Keswick for a few days, to visit her parents.

'I just can't believe the way that man has behaved, to his own flesh and blood. I know it's not unheard of, men abandoning their children, but *fancy* not so much as a Christmas card, a letter . . .'

Brenda is standing at the sink, washing vigorously, handing the soapy dishes to Lily, who stands dutifully with a tea-towel, knowing her mother is referring to Alan, but having little comment to make. From the living room rumbles the sound of the TV, a cartoon, punctuated with hearty belly laughs from Bob and the odd squawk from Matthew. Thankfully, this year, the Queen's Speech has been forgone and replaced with one of Matthew's videos.

'He did send a letter,' Lily interjects, thoughtfully. 'A parcel. A letter of sorts.'

Brenda peels off a rubber glove, raises her eyebrows in surprise.

'What did he say? What's his excuse then for not finding the time to keep in touch with his own son . . .'

'He didn't have one. He didn't say anything. I think it was a goodbye letter.' Brenda lets out a short sigh, angry, it seems, as much with Lily as with her ex son-in-law.

'There's always the Child Support Agency. Make him pay you know, isn't that right Bob?'

She calls through the open kitchen door to Bob, who is now snoozing, on the sofa, the Christmas *Radio Times* balanced across his stomach.

'I don't really want him to *pay*,' Lily mutters, filling the kettle with water and setting it to boil.

'Well, someone has to look out for Matthew . . .'

Lily turns to her mother, her back against the kitchen counter-top, her eyes straying despite herself to the neatly arranged glass ornaments on the top shelf; a tiny blue and white horse, a pink and silver elephant. That was the one Lily bought her mother, when she was eight. How astonished then Lily had been, to think an elephant could be spun glass; this tiny, this delicate.

'Mum, I'm doing all right. *I* can look out for Matthew, I've discovered I'm good at it, I like it even. I have two jobs now – no, not at the library – one is for this woman, Isobel, doing some admin, the other for her friend, helping out with typing and her business. And there looks like being more work, for both of them. I'm not coming back to Yorkshire Mum. You know that, don't you?'

Brenda sniffs, carefully hangs the rubber gloves from a hook inside her kitchen cupboard.

'D'you hear that Bob? Our Lily's got two jobs and she's doing okay thank you very much without *our help* . . .'

'Mum, that isn't what I meant. I do appreciate your help. It's been lovely coming home these few days, and Matthew's had a great time. We loved our presents. But we're going back the day after Boxing Day, okay? I've booked the train.'

Brenda nods, a sharp nod, her eyes averted. A nod of defeat, Lily thinks. She thinks of Brenda reading to her, as a child; how sad Brenda's voice sounded when she described to her daughter the lilypad floating down the river, with Thumbelina's white butterfly tied to it. Sad always for the loss of the beautiful butterfly. It never occurred to Lily until now, how odd it was that Brenda didn't mention once to her daughter that because the butterfly was tethered, it would certainly twirl to its death.

Lily, Josh and Matthew are walking in the park towards the canal, heading for Matthew's favourite spot, the filter beds. Matthew is learning to ride the bike that Lily bought him for Christmas, from Wishley Street Secons, a rusty red number with a cranky bell. He has the cycle upright on the green cycle track with Josh walking beside him, holding the handle, but Matthew is only erratically pedalling, mostly he keeps his feet on the ground. Lily is obsessed with dog shit, with avoiding it and the pigeons that dot the grass. She walks behind them, dropping a cigarette-end into the fancy wrought-iron litter bin with its gold lettering, *Millfields*; shuddering at the smell.

'Don't you want to go off on your own for a little try?' she asks Matthew.

'I want Josh to come. Josh can take me . . .'

Lily is about to protest that Josh's back must be aching, leaning over the bike like that, supporting it while Matthew pedals, but Josh gets there first, insists: 'No problem. Let's take a little ride, boy.'

It's sunny, January, cold and blowy, leaves littering the grass, the trees mostly bare and stumpy, or else thin and pathetic, surrounded by their short metal fences, their feeble defence against vandals. Lily finds a bench, stares out across the park to the treelined edges, aware of the drone of traffic, and the distant barking of dogs. She can hear Matthew's voice, rising and falling, the tone plaintive.

Although she can't make out the words she knows him well enough to understand that he will be frustrated, want to do this cycling thing instantly, without falling off once, without any humiliation in front of Josh, without in fact any difficulty at all.

Lily watches the tall figure of Josh in his bulky winter jacket running next to her son and every few minutes Matthew is flipping over to one side with the bike between his legs, as if something knocked him down, or the wind blew him over. Two enormous pylons overlook the cycle track, like stalking metal giants. Matthew has already nicknamed them The Big Mum and The Big Dad, everything in pairs, Lily thinks, he has not adjusted his paradigm one jot, couldn't conceive of The Big Mum, all by herself.

Eventually she realises that Matthew is crying, that the bike has stayed down and so has he, that he is lying sideways and refusing to be pulled up, his legs still on the pedals, his elbow awkwardly hooked beneath him. Lily hastily puts out her just-lit cigarette, runs over to Josh and Matthew, but by the time she reaches them, Josh is pulling him up, his tone is teasing.

'No good falling down and staying down. You have to get yourself up again, you nearly had it then. What, am I wasting my time here, with you, pic'nee?'

Lily thinks this tone will rattle Matthew, she wouldn't use it herself, she kneels at Matthew's face, pulls the bike gently upright, asks if he is all right. Matthew doesn't answer. His bottom lip is tucked beneath his teeth. His knuckles are rigid on the handlebars. He is staring over Lily's head, at Josh.

Tears glitter in his eyes. 'Don't tell me what to do! You've got stupid hair and a stupid nose and I hate you!'

'*Matthew!*' Lily's tone is shocked, severe. She turns imploringly to Josh, ready to apologise, but Josh isn't looking at her either, and his expression is not angry. His eyes are fixed on Matthew. He steps a little closer, his voice low and calm.

'Cycle towards that big blue and black building,' Josh suggests. 'I need you to go read that sign for me, and tell me what it says. *Me cahn read, you know, me an old man now.*' (This bit sotto voce, but well within Matthew's hearing.)

Josh indicates a huge electric power station, a hundred yards away in the park. Matthew hesitates and Josh moves an inch closer, his hand on the back of the saddle.

'Push now boy, push down hard, that's it now, keep going . . !'

Josh is yelling, excited, and Matthew, wobbling, determined, shoots away from his grip, his feet pedalling frantically, gathering speed, his back hunched in the shape of a large insect, a beetle flying across the grass, his jacket filling with air like wings about to open. Josh, running beside him, continues to yell encouragement, he whistles, he is breathless and laughing and saying, *that's it, that's it boy, now you can do it!*

Lily is frightened, she is struck at once by something terrible, something she should have thought of sooner, she could have prevented: Josh and Matthew, Matthew and Josh, their need for one another. They are about to snap shut like two sides of a clam, never to be re-opened, never that is without trauma, a hammer, a devastating wrench. Only if Lily slips in there now, slides herself between them to keep a fissure open, only then can she keep her son, keep Josh, safe.

'Matthew!' Lily calls, her tone playful, light, betraying nothing. Matthew cycles back to her, unsteady, a bit sharp on the brakes, but grinning.

'What did the sign say?' Lily asks. 'Did you manage to read it?'

Matthew jumps off his bike, too excited to speak, and begins mimicking the yellow triangular sign he found there, with its image of a man sideways, in the throes of agony. When he stops laughing and recovers his voice, Matthew screeches hysterically, loud enough so that Josh, striding back towards them, can hear it too: 'It says sixty-six thousand volts, or sixty-six million or something. *Danger of Death! Danger of Death!* and there's a man doing this (giving his impression again) and did you see me Mum I can do it, I can ride my bike!'

'Danger of Death, Danger of Death!' Matthew chants it all the way home, sing-song style, and he wants Josh to steady the bike again, with his hand on the handlebars. Lily walks behind them, across the park, towards the road, puffing on her cigarette. She is sensitive to Josh's feelings, would like to tell Matthew to shut up, but finds herself listening in a compulsive silence to the squeak of the pedal and the little voice singing *Danger of Death* until its rhythm is more than a song, it's like breathing, it's something she's taking in, whether she wants to or not.

Josh wants to tell Lily that he can't bed her any more. He thinks of ways to say this, ways which won't hurt, won't make her spit flames. He's choosing his moment. She's here, in her kitchen, pouring water from the kettle on to herb teabags, late at night, the child asleep, the music on low.

'You post my letter to Daphine?'

The girl looks startled. She has on a white robe, cotton with a sprig flower pattern, a gift from Isobel after it shrunk in the wash. The robe is tightly wound and Lily's slender frame beneath it is well defined, the curve of her back, the dip of her waist. She no longer flutters in front of Josh like something phosphorescent, ephemeral. The lines are properly drawn, with no blurred edges. She is as separate and solid as a slim white vase.

'Yes,' Lily replies, cautiously. Then, 'Did you hear from her?'

'No,' Josh mutters, wondering how to get the conversation on the right track. It isn't about Daphine. He doesn't know, actually, what it is about. Just that he no longer feels drawn to Lily. He feels full, he thinks night and day about Neville, he never wants to stop the pictures, he can't now imagine why he once struggled to keep them at bay. Even the worst, even picturing his own son in his leather jacket, standing with his friends, arguing with the boy who stabbed him, gesticulating, waving his arms, ducking his head that way Neville has, sticking his chin out. Even picturing Neville in the moments before the ambulance arrives, sliding down the glass window, crumpling into a heap, girls suddenly swarming around him, onlookers. Even straining to imagine what Neville is thinking, *feeling*, as the white-lit world of the shopping arcade retreats into a tiny circle in front of his eyes, and the boy knows – *did he know?* – that he is dying, the wrong death, the too-soon-come, accidental death . . .

Even that, Josh wants to hold on to. This is my boy, *my boy*: at this moment he hangs here by a thread and there is nothing on this earth I can do to peel back time, to save him.

Timing is everything. *The moment to hold tight, the moment to let go.*

When he feels close to Neville in this way Josh has the broadest feelings, the wildest feelings, he feels as if his body might burst with the effort of holding such enormous feelings inside him, as if his own ribcage holds a waterfall, a landscape, something powerful that just keeps running, that runs right on, no matter what he or anyone else does to stop it. He can't say what it is, but Neville has taught him everything. He could never explain this to Lily, but he feels a tenderness towards her, something that wasn't there in the beginning, and his agitation, his compulsion for her has flown him. He feels calm and ready. He has no desire to fuck Lily. All desire to fuck Lily senseless has ebbed away.

'Maybe we should stop making love,' Josh says, sipping his tea.

Lily blows on her own hot tea, the air raising a tiny skin of the green surface. She stares at Josh's mouth, his beard, his profile. She remembers him yesterday with Matthew, running beside the bike, laughing. Tears slip down towards her cup. It's not that she didn't anticipate this, not that she hasn't somehow managed to catch Josh's reasoning. How can they go on? They aren't going to make a couple, a new family, it was never on the cards. Carrying on will only confuse Matthew, make life impossible for themselves.

'Are you bored with me?' Lily asks. Josh puts his arm around Lily's bony shoulder, nestles his chair beside hers at the kitchen table.

'No, that's not it.'

'What then? A New Year's Resolution? Not to sleep with me? Or other women generally?'

The overhead light strip in the kitchen is too bright,

he would like to reach up and switch it off. He doesn't fall in with her tone, he doesn't smile bitterly. His voice is gentle. 'Bored with myself, maybe,' he offers. He wonders what else to say.

Bob Marley playing again on the cheap cassette player by the window and this time it's his favourite. *I kept this message for you girl . . . but it seems like I was never on time . . .* Being on time, Josh decides, is everything. He can't afford any more mistakes.

Lily continues to watch for Josh, she can't help herself. She watches him leave for work in the mornings, the big wool hat pulled down low, the top of his head from her position on the fifth floor a brightly coloured pom-pom; red, green and gold. He walks stiffly, self-consciously she thinks, almost as if he can feel her gaze, her eyes burning a hole into the top of his head. One time she gives in to an urge to take the lift downstairs when she knows he is about to enter the flats, so that she emerges just as he is unlocking his front door. He has a letter in his hand.

Lily blurts out to him: 'Do you need me to read that?'

Josh looks up slowly, stares at the letter as if he didn't know he was holding it. He pushes a lock of hair away from his eyes.

'I'm going to a class. At the college. For adults.'

He grins, a little sheepishly, Lily thinks, as she gets his meaning.

'Oh. Adult literacy. Oh. Great. Oh. Well – good luck.'

'Thanks,' he says.

Tanks, Lily hears it. Tanks. She loves the way he says that. She loves the way he tilts his head slightly, walks with his shoulders back. She loves how slowly he walks. Even his back, turning away from her, the sound of his shoes. The squeak of his iron security-door, beginning to swing shut.

'Josh,' she says, suddenly. The name feels odd in her mouth, then in the air all around them. He turns his face to her, he is half inside his flat now, his expression is not what she expected, not smiling, not playful, not at all. He stands expectantly but he doesn't speak. He rests his brown eyes calmly on hers.

She has nothing to say, nothing at all. She stares back at him until he gives her a half-smile, releases her. Then she drops her eyes, and Josh nods at her, closes the door behind him.

She has been spending too long lying in bed, making Matthew late for school. Yesterday she had a phone call from Tanya Mathers, the Ed Psych, inviting Lily to make another appointment, to come and 'meet with her' again.

'I feel we got off on the wrong foot last time,' suggests Tanya, politely, and Lily has to agree.

She is touched, oddly, by the other woman's willingness to persist with her. She remembers something now, from that day: a photograph on the desk. Suzanna James, the social worker, smiling in the sunshine in a park somewhere with her arms around two round-faced children with big eyes, unsmiling. No man in the photo. Of course he could have been the one taking it but that isn't the impression Lily has. She is thinking, perhaps she's a single parent too. Perhaps both women are. In any case, why should I be so defensive, all the time, act like I did something wrong; presume I'm the only one suffering?

She agrees to meet Tanya. She agrees they could talk about some 'common goals' for Matthew, adding, 'I know Matthew's father isn't *dead* or anything, but I know Matthew has to grieve somehow, it's such an enormous loss, unimaginable . . .'

'I know,' says Tanya. The phone line goes dead with a soft click.

Nine's a Kiss

How would it be, Lily wonders, to write a letter to Josh, a letter that he would one day be able to read, that would communicate itself slowly to him, unfold a little more each time he looked at it, until, finally, he could understand everything. She considers this. What she would say? *Dear Josh*. But she can't get any further. A letter wouldn't do, even if she did have the satisfaction of knowing that he might read it himself one day. No. Letters have some power, but even they're not magical, they can't do everything.

Next she imagines seducing him, her winter coat over her nightdress, slipping downstairs to his floor in the lift, knocking on the door, falling in on him when he opens it. Like that other time, that early time, the time that now that she remembers it makes a catch in her breathing, like an air-pocket in her lungs. How to be back in that time again, only this time to know, even while it is happening, how special it is, how it won't come back, how flawed is everything she struggles for.

Did I ever thank him for the present, for the sweets? she thinks, suddenly obsessed with the idea that she hasn't thanked him, hasn't thanked him enough. Maybe she should go downstairs right now, tell him how much she appreciated that gesture. Appreciated all his kindnesses in fact, the food, the drinks, the money . . .

This feels worse, far worse than losing Alan to Gaynor and Lily can't work out why. That was a marriage of nearly six years, this a relationship of only a few months. Lily is smoking one cigarette after another, it's not late at all, it's only 11 p.m., the bloody police helicopter is hovering again, the whirring blades so noisy that she's amazed Matthew can sleep through it. She goes to the window, stares out at the Flanders Estate, watches the red light of the helicopter for a while until it slides out of view, behind the flats. Lily looks down at the roofs of cars, at the dull-violet night sky.

Those two weeks between Alan moving out and the fire, what happened to her? The shock of him telling her about Gaynor, of him moving out, taking his small sportsbag, packing his underwear, she remembers vividly, like a blow, like someone taking her in their arms and shaking her, shaking sense into her. *You never really loved me. You just needed me.* But she continued to resist his words, she let smoke curl up the stairs and into her nostrils, she made one last ditch attempt not to know, to keep knowledge cloudy and swirling, unclear.

You needed me too Alan. I am not the only one to blame.

She hears a car slam, the sound of high-pitched laughter. Teenagers. When she lived in Yorkshire she could not imagine being comforted by the sight of so many other human beings, not sleeping either. Some of the windows still have Christmas lights in them, most of the block directly opposite are boarded up. She watches as Sherry appears from the entrance-way, hurrying, pushing the child in the buggy, huddled inside her furry sleepsuit.

She found out from Josh that Sherry was not seriously hurt, she spent a week in hospital, some guy was arrested. Sherry and her daughter are fine, and although Lily has not plucked up courage yet to admit to Sherry that she was the one who phoned the police, she is deeply glad that she did, glad to see her neighbour up and about, tripping on her platform soles, joking with the cleaner in the mornings.

It's astonishing to Lily that women would be out at this time, but she is growing used to it. Flanders Estate is rarely quiet and Lily has the distinct feeling that whatever happens, because of the design, because the buildings all look inwards towards one another, around their central court, someone is always watching. She can't see Josh's flat from this angle, although if she leaned out of the window she could see if his light was on, or if his window was open.

There is the sound of another car entering the estate from Wishley Street, a black cab, the engine noise unmistakable. Lily watches idly, without particular interest, drawing on her cigarette, opening the window to let the smoke out, as the cab negotiates the curve of the road, pulls up at the entrance to Bridge House. The cab door opens, and a woman gets out, steps to the cab window to pay the driver. She is wearing a hat, dark in colour, she is small, perhaps a bit on the stout side. Lily can't see her face but she hears the voice, hears the woman call thank you to the driver, and pick up the two cases she has at her feet. Lily opens the window further, leans right out. The woman is wearing a camel coat, she is black, she might be around forty.

She has a London accent but a rich, fruity voice, loud. Lily's heart hammers faster, the bottom of the window-ledge cuts into her flesh in the flimsy night-dress, the night air whips goose pimples all over her skin. The woman heading into the building does not press the button for the lift. Lily listens, straining, waiting to hear the lift engage, a sound she hears every night, over and over, a droning, mechanical sound, the comforting evidence of other lives, of coming and going, of the endless possibility for visits, for surprises. But the lift does not engage. That means the woman is going into flat number 1 or number 2. Flat number 1 is empty, boarded again yesterday by the council, slamming a metal door over the wooden, to keep out squatters. There's no doubt, then. Daphine is back.

Bitterly cold. Lily's shoulders are cold inside her coat, her hands inside her gloves, the wind licking nastily around her bare neck. Matthew, cycling on ahead of her, squeezes his bike through a blue-painted cycle gate, then whizzes over the bridge and is already on the other side of the canal, pink-cheeked, probably warm as toast. Lily hurries to catch him up. The wind makes dimples on the surface of the canal, dull silver water, raised like the surface of a cheese grater. Matthew pauses, a few yards away from Lily, watching a huge British Waterways dredger plough noisily down the canal, driven by a guy with headphones who doesn't respond to Matthew's waving, stares glassily at the scoop of the dredger, churning up its green slime.

Lily catches Matthew up, stands beside him, follows his gaze. The dirty-water smell whirls around them and the engine dies out as the dredger continues down the canal, towards Lee Valley Park. Lily and Matthew stare at the water, clean and dark in a strip in the middle, green and scummy at the edges, a soup of beer cans and puffed up plastic carriers.

'Cycle slowly. Then I can walk beside you.' Lily lights a cigarette. Matthew pedals a little slower, but not much. The pylons dominate the skyline, that and a second rusty bridge, this one not for pedestrians, it's covered in signs like the Supergrid, *Danger: 66,000 volts*. Lily has long stopped wondering why this is Matthew's favourite place. It has the widest open spaces. The biggest football pitches in Europe.

'I've got something to tell you!' she yells after Matthew.

He circles along the stony path beside the canal, cycles back.

'I have a parcel at home for you. It's from your Dad.'

Matthew is wearing a woolly hat. Red. His coat is pulled up to his chin where he can chew on the collar, now turning soggy with saliva. He stares at Lily.

'Is it a Sony Playstation?'

'No. It's not that kind of parcel.'

Matthew bites the collar hard, his top teeth appearing like the teeth of a rodent. 'What kind of parcel is it then?'

'Just some things. Things of yours mostly, your Dad must have kept. He – I think he – wanted you to have them. A toy sword. Some plastic sandals. A cap. I don't know. I'll show you when I get home.'

Matthew says nothing. The pylons fill the silence on this side of the canal with a faint hum, an occasional tiny weird hiss. Lily scuffs her shoes in the pebbles, looks down at the ground, waits.

'Okay,' Matthew says, turning his bike around and cycling in the direction of the Filter Beds. His okay is neither excited nor pleased nor disappointed nor even surprised, it's not in fact anything that Lily can work out. Lily runs after him, she's breathless, her chest is hurting, her cheeks sting in the cold January air.

'Matthew! Don't go so far! Come back! It's cold, I want to go home.'

He turns his cycle around, deftly, he has confidence now, his knees pump up and down, his small hunched form cycles towards her, overtakes her, passes the bridge before her, only stops when he gets to the main road, and then he is too out of breath to speak.

'Do you think after I die I might come back as a cyber pet?'

The bike is propped against the window, they are in McDonald's, sipping two huge, wickedly cold milk-shakes. Lily's mouth, her skin, her eyeballs in her head feel freezing, but it was Matthew's choice, he says they eat ice-creams in Russia, Mrs Jalil told him that.

'No, I don't think you'll come back as a cyber pet.'

'What will happen to me then?'

'I don't know . . .'

'Maybe I'll live to be six hundred and be the oldest man on Earth.'

'I don't think so, Matthew.'

Matthew slurps noisily, finishes his drink, pulls his hat down close to his eyes. Lily feels for her cigarettes. 'Is this about Dad, Matthew?'

'No. He's out of here.'

A young woman in her uniform comes close to their table, swishes the mop around the low red toadstool chairs. A noisy party of five or six children are screaming with delight at a nearby table, blowing Coke at one another, through straws. McDonald's is steamy, warm, red and blue, scented with chips and cold winter breath, heaving with children. Matthew is distracted now, watching a small scene unfold; a homeless man, bundled inside several coats, is being shown the door by the branch manager, a young man with acne, who looks deeply embarrassed.

'Your Dad's not "out of here",' Lily says, firmly. 'He's only in – Wetherby. I don't have an address for him, but I could try to find out. Then you could write to him, you know . . .'

The months after the fire, while Lily stayed with Brenda and Bob, waiting to hear from the council, waiting to be rehoused, she still believed that Alan would persist as Matthew's father. She was truly astonished at the way Alan unravelled himself from fatherhood, inch by inch. He was slapdash with the maintenance payments, late for Saturday visits with his son, then one week he didn't turn up at all. That was the week she decided. The flat came up in London and there was no reason to stay. Lily tried to phone Alan, to let him know, and Gaynor's spry voice came on the answerphone asking her to leave a message. Despite all the messages she had inside her, all the things she longed to say, she fell silent, she let the phone go dead.

Alan is not the person she thought he was, nothing like that person. But Matthew doesn't know that. He's six years old. It's Lily's job to be the adult, not to lie to Matthew. Lily's painful job to be the one bearing the full brunt of the truth, until Matthew is big enough to hold it, carry it by himself.

Now Matthew spots a friend, at another table; Tyrone. He turns away from his mother, yelling '*Tye! Tye,*' knocking over his empty cup in his haste to get Tyrone's attention.

Lily puts the straw between her lips, sucks up the cold, head-chilling milkshake. She knows Matthew has heard her, taken it in.

Ten for a Bird You Must Not Miss

Bob is making himself a sandwich, a *best butty*, is how he thinks of it. He knows the child is watching him, feels Lily's eyes follow him around the kitchen, but when he offers her some she says tartly, *No thank you Daddy*.

First he cuts the bread: white, thick slabs, doorstops. Then he spreads the butter, butter Brenda helpfully keeps out so that it spreads smoothly, easily. Next, two slices of tomato, two wafer-thin slices of ham. Then mustard, Branston Pickle and HP Sauce. He squashes the top slice of bread down, sighs hungrily in anticipation, takes the sandwich into the living room.

The TV is on in the corner. Something like *Match of the Day*. He's not really watching but he likes the theme tune. He settles himself into his armchair, Bob's chair, no one else sits in it; his paper is stuffed down one side, the remote control down the other. He stretches his feet out on to the pouffe Brenda thoughtfully keeps at exactly the right distance, so that he doesn't have to bestir himself too much. Because of her agoraphobia he knows where his wife is at any given time (you might say that it even works to his advantage, but Bob wouldn't say that, of course, because he loves that lass and he wouldn't want her to suffer unnecessarily). For example, he knows that right now she is ironing, upstairs in the bedroom, where she always irons, close to the airing cupboard. She sings when she irons, he can faintly hear the foot-tapping from the room above. And a good smell, clean ironed shirts, floats over the house.

When he bites into the butty he notices Lily again. 'What's up with you, lass?' She's staring at him. He offers the sandwich over to her but again she shakes her head.

'Go find summat to do,' he says, suddenly irritated with her big eyes, her silence. He rests the sandwich comfortably on his belly. He opens his mouth wide. *An Englishman's home is his castle. There's food in the fridge and all's right with the world.*

That sandwich he loves so much, Lily is thinking. That's him and Brenda with me in the middle. And he's just about to eat it right up, to open his mouth wide as a cave and swallow us whole.

She's eight but even now – especially now – a phrase is forming in her, she is questioning, wondering: Brenda and Bob, Bob and Brenda – book ends, pressing something tightly together, holding something else at bay. The phrase is this: *Is that all there is?*

She dreams again the dream of Mother Shipton's Cave, she follows the dream knowing every step, knowing the drip-drip and the lurid green light inside the cave, the wet, dank smell, Matthew somewhere in the dream beside her, but out of sight. This time, she feels light, light and not frightened at all. She knows what she is about to find. She plunges empty arms into the wishing well and brings up the stone gargoyle. It is not Matthew. It's heavy, grey and the face on it is distorted but not terribly. It's Lily. The face is grimly plain, a mirror. Lily dunks it again. Lifts, dunks. *Dunk it with authority!* says Matthew, somewhere (a TV ad, one of Matthew's favourite jingles). Lily lifts, dunks and the gargoyle smiles at her: what makes you think you're so special? What makes you think you're *immune*?

'Okay, okay, fine, fine, I get it,' replies Lily. Then she wakes up.

Josh knocks lightly on Lily's door. He thinks this knock sounds a bit too timid, *scared* even; tries again, rapping this time, a little harder. He has something heavy, partially covered in a black bin-liner behind him on the floor, bends to pick it up.

The girl when she opens the door is smiling at him, pushes a tuft of hair behind her ear, where it bounces out again instantly. He notices her hair is a little longer. Notices her perfume, that she is wearing a soft blue cardigan, with several of the pearly buttons undone. He can't help himself from smiling back.

'You have a carpet then?' he says, stepping over the threshold without being invited, carefully carrying the box in front of him.

The flat is warm, smells good, of something cooking. Lily's bare feet pad along the corridor in front of him, leading him to the kitchen. She has hardly spoken, seems smaller even than he remembers in her tight black jeans. And prettier. He is relieved that she asks no questions.

She looks at the box with curiosity, her face friendly, her welcome unspoken.

Josh lays the present on the kitchen table, unwraps the bin-liner and smooths down the front of his cotton sweatshirt. 'I brought something for the boy.'

Matthew is watching TV in the living room; his mother steps into the next room and calls him. The child too is pleased to see him and grins and grins when he lights his eyes on what Josh has brought for him.

'A fish tank! A fish tank! You brought me a fish tank!'

'Only a small one,' Josh says.

The tank has been filled with a few inches of water and two silver-coloured fish.

'You shouldn't have . . .' the girl begins.

'It was Neville's,' Josh interrupts her. 'Been doing some clearing just lately of Neville's room and things like that.'

Lily and her son are smiling at him, the room is scented with the good cooking and the girl's perfume and both of them grinning at Josh, delighted, fussing around the tank.

'You need water purifier and things like that. Your mum can get you that stuff. I just brought you the simplest thing. This fish make me think of your mum. Silver Dollar. You can get more. When your mum have the money or the time . . .'

'Matthew, what do you say?' Lily prompts.

Now Josh feels shy, choked up, he doesn't want the boy's thanks, or the fuss. Daphine is waiting in the flat downstairs, also cooking. She knows he is up here, but he's unsure what she makes of that. He told her he grew friendly with Lily and the child. She seemed to accept this, to think that it helped him, but you never know with Daphine. She knows a lot of things. It was Daphine who mentioned that maybe it's high time they go through some of Neville's belongings, go into his room, sort things. And now they have begun.

'Thank you Josh!' yells the child, excited, his face at the edge of the water, staring down at the two flat fish, slightly lost in their oversized tank, their small amount of water.

'You need a few more fish . . .' Josh says, backing towards the corridor, peeling his eyes from Lily as she stands behind her son, one hand on his shoulder.

'Yes. Thank you,' Lily says.

He shifts his eyes from her with some trouble, staring instead at the two Silver Dollars swimming a dramatic loop, a watery figure of eight, chasing each other in a slow, silvery celebration.

Lily Waite is standing at the window of her bedroom, her favourite place. The half-hour in the afternoon just before Matthew comes home from school, her favourite time of day. Steam rising from a cup of black tea in her hand.

Tiny birds wheel in the distance, over in the direction of St Paul's Cathedral. She is watching the sky slide past in a deep smeary blue, mixing with silver like paint in water. The way she used to watch the sky as a child. Sky, like flame, never seems to be still. Like watching time slip past in front of you.

She likes the fact that what she can't see from here very easily is the ground.

The light is special, deep, orange. The buds on the skeleton twigs of tree are coated in it, fine finger biscuits, half dipped in chocolate.

The bins are still overflowing. The doors of the flats

in the estate look in on each other, as if there were nowhere else to look. Two out of three doors opposite are boarded up. New leaflets have been dropped by for tenants, leaflets letting them know that a housing association will soon be their new landlord and inviting them to consider other housing options, not *Right to Buy* any longer but *Do It Yourself Home Ownership*, with the help of the housing association.

Lily thinks that this will probably only help a few people, those who can get a mortgage, those who have a job, good credit, those without long-term debt problems or a criminal record, those who have people in their life whom they can borrow the deposit from. It is a system that will probably help her, for instance. That and the letter from the loss adjuster she had recently.

On the one tree in the centre. A magpie with its pendulum tail, sharp as a fountain pen, its inky head constantly agitated. The bird jumps a branch, opens its wings in a burst, a flapping cloak. Lily watches it carefully, trying to remember ever looking at a bird this closely before. Now she thinks of waitresses, bell-boys, uniforms. The velvety blue-black head, wing, the tail, swinging beneath the branch. The creamy underbelly.

One for Sorrow. She knows she will never be with Josh again, never in the way she wants to be; in fact she can scarcely imagine a way for their paths even to cross in future, if she moves out. But then again Brenda's superstitious clap-trap – don't open an umbrella in the house, cross your eyes if you see a magpie so you can see double – how did that ever help Lily anyway? Wasn't it as bad as everything else, religion, superstition all of it, a way to fend off knowledge, the knowledge we all possess? So simple but so frightening. That there is only this, only this.

'I never crush a relationship dead,' Josh tells her. Letting her down gently. She turns this phrase over for a long time, until it's smooth as a pebble in her hand. She recognises many things all at once: that Josh is kind, that he was rearranged by grief, that the heat between them was real, maybe unique even, that he probably loves his wife very much. That he will hover around in Lily's life for some time, singeing the edges, making paper or flammable things crackle once in a while. Making second best no good at all, which is fine, which is as it should be. Reminding her.

The bird opens its wings, ceases for a moment its agitated head bobbing, its watchful paranoia. She sees its frilled underbelly spread itself as it sails high above the lace of tree branches, disappears into a dot, an ink dot on a sliding sky.

JILL DAWSON
Wild Boy

'A 12-year-old child is found, naked and with the scar from an
attempt to cut his throat, living wild in the savage hills of the Tarn.
Post-revolutionary France is ablaze with rumour, and with curiosity to
see whether Jean-Jacques Rousseau's theories on childhood and the
"state of nature", in which primitive man was superior to the civilised,
are vindicated. The boy is brought to Paris, where Itard, a young
ambitious doctor, attempts to teach him at the Deaf-Mute Institute.
Out of this true story Jill Dawson has created a fascinating work of fiction.'
Amanda Craig, *New Statesman*

'Intriguing and deeply moving'
Mark Sanderson, *Sunday Telegraph*

'An accomplished novel, rich with ideas and vivid
characters, which is, above all, a lucid and moving
exploration of the nature of autism.'
Laura Baggaley, *Observer*

'Fascinating and deeply sympathetic . . . Ingenious, well-crafted
and carefully researched, this novel questions what makes us
human and leaves one a little wiser for it.'
David Shukman, *Daily Mail*

'The damaged child's frantic little body and fragile heart are an insistent,
vivid presence on every page of [Dawson's] fine novel . . . Dawson's prose
is graceful, her approach deeply intelligent and persuasive.'
Hilary Mantel

'Excellent . . . Dawson takes what is already a compelling tale
and successfully fleshes it out into a convincing and highly moving
book . . . She revivifies a piece of history with emotional
intelligence, fleshing out the few documented facts with an
admirably perceptive grasp of human nature.'
Michael Newton, *Guardian*

'As interesting anthropologically as it is engaging, examining
notions of civilisation and wilderness and, as the story unfolds,
the fine line between savant and savage.'
Elisabeth Easther, *Time Out*

SCEPTRE